SLEEPING BEAUTY

Isabella stared in wonder at the man who lay unconscious on the bed. She judged him the hand-somest man she had ever seen.

Strong, and evenly cut, each of his features fit perfectly with the others so that the man's straight nose complimented his lean jaw which, in its turn, set off his square, firm chin. Isabella saw that the Creator had also seen fit to give him thick, waving hair the color of antique gold, and a tall, lean body, a picture of strength and grace.

If this gentleman cast so seductive a spell over her now, what would happen when he opened his eyes—especially if he chose to wake her . . . ?

EMMA LANGE is a graduate of the University of California at Berkeley, where she studied European history. She and her husband live in the Midwest and pursue interests in traveling and sailing.

SIGNET REGENCY ROMANCE
COMING IN JANUARY 1991

Marjorie Farrell
Autumn Rose

Amanda Scott
Bath Quadrille

Gayle Buck
Hearts Betrayed

The Reforming of Lord Roth

Emma Lange

A SIGNET BOOK

SIGNET
Published by the Penguin Group
Penguin Books USA Inc., 375 Hudson Street,
New York, New York, 10014, U.S.A.
Penguin Books Ltd, 27 Wrights Lane, London W8 5TZ, England
Penguin Books Australia Ltd, Ringwood, Victoria, Australia
Penguin Books Canada Ltd, 2801 John Street,
Markham, Ontario, Canada L3R 1B4
Penguin Books (N.Z.) Ltd, 182-190 Wairau Road,
Auckland 10, New Zealand

Penguin Books Ltd, Registered Offices:
Harmondsworth, Middlesex, England

First published by Signet, an imprint of New American Library, a division of Penguin
Books USA Inc.

First Printing, December, 1990
10 9 8 7 6 5 4 3 2 1

Chapter 1

A late winter storm lashed Suffolk. Driving rain rattled the panes at Marsh House, while the wind screamed like a thousand banshees as it assaulted the eaves.

Sorely vexed by the tumult that had kept her home that night, Liza Ramsey flung open the door to her sister's small study without knocking and was further displeased with what she found within. "I knew I should find you in here, Bella!" she cried, her hands going to her dainty hips. "Though Nell is soon to bring up the tea tray, here you are with your absurd spectacles on your nose poring over those infernal books like some clerk! Oh, I do believe I see a line on your brow!"

Isabella Ramsey did not seem terribly affected by either her sister's vexation or the discovery of a wrinkle on her brow. Indeed, she chuckled. "Value that line, Liza. It is a token of success. The accounts for January have come out even at last."

"Oh, Bella!" Liza stamped a tiny foot. "You are hopeless! First this storm keeps me from dinner at the Bashams', and then you must work into the night, leaving me with only Papa and Lady Prim for company. Oh! I cannot wait to go to London!"

Isabella closed her ledger and rose to move closer to the fireplace. "You've only a little over a month more, my dear," she said, putting out her hands to the fire.

Liza tossed her glossy curls. "A month!" she wailed as if it were a century of waiting she faced.

Smaller, more voluptuous, and prettier than her sister, Liza was given to excess in her moods. Having been cosseted from birth by both her mother and her elder sister, she was best pleased when matters were arranged precisely to suit her. When they were not, she could reproduce to a nicety the effects of a tempest.

After her approaching Season, her greatest interest in life was young men, and they returned the favor. One or another of her beaux was forever penning a sonnet in praise of her alabaster skin, her Cupid's bow lips, or the long, thick lashes she could bat to decided effect.

Those thick lashes were the only feature she and her sister, at twenty, two years older than she, had in common. Isabella's face was merely pleasant, not pretty. Her eyes were hazel while Liza's were a dramatic green, and her hair, though abundant, was only a soft brown. Liza's was almost black it was so dark. Had one of the young gentlemen in alt over Liza been given to looking ahead, he might have imagined the shorter girl turning plump in her middle age and her temperament wearing a bit when she was not in the first bloom of youth; but young men are seldom given to looking ahead.

To be fair, even had a young man wished to judge Isabella more favorably, he'd have had little opportunity. She had never gone with her sister to the Assemblies in Ipswich and only on occasion had attended smaller affairs closer to home. She had had little time for flirtations and dances and new dresses since she had come of age.

When her mother had been struck by illness, it had been Isabella who had assumed the responsibility for nursing her. She had been the eldest, though only sixteen, and eager to do what she could to ease first her mother's suffering and then, after two years, her death. Liza and their brother, Peter, had been too young to do more than sit with their mother occasionally. Their father, the squire, though he had dearly loved his Betsy, had had little heart for the task.

Nor had he much heart for managing his finances. Never the most capable of stewards, his wife's passing had left the squire so adrift he had embarked upon a prolonged profligate fling that had put him and his family in very serious debt. Not a bad man, he had reacted rather like a small boy who realizes he is in need of restraint when Isabella, after a look at his books, had suggested she needed an endeavor with which to occupy herself. In truth, flirtations and parties and breathless considerations of the newest styles, had never precisely riveted Isabella, but after her mother's death she had been obliged to put such girlish things aside altogether, for all her energies were required to master the quite difficult task of putting her father's estate in order.

Aware how many depended upon her, Isabella took her duties as estate manager seriously, an attitude she did not, as a rule, extend to her sister. Just then, in response to Liza's mournful complaint, she smiled, causing a remarkable change to occur in her appearance, for she'd a luminous smile. "Ah, yes, alack and alas," she sighed extravagantly. "An entire month, Liza—and a little more even—before you are in town shopping at the Pantheon Bazaar, crossing Almack's hallowed portals . . ."

"Oh! I shall adore it all!" Liza exclaimed, succumbing, as usual, to her sister's smile and humor. "And I do know that I am the silliest wigeon, Bella! I ought to be consoling you, not the other way about. I tell you, had Papa betrothed me to Lord Wrexham without granting me even one Season, I should have been too furious for words!"

"The viscount is to be my husband, Liza," Isabella admonished, a little stiffly, as she looked back to the fire.

The younger girl pouted a long moment, then burst out with, "Truly, Bella, I cannot think why you would fall in with Papa's plans! Surely you must see he weds you to our nearest neighbor, a man more than twice your age, because he wishes to have you near enough to continue managing his affairs for him!"

"I do know Papa, yes," Isabella said, a half smile lifting the corner of her somewhat too generous mouth. "But in this instance what suits him suits me as well. I would be a fish out of water in town where there is nothing to put one's mind to but balls and routs . . ."

" . . . and soirees and theater parties and breakfasts!" Liza finished, her eyes taking on a sparkle. "I, on the other hand, shall get on famously there!"

They laughed together at the truth of the remark, then Isabella nodded down at the dress her sister wore. "Your new dress suits you very well, Liza. It is the one Lady Prim helped you choose?"

Reminded of the original reason she had sought out her sister, Liza twirled about, holding out the hem of her dress as if she were dancing. "Is it not quite stunning, Bella? And yes, it is in the style Lady Prim suggested. I confess I thought you mad when you invited Wrexham's aunt as well as his child to live with us at Marsh House, but I admit I have become marvelously fond of Lady Prim. She knows so much of town!''

"She did live there some thirty years," Isabella observed, but Liza did not hear the dry note in her voice. A great streak of lightning ripped across the sky, distracting her.

"Oh!" Liza wailed as thunder shook the house. "I hate storms! But look at you, Bella! You look almost radiant!"

Isabella's hazel eyes, quite her finest feature, did indeed glow as she looked toward the window. "The rain means a good deal to us," she said calmly enough, though when she had heard the first drops lash the windows, she'd had an impulse to run outside and fling her arms wide in welcome. "Another year of drought, and I am not certain what we'd have done."

"Would not Lord Wrexham have helped us?" Liza asked curiously. "After all, he was generous enough with your marriage settlement. To my mind, it was the one good point about him."

"Liza!" But Isabella got no further in her reprimand. A knock at the door interrupted her.

At her call, a young maid, balancing a tray on her broad hip, entered. "Ye did say to bring the chocolate here, Miss Bella?"

"I did, Nell, thank you. I can carry it up to the nursery while you attend to Papa and Lady Prim in the drawing room. Liza . . .''

"I protest, Bella!" Liza cried before her sister could frame whatever had been her question. "It is not done to take on servants' chores. First the books and now this!"

She gestured vexedly at the laden tray Nell held, but Isabella was already taking it from the maid. "Did you not know Annie has taken ill, Liza?" she asked over her shoulder. "Cora says it is influenza, and I fear she is right. It is the time for it."

"Cora Geddes reminds me of a witch," Liza said then, rather petulantly.

Nell glanced up and was not surprised to see irritation flash in her mistress's eyes. "Cora is only an old woman who learned healing from her gypsy mother, Liza. She is no witch."

"Oh, perhaps not, but she is a crone, and she does put me in mind of those stray animals you were forever bringing home when you were younger."

Isabella gave her sister a brief, acknowledging smile, for she had brought home her share of strays, but she did not allow Liza's attitude toward Cora Geddes to go unremarked. "Cora relieved our mother's suffering enormously when Dr. Davies, addled as he is with age, had no thought what to do. Providing her a warm home in her old age is the least we can do."

Nell hid a grin as she turned to go. Miss Liza's lips were buttoned tight, for no matter what she thought of Cora Geddes, she'd not gainsay her sister, not when there was that light in Miss Bella's eyes. And thank the good Lord, Nell added to herself as she hurried back to the kitchen, that it was Miss Bella who had charge of them all. Miss Bella was quality and never one to be thinkin' only of herself like some others Nell could name but would not. After all, weren't she weddin' that cold Lord Wrexham just to see Miss Liza sent up to Lunnon town and Master Peter off to school?

"Will you come and have chocolate with Sarah and me, Liza?" Isabella asked as she waited for her sister to open the door for her.

The invitation had the effect of soothing Liza, but after a moment's thought she shook her head. "Sarah becomes so fearfully shy when I am about, Bella, I should prefer to return to the drawing room and bedevil Lady Prim for stories of town.

"But, of course!" she cried suddenly, as they stepped into the corridor together. "The true reason you agreed to wed Wrexham is Sarah."

"There is no 'true' reason, Liza. The viscount did me honor to offer me his name."

"But he is so different from you, Bella. You must admit it! Phew! I found him cold as ice at your betrothal supper!"

Isabella disregarded a sudden feeling of heaviness in her chest. "I found the viscount very courteous and dignified . . ."

"He has not written to you above twice in all the nine months since he left for London—and that was only a week after you became betrothed! That is not very lover-like behavior to my mind."

"The viscount and I are not in love, Liza," Isabella replied in the tone of one repeating a lesson. "Wrexham proposed a match of good sense to me. We shall have children together and build up his estate. And," she added, smiling a little, "it is true I shall be pleased to look after Sarah. She is doing much better now that she is free of that martinet of a governess. Imagine anyone telling a child they were wicked for stammering! It is a great wonder Sarah is not shier than she is.''

Seeing the flame of wrath kindled in Isabella's eyes, her sister laughed aloud. "I wish I had seen you turn the dragon out, Bella. Lady Prim says you were quite magnificent.''

"It was a most satisfying moment," Isabella allowed. "Ever since I first stumbled upon Sarah cowering behind a tree in the woods because she thought I was her governess come to drag her home, I had nursed a desire to send that woman on her way. Happily, Wrexham gave me the authority.''

After you importuned him twice, Liza might have added but found from someplace or other the wisdom to forebear. Instead she bid her sister good night and went off to the drawing room while Isabella proceeded to the nursery.

She arrived none too soon, she found, for Lady Sarah Farley, her betrothed's only child, sat huddled in the middle of her bed, her knees drawn up to her chest and a blanket drawn about her so that only her dark, brown eyes showed.

"Oh, Sarah, are you afraid of storms?" Isabella cried, settling the tray quickly, as the six-year-old bounded off the bed and ran to her. "There, there. The thunder is loud, I grant, and though Marsh House is solid, even Liza was a little put off." Sarah freed one eye to measure the truth of that remark, and Isabella nodded firmly. "You are not alone, my dear. And in the future if you are afraid of anything, I wish you to come to me. Will you, Sarah? I do not want you to sit here in the nursery all alone.''

Isabella's clear, direct, compassionate gaze had its effect. On a little intake of breath, Sarah nodded.

"Good girl." Isabella smiled and dropped a kiss on the child's brow. "Now, I think it is time for our hot chocolate.''

As the beverage was Sarah's favorite bedtime treat, she was more than willing to adjourn to the table, but was not so amenable to returning to her bed when they were done.

Isabella assured the child she intended to stay, however, and after tucking Sarah in, sat by her bed, holding her hand and singing lullabies slightly out of key, while the wind continued to make its eerie sounds.

Even when Sarah fell asleep, Isabella remained awhile to be certain she would not awaken again. As she gazed at Sarah's flaxen hair, she was reminded of the child's father, whose hair was of like color, though not of similar thickness for he was fifty at least.

She had been as surprised as anyone that the Viscount Wrexham had approached her father for her. They had been neighbors all her life but had met only infrequently, for Wrexham had long preferred the pleasures of town to ccountry life.

But they'd encountered one another at a birthday party the Bashams, other neighbors, had given for their daughter of Liza's age. A great many young people had been present, and the affair had been quite noisy. There had even been a play staged by the young gentlemen of the neighborhood in honor of Miss Basham's eighteen years. A very silly thing about star-crossed lovers, it had sent the young ladies in the audience into giggles, but Isabella, while she had chuckled at the more outrageous mishaps, had grown weary rather soon.

Turning her eyes to the window and the moonlit summer night beyond, she found the viscount's gaze upon her. She could not quite credit the approval she discerned in his look, but he had come later, after the play, to assure her of it. Bowing over her hand, he'd told her, "You are a steady lamp, Miss Ramsey, among these wavering candles."

A steady lamp sounded rather an unglamorous thing to be, but she had smiled. "I suppose I am glad, sir, not to be thought a wavering light. They are so difficult to read by."

Her reply had amused him. He had not laughed. He was not given to such display, but he had smiled faintly.

Throughout the month he had courted her, he had been much the same, considering her with muted admiration and awarding her faint, but amused smiles. His attitude toward the rest of their neighbors was not quite so benign. As he looked out at them, his pale, heavy lidded eyes often gleamed with a rather more enigmatic—some might even say cold—light.

Her brow knit just a little then. He was, in all, a cool man. And he would be her husband. The thought of their marital bed . . . but she restrained those thoughts. She had not agreed to wed Wrexham for warm reasons. She ought to own that.

She had betrothed herself to the viscount for the coolest of reasons, in fact: a generous betrothal settlement. The Ramsey purse had been in dire need of it. Only she and her father knew how dire. Liza and Peter had not been told of the staggering debts the squire had managed to run up in a mere three years. He had repented his bad behavior and quit wagering so deeply, but too late. Leaving aside a healthy sum to finance Liza's come-out and Peter's schooling, they had had enough left from Wrexham's largess to cover only the greatest part of the squire's losses.

Isabella sighed a little raggedly then. It was not the betrothal or the marriage of her dreams. It was, however, a marriage, and there had been no other man asking for her hand, particularly not one with ten thousand pounds.

She would have her own home. Granted, Wrexham Hall was a rather grim old pile of stones, for it had never lost the appearance of what it had originally been, a fortress built on the only land that could pass for high in their low, marshy country. But it did have a view of the sea. Below it was the only deep-water bay for miles along their coast. And, if she liked rather better to watch the activity in the marshes stretching out from the dikes protecting her father's estate, Isabella did also like to observe the sea.

And she would have children, beginning with the fragile one whose hand she held and whom she loved. In that she and Wrexham were united, for he had made no secret of desiring a male heir. Old enough so that he'd begun to feel time's pinch, the viscount had looked around for a suitable second wife and settled upon her, primarily, Isabella thought, all her pleasing steadiness aside, because she was of good lineage. A man as proud as Wrexham would be pleased to form an alliance, not with her father's family, all squires and no more for generations, but with her mother's. Betsy Ramsey, a Carrington, had been daughter to the Duke of Carlisle.

So the marriage benefited them both. And she would not have to spend a great deal of time in town. Wrexham had agreed, rather quickly she fancied, to that. She would stay at home, minding the house and the children, visiting her friends, taking walks along the dike, and she would be content. She would.

She had given her word after all, and she owed the viscount loyalty for the generosity he had shown her family.

Isabella straightened suddenly. Something was not right. Frowning, she glanced to the candle by Sarah's bed to realize she had fallen into a doze, for the thing had nearly burned down. There! That was not thunder, though the storm still raged. Again! She was certain now. Though it was the middle of the night, someone banged at their door.

Chapter 2

Isabella harbored no expectation that Dobson, butler to her father since before she was born, would hear the summons and stumble out of his bed to see who could be desiring admittance after midnight. The old man's ears heard little enough when he was wide awake.

Happily, their footman, Jack, was younger and slept more lightly. When she reached the stairs, Isabella saw the young man hurrying along the hallway below her, holding a lantern in one hand as he attempted to tuck in his shirt with the other.

"Jack. I am glad you heard the knocking," she called out to him. "I cannot think who could be at our door at this hour in this storm."

Having not heard his mistress's light step upon the stair, Jack looked up with a start, then, making out her warm smile, ducked his head shyly. "They've heavy hands, Miss Bella. Woke me easy, they did."

Another surge of clamorous banging returned their attention to the door, and Jack, his lantern held high, ran to unbolt it. At once, seeming to be lifted by the wind, two men surged forward into the hall, their sodden cloaks scattering water everywhere.

Rain blew in the open door, but Jack, like his mistress poised upon the bottom step, her gutted candle forgotten in her hand, stared with wide eyes from the two strangers to the rough pallet they carried between them.

A man lay on it. He was so still Isabella thought him dead until, with a flood of relief, she saw his chest lift then fall. Her gaze went flying to his face. Despite the flickering light Jack's lantern threw about the hall, she saw he was chalky pale. Before the shadows returned to veil his face from her, she also received an impression of handsomeness.

"Jack, the door," Isabella prompted the mesmerized boy, then she looked up at the nearer of the two strangers, a giant of a fellow, who seemed to tower above her.

"Is he badly hurt, sir?"

The large man's response, at least as to the extent of the other's injuries, did not surprise her. "I fear so, miss," he replied in a gruff voice that fit with his rough-seamed countenance. "Lord Roth was drivin' 'is carriage, when it o'er turned. Thrown to the ground, 'e was, 'ittin' 'is head bad. 'Ave ye a room for 'im, miss?"

"Yes, yes, of course," Isabella assured him, the direct question restoring her ability to think clearly. "My brother's room is free. I will take you there. Jack, you go and rouse Cora. This gentleman's injuries will require her skills, I think."

The boy nodded, and after relighting Isabella's candle with his lantern, hastily returned the way he had come while Isabella mounted the stairs before the two men straining to carry their heavy burden.

"You may lay him here," she said, throwing back the covers of Peter's bed as the man carefully lowered the pallet to the floor.

While they removed the man's wet outer garments, their soft grunts indicating the task was not easy, Isabella hurried to light the room's candles. Next, she knelt to put a match to the kindling some thoughtful soul, likely Nell, had laid upon the hearth, and when she had the robust beginnings of a fire, she turned around.

The injured man was laid out upon Peter's bed, and the large fellow who had spoken to her was struggling to remove his boot. Glancing down, Isabella saw that the other boot, tall, black, and tasseled, lay upon the floor. Though spattered with mud, she could see its cut was very fine.

Accepting the notion that the injured man truly was a lord something, she could not think what name the giant who served him had given. Isabella looked more closely at the man and had her earlier impression of him utterly vindicated. With a sharp intake of breath, she judged him to be, even gravely injured, the handsomest man she had ever seen.

Strong, and evenly cut besides, each of his features fit

perfectly with the others so that the man's straight nose seemed
to complement his lean jaw which, in its turn, set off his square,
firm chin. Glancing up, Isabelle saw the Creator had also seen
fit to give the gentleman, who looked to be in his late twenties
or early thirties, quite thick, waving hair the color of antique
gold.

In the next moment, however, as her eye lit upon his blood-
stained shirt, Isabella quite forgot the man's startling looks. "Is
he bleeding badly?" she demanded, hurrying forward.

"Not so bad, miss," said the large man, who seemed the
spokesman of the pair of servants. " 'E's 'ad worse afore an'
lived."

Isabella ignored a sudden flaring of curiosity about the
wounded man's history. "I shall go at once and get some
bandages," she addressed the giant. "Our, ah, nurse, Cora
Geddes, will be here shortly to tend to your master. I hope you
will not be put off by her, sir, for though she may look the part
of an ancient crone, she is the best healer we have in this part
of Suffolk. Dr. Davies would not do half so well by your master,
for he is in his dotage."

To Isabella's surprise the man's lined countenance split into
a great smile. " 'Appen it'll take more'n a crone to put fear
in me, miss. And 'tis Jepson, I be. I was 'is lordship's batman
'til last year, when 'e come 'ome and now I'm 'is man's man.
This 'ere be Jennings, coachman to 'is lordship."

The other man, shorter and plumper than Jepson—surely the
most unlikely valet Isabella had ever imagined—turned to pull
his forelock in her general direction. A thousand questions
hovered on her tongue, but Isabella did not waste time asking
why they had traveled in such a storm, nor why the master and
not his seemingly fit coachman had been handling the reins,
nor even what their destination was.

"Come with me, Jennings," she said instead. "You can help
to bring up the things Cora will need."

Docile as a lamb, the coachman followed her out of the room.
They met Cora on the steps, and Isabella stopped to describe
what she had seen. The old woman, wizened and bent with age,
listened without speaking, her gypsy-dark eyes taking in the
coachman, who stirred uneasily as a result, before returning
to Isabella.

"I shall send up some bandages, hot water, and tea for Jepson. What else will you need, Cora?"

"The root salve for 'is wounds, basilicum powder, too, an' a poultice to keep off the fever. Naught else, but 'urry with the bandages an' water, lass. We'll be needin' 'em most."

Shooed like a chick, Isabella hurried off toward the kitchen, the coachman following in her wake. She found Jack at the hearth putting on water to boil, and after nodding to him, she continued on to the little room where Cora supervised her efforts to make medicaments from the herbs and roots they gathered in the nearby woods and fields. Thrusting a stack of bandages into the coachman's hands, she sent him back upstairs, and then went to gather the ingredients for the poultice Cora would need.

"Do go and take the water up, Jack," she directed, when it was sufficiently hot. "I shall stay here to make the poultice and some tea for us all."

Jack departed at once without giving any thought to waking Nell to help. He had been at Marsh House since the year before Mrs. Ramsey had died, and he knew Miss Isabella would forbid disturbing the maid whose chores began just after dawn, when she was already awake and could sleep as late as she pleased.

When Jennings returned to the kitchen, Isabella gestured toward a chair she had placed by the fire. "Sit down there, Jennings. I've a cup of hot tea for you."

The coachman darted an uncertain look at the chair, but Isabella would have none of his reluctance to be served by her. "I imagine you have had a dreadful night riding in that storm, Jennings. Go on, now. You deserve a seat and a hot cup of tea."

Isabelle gave him such a gentle smile, the coachman's stiffness drained from him. "Thank 'ee, miss. 'Twas bad, right enough," he said, sagging tiredly into the chair.

"Did you come from London today?" Isabella asked as she returned to stirring the brew for the hot poultice.

"Aye, miss," Jennings nodded slowly. "We set out late. Evenin' it was, but no rainin', though wouldn't 'ave mattered much, if it 'ad been. In the devil of a temper 'e was." The coachman dropped his voice as if he thought his master might hear and rise from his sickbed to direct that temper at him. "Drove the 'orses like a madman, 'e did, miss, and wouldn't hear of stoppin' when the storm come. Nae, on and on, 'e'd go with the wind 'owlin' and the rains lashin' us. The coach were like a prison," he confided, grimacing as he recalled the hours he had spent in the small, enclosed space of the lurching carriage.

With a shiver Isabella thought how the powerful winds and the lightning and the thunder even now made Marsh House itself feel vulnerable. "I do not doubt it was a very grim trip," she said with conviction. "But what was your destination, Jennings? There is not much out this way, you know."

"As to that I can't say. Never been this way afore, miss. But we was to Wynchley Abbey."

"Wynchley Abbey?" Isabella echoed, her surprise such that she waved her spoon in midair. "Are you certain, Jennings? It is owned by a gentleman who lives in India."

"That one's passed on, so Jepson says. 'Is lordship's to take the place now by 'is da's order." Under his breath Jennings muttered. "An none too 'appy about it, 'e is, I'd say."

Isabella heard, but did not press the coachman for further details. He had turned half from her so he faced the fire, and she guessed he regretted having been so talkative with a woman more of his master's station than his own.

Mulling over what she'd learned, Isabella could come to little conclusion. She knew nothing of the landlord who, though he had owned the estate next to her father's on the south ever since she could remember, had never once visited. As a child, Isabella had used the deserted abbey almost as a playhouse. She had imagined herself mistress of the great, old house and had run about curtsying to the two dusty suits of armor that stood in the great hall. Later, when she had grown older, she had made herself at home in the library.

Isabella frowned. She could no longer borrow from the extensive collection. Indeed, she could not even visit the estate. Quite suddenly the summer before, the land agent at Wynchley had forbidden her access to the estate. And Cora as well, though his tenants all relied on the old woman when they were ill. Isabella had protested the unprecedented move, sitting on the seat of her trap while the odious man glared down at her, but when Jaspar Willis had lifted his whip menacingly and growled, "I'll not have you an' that old witch pokin' around Wynchley matters again,'' she had had little choice but to turn her trap about.

Perhaps the gentleman above would not retain Willis. The thought pleased her, until she recalled how the agent could play the toady when it behooved him. She had seen him do it with her father. As a result, when she applied to the Squire to intervene with Willis, he had shrugged his shoulders and said Wynchley was none of his affair.

Jack's return interrupted Isabella's speculations. ''Cora says the gentleman's feverish but not mortal wounded, an' she'll be needin' the poultice now.''

''Very well, Jack. Help yourself to some tea, and then show Jennings and Jepson, if he wishes, to the spare room in the attic.'' Isabella turned to address Jennings directly. ''The room may be a trifle musty, I fear—we have not had a use for it in years—but it will be warm and dry enough.''

Jennings said gratefully he would be glad for any bed, and Isabella bid him good night only to turn back suddenly at the door. ''Dear me, Jennings! I forgot your horses. Will you need help getting them up from the road?''

''Nay, miss. We carried 'is lordship 'ere with their 'elp. I'll go 'n stable 'em now.''

''Good night, then.''

Isabella's soft knock on Peter's door brought Cora. ''Cracked 'is 'ead more'n a bit,'' the old woman answered Isabella's question before it was voiced. ''An' broke two, mebbe more, of 'is ribs. Cuts and bruises aplenty, too. Aye, 'e'll be sore as the devil tomorrow. But 'e's a strong 'un, lass. Ye needn't look so worried. 'E'll not die young. Now do ye go ter yer bed. 'Is man and me'll stay 'ere wi' 'im. Get yer rest.''

Weary to the bone, for she had been up since early that morning, Isabella trudged off to bed, but at first her sleep was fitful. Dreams of abbey disturbed her. Jaspar Willis was there with, of all people, her husband-to-be, Wrexham by his side. She was afraid until she saw the man of the carriage accident coming toward her. He was hackng at trees that threatened to strangle the drive when she came awake.

She smiled a little then, the vague sense of menace dispelled. Dreams could be fanciful, but it was true the gentleman would have difficulty getting his carriage through the overhanging trees. Like most everything else that did not profit Willis, directly pruning them had been neglected. Poor Lord Whomever. He'd take one look at the mess at Wynchley and hie back to town in as bad a humor as he'd left.

Chapter 3

"Why, it must be nearly nine o'clock, Nell!" Isabella blinked as the maid pulled back her draperies and bright sunlight flooded her room. "Whyever did you allow me to sleep so late?"

Hands on her broad hips, Nell assumed the air of a nanny addressing her charge. "Cora said ye was to sleep to nine, if ye could, Miss Bella. Said ye was up half the night with that gentleman what's in Master Peter's room. An' why ye did not call for me, I'll not know. 'Tis I'm the maid at Marsh House!"

As she threw back her covers, Isabella smiled, for Nell was her own age. "You sound more like Liza every day," she teased, prompting the maid to give a short, pithy snort. "And I did not awaken you, because I was already awake with Sarah. Now you understand, I do hope you'll leave off looking so grim and tell me how our guest is this morning."

Nell rolled her eyes to the ceiling as if she must ask for patience, but she was not proof against her mistress's smile. As she held out a dress, she reported that though the gentleman was sleeping, he had opened his eyes and spoken briefly just at dawn.

Isabella expressed her relief. "That is good news! His head injury cannot be too severe if he has regained his awareness. How are his other complaints?"

However, as Tuesday was baking day and Nell had been kneading dough all morning, she had nothing to add to Isabella's scant store of knowledge about the gentleman or his injuries. "I only know the coachman patched up the carriage good enow to return to Lunnon," she announced, then added, in answer to a query from her mistress, that Lady Prim was, indeed, at the breakfast table.

Eager to question the best source of information she had

available to her, Isabella hurried below. Lady Prim, or more fully Lady Millicent Primley, was the Viscount Wrexham's aunt. Left without two pennies to rub together after her husband was taken by a fever, she had appealed to her nephew for assistance, and he had sent her, forthwith, to Wrexham Hall. Accustomed to a life in town where she had a wide circle of acquaintances, Lady Prim had been close to wasting away from sheer loneliness with only her shy great-niece for company, and when Isabella had suggested that Sarah come to live with her at Marsh House so that she and her future daughter might come to know one another better, Lady Prim had been in alt to be included in the invitation.

As she approached the breakfast room, Isabella heard not only Lady Prim's gentle tones issuing from within, but her father's robust rumble as well. In counterpoint to both came a shrill, high-pitched bark. That was the voice of Lady Prim's dearest companion, Mr. Buttons, a fluff of Chinese extraction who had taken the squire into intense dislike from the instant of their first meeting.

"Madame! This infernal mutt will not cease and desist chafin' at my ankles!" The squire's protest sounded strangely muffled as if he spoke through clenched teeth. "I demand you bring him to heel!"

"But Mr. Buttons means you no harm, I assure you, William!" Lady Prim's voice conveyed real distress. "It is his intent merely to greet you. He quite likes you, you know."

"What he'd like is a taste of my skin, Millie! That's what he'd like!" The squire ws roaring now. "If I came rigged out only in my stockings, the beast would cheerfully breakfast on me!"

"In only your stockings, William! Why, never say you would come to the table half dressed."

A muffled exclamation that Isabella interpreted as an indication of possibly terminal frustration produced pity in her breast. Renouncing her position as eavesdropper, she entered the breakfast room.

At once Mr. Buttons raced to greet her with a series of piercing barks and excited leaps into midair. Bidding the tiny animal a good morrow, she swept him up and delivered him to the lap of his mistress, where she wished he might remain endearingly ensconced.

"Good morning, Lady Prim, Papa."

Lady Prim, her plump figure quite styllishly turned out in a blue silk, for she and her husband had lived well if not within their means, returned Isabella's greeting with a sweet smile. She was just about to ask if Isabella had managed to sleep well despite the storm, when the squire, having finally attained his place, exclaimed loudly, "Bella! What the deuce is all this nonsense about a carriage accident occurin' in the middle of the night?"

Before Isabella could reply, Liza burst through the door, crying, "Whatever can Nell mean saying there's a wounded gentleman in Peter's room, Bella?"

Isabella laughed as Jack put her breakfast plate of toast points and a rasher of bacon before her. "And to think that I thought I might be the one to announce the news," she said with mock chagrin. "But yes, Liza, before you burst with impatience, a gentleman was seriously hurt when his carriage overturned during the storm. I put him in Peter's room," this to her father, "where Cora and his valet, who, I warn you, is a great shaggy bear of a man, are tending to him." Isabella took in the four pairs of eyes—Mr. Button's bright, black ones gleamed with as much intense interest as anyone's—trained upon her and gave a rueful smile. "I am afraid I cannot tell you much more. The gentleman's name was given, but I heard little beyond Lord something or other and in the confusion forgot to inquire further. I only know his destination, which is curious in itself. He was bound for Wynchley Abbey. The man who has owned it so carelessly all these years has died, it seems."

"The abbey!" The squire's outburst startled Isabella. He seemed quite taken aback to learn the abbey would be in new hands, but she had not time to think on the oddness of his response, for Lady Prim spoke a man's name on a sigh.

"James Montcrief, poor thing! Odd to hear of his death this way," she murmured, shaking her head so the lacy edges of the little cap she wore over her gray curls fluttered. Then, seeming to realize she had spoken aloud, she looked up with an apologetic smile. "I am sorry, I did know James rather well once, but I wonder who can be above, then?"

The Ramseys waited in respectful silence as she gave thought to the matter, for she was only one of them who had the least hope of divining the answer. "Is he in his late twenties, Bella?" Lady Prim asked after a moment and when she received an affirmative response an excited light animated her very nice blue eyes. "Then, surely, it must be Julian Montcrief!"

"Who is he, Lady Prim?" Liza demanded, her enthusiasm sparked by Lady Prim's expression. "And who, for that matter, is James Montcrief?"

Lady Prim, seeing how attentively her answer was awaited, turned a pleased pink. "Well, now," she began, tipping her head to the side. "James Montcrief was the owner of the abbey, and the brother of Anthony Montcrief, the Duke of Chandley."

It amazed Isabella to learn that the abbey's remiss landlord was so highly connected. Like everyone in England who received a London journal, she had heard of the Duke of Chandley. She seldom read the several columns devoted to the doings of the *ton,* for she found tittle-tattle about people she had never met quite dull, but Liza always read them and often aloud whether her sister cared to listen or not. Having heard their names float by her ears innumerable times, Isabella knew the Duke of Chandley and his duchess were leaders among the highest society in town.

Somewhat to her surprise, she found her father had been as ignorant as she. "Never knew the man was Chandley's own brother," he muttered in an oddly fretful tone.

"James was younger than you, William," Lady Prim explained helpfully. "By the time you made your too infrequent trips up to town with Betsy, he had already left England for India, I believe it was."

"Then who is this Julian Montcrief we have upstairs?" Liza was more concerned with the present than the past. "Is he James's son?"

"Oh no, my dear!" Lady Prim exclaimed and wagged her head so firmly the curls peeking out from beneath her lace bobbed. "Julian Montcrief is son and heir to the Duke of Chandley. By title he is the Marquess of Roth."

"The Marquess of Roth!" Isabella looked at her sister in amazement. Liza's rosebud mouth had formed a perfect, astonished "O." "Roth!" Liza repeated, in the same breathless voice. "But he is the greatest rake!"

Lady Prim looked most unhappy. "I think that is a trifle harsh, child, though it is true. I admit, that Roth does not have a blameless reputation."

"They say no lady can resist him!" Liza cried, undaunted. "Ellie Basham told me he even fought a duel last Season and might have fought more, had the other husbands in town not feared his ability with a pistol."

Isabella realized she was not surprised to learn the man collected hearts. He was too handsome not to, but she did not like to hear her sister broadcast unfounded gossip. "I hope you do not repeat everything Ellie tells you, Liza. I do believe she would be hard put to tell you accurately what she had for dinner last evening."

The dry remark made Liza whirl to Lady Prim. "It is true is it not, Lady Prim?" she demanded.

Lady Prim cast Isabella a most apologetic look. "I fear Miss Basham did not exaggerate in this instance, Isabella." Liza shot her sister a triumphant look as the elderly lady continued, "Lord Roth has ever enjoyed success with the, ah, ladies, and I regret to say he did engage in a duel last Season, though in fairness I must add, he did not wound Mr. Markham, only sent his pistol flying from his hand."

The squire, having made short work of the sausage and eggs Jack had put before him, gave a dismissive grunt. "He's a town dandy then, Millie? The sort that frets over his neck cloth and his snuff and naught else?"

Isabella thought her father sounded almost hopeful, but if he was, and she thought it strange he would want such a fribble for a neighbor, he was disappointed. Lady Prim shook her head. "No, no, William. Roth is no dandy, though, of course he is ever dressed as . . ." Lady Prim's gaze slipped to the squire's rumpled coat, and Isabella watched, amused, as the impeccably attired elderly lady seemed literally to swallow whatever she had been going to say. " . . . Well, that is to say, he dresses as befits his station. He's more a Corinthian, you see, though some say he is too untamed to be called so. Still, however reckless he may have been as a younger man, it must be said to his credit that he served on the Peninsula. It was when his elder brother, Richard, died of an inflammation of the lungs, that he sold out his commission and returned to assume his duties as heir.'' A slow frown formed to mar Lady Prim's smooth brow. ''I cannot doubt the two years since have been a difficult time for him. He and his father have ever been at odds, Chandley being rather a stickler, you see, and as for his mother . . .'' Lady Prim sniffed. ''Caro Montcrief is too seldom in the habit of thinking of others to think to smooth relations between the two.''

Isabella's brow lifted in surprise. She had never heard Lady Prim speak so harshly of anyone, but the elderly lady, her cheeks rather flushed, was busy wiping crumbs from her lap though Isabella had not seen her eat a bite of toast.

Liza, who had no interest at all in either Roth's parents or Lady Prim's unspoken thoughts, bounced excitedly on her seat. ''Lady Prim, do tell! Is Lord Roth quite, quite handsome? Ellie said he made her feel faint when she was presented to him!''

''I cannot say I ever heard of a lady fainting before him, my dear,'' Lady Prim replied, looking up from her lap with a rather merry gleam in her eyes. ''But I will say this: in my day, we'd have termed Julian Montcrief a 'dangerously handsome' man.''

''Is the boy married off, Millie?'' the squire demanded, abruptly. When Lady Prim shook her head, he frowned upon his younger daughter. ''You are to behave yourself with him, girl! There'll be no goin' to his room on any account, unless you've your sister or Lady Prim with you.''

Liza looked quite put out at being told so obvious a thing, as if she were a scatterbrained child, and turned with a distinct flounce to address her sister. ''What of you, Bella? Did you think him monstrously handsome?''

''It was dark, Liza, and there was a great deal of distraction, but,'' Isabella smiled as her sister's brow lowered in vexation, ''I should say Lady Prim had it precisely right.''

''Why, thank you, my dear.'' Lady Prim gave Isabella a pleased smile. ''I do try to be accurate.''

Though Lady Prim had not meant to be ironic about her tendency to gossip, Isabella laughed. ''And you generally succeed,'' she said with affection.

"When do you think I shall be able to meet him, Bella?" Liza would know.

A vivid picture of the bloodstain on Lord Roth's shirt flashed in Isabella's mind. "He was badly wounded, Liza, and I cannot say how long it will take him to recover." Then, with some humor for the impossibility of what she would suggest, for after all it was not every day they'd a notorious, rakish—and handsome—peer of the realm languishing in their very house, she added, "I fear we shall simply have to be patient."

Chapter 4

"Do you think last night's rain heralds an end of the drought, Mr. Cummings?"

Isabella's principal tenant and most valued advisor rubbed his broad, weathered brow with a blunt hand. "I dunno, Miss Bella. Could mean an' end ta it or might not. This next fortnight should tell."

"And even then only God will know for certain?"

They both chuckled, though the issue of rain was, in fact, dreadfully serious. Were the drought to last another year, Isabella would not be able to pay off and last and final round of debts her father had incurred and that Wrexham's largess had not covered.

As it would not do to dwell on the unhappy possibility, however, she joked lightly with Mr. Cummings and he, aware of the lines of strain about her eyes, replied in kind. Knowing there was nothing for it but to gamble the rains would come as they ought, they then went on to decide where and when they would plant the oats and barley that were the mainstays of their produce.

Just as he was to go, Mr. Cummings paused. He knew his news would be an added burden upon the shoulders of the courageous girl, but he knew as well she would want to know. " 'Tis one more thing, Miss Bella. That family old Cora did nurse at Wynchley last year? The Prewitts they were?"

"Yes?" Isabella looked at him over the rim of her half spectacles. "Of course I remember the Prewitts. I'll not soon forget how brave their little Billy was. I truly thought Cora had lost him half a dozen times, but he fought the fever valiantly."

"Aye, I recalled how ye thought him a right sweet lad, and

believed ye'd want ta know his mother and two of his brothers have this influenza as is sickening everyone it seems.''

"That is bad news, Mr. Cummings! Mrs. Prewitt and the other boys will suffer, but they've the strength to recover. If Billy should contract it . . .''

Though Isabella left unfinished what might occur in that case, Mr. Cummings nodded. "Aye. The lad's been weak since his birth, for all he's a rare child. They're not able to go in to Dr. Davies in the village, as ye know, Miss Bella, but I'll see they get a basket from Cora, if ye have her ta make one up.''

"I'll do so at once, but how will you get by Willis?''

Mr. Cummings had as little liking as Isabella for the petty tyrant who ruled the abbey. "I've a boy can run it along to 'em quiet-like,'' he explained with a shrug, then frowned. "The Prewitts be a good family. Why, one of that name ha' lived at Wynchley time out of mind. 'Tis bad for 'em now they're under that man's thumb.''

"Why do they stay, Mr. Cummings? Why do any of the tenants endure him?''

Mr. Cummings shook his head. " 'Tis a question to study, Miss Bella. I dunno, but that he got 'em in his debt at the first somehows, and they've no choice but to stay on. Mayhap this lord's come to see to Wynchley, will improve their lot.''

"Yes, I hope so.''

But Isabella's hope was thin. From what she had heard of the marquess, she could not imagine he would wish to give up his mistresses and duels for long. How convenient to leave the long-neglected estate in Willis's hands and be gone. The thought brought her to the realization there was nothing for it but that she speak to her father. Though she did not care for the fact, she knew he was almost the only person in the neighborhood on any footing at all with Willis, and she hoped he might persuade the estate agent to allow Cora to make a visit to the Prewitts.

She found her father in his study as was usual after luncheon, for he often dozed there under the cover of reading the *London Journal*.

He was pleased to see her as ever, when she first settled herself on the ottoman at his feet. "Come to ask a favor have you, Bella? A new dress, perhaps? You've not asked for a single one, while Liza demands more than she could wear in her lifetime.''

''You mustn't fuss at Liza, Papa. She is going to town and will need them. I've come for something else altogether. It is about the Prewitts, the tenants at Wynchley whose little boy, Billy, I thought so dear. Do you remember? He'd have died of fever last winter, but that he was so brave and Cora a good nurse.''

Her father did not seem well pleased by the turn of the conversation. ''Mayhap,'' he grunted, his eyes shifting away from her.

Isabella felt her heart sink. Her father's tolerance for Jaspar Willis was entirely unaccountable and, it must be admitted, suspicious to her. She could not remember her father ever having the least patience with so harsh or crude a man.

''Billy Prewitt is in some danger again, Papa. He, himself, is not ill, but his mother and brothers have all contracted the influenza. I am afraid, if they do not recover quickly, he'll contract it from them and being as weak as he is, that he will not be so lucky this year as he was last.''

The squire's singularly thick eyebrows formed a belligerent ''V.'' ''And what have I to do with the abbey, pray tell?'' he demanded. ''It ain't my estate! Belongs to that buck lyin' upstairs, though I doubt he'll do more than glance once at it and be gone.''

''Papa! The marquess is no help, because he is ill. You cannot wish Billy harm, surely, and you are the only person in the neighborhood on any footing at all with Mr. Willis.''

The squire looked away from his daughter's expressive eyes. ''There's naught I can do, at any rate, missy,'' he grumbled. ''The man's away just now. But don't you go gettin' the idea to trespass! It's Willis's right to do as he pleases at the abbey.''

''Will you speak to him when he does return?'' Isabella persisted, the thought of Billy Prewitt's brave smile and quite pitifully thin body giving her little choice.

''We'll see then!''

Aware she would only anger her father if she said any more, Isabella took her leave. She would press him again later, when Willis had returned, and in the meantime she would send what she could of food and Cora's herbs through Mr. Cummings.

She was en route to the kitchens to ask Mrs. Hobbes, the cook, to save back food for the family, when she encountered Dobson in the hallway. His old face had always reminded her of one of her father's hounds, but now his look was even more sepulchral than usual.

"Sorry to say, Miss Bella," the old butler intoned grimly. "But Mrs. Smithby's come to call."

Dobson had dangled Isabella on his knobby knee when she was a child and had not thought it necessary as time passed to adopt a more formal attitude toward her. For her part, Isabella never thought to question their entirely comfortably relationship and now sighed, giving Dobson to understand he had been quite correct to suspect she would not be eager for a coze with the vicar's formidable wife. As stout and robust as her husband was thin and wispy, Mrs. Smithby had the officious habit of bustling, broad bosom forward, into the midst of her husband's parishioners' affairs—for their own good, of course. When she was not so altruistically engaged, she was with equal energy promoting the interests of her only daughter. Lettice, a pretty enough girl of about Liza's age.

Isabella guessed they could thank both traits for her prompt visit. Having heard through the servants' grapevine of Lord Roth's accident, Mrs. Smithby would think it her duty to make clear her recommendations for his care, and having heard in the same way of his title, she would think it her duty to Lettice to find out all she could about him. It would be a long visit, Isabella thought, unable to summon even a weak smile.

"Mayhap you'll want to know, though, Miss Bella, that Lady Prim has gone in with Mrs. Smithby, and Cora did send word down she's in need of you."

"You rogue!" Isabella admonished, causing Dobson's face to contort into the grimace that was his smile. She ought to have trusted that the old man, who had never cared for Mrs. Smithby since the first time she had looked down her thick nose at him, would have some excuse at hand for her. He generally did. "Well," she gave the old butler a cheerful smile, "I do hate to desert Lady Prim, for she is as fond of Mrs. Smithby as I, but I shall do her some extraordinary favor in the very near future. You must remind me, Dobson, if I should forget."

And so saying, Isabella took herself upstairs to the marquess's room, while Dobson creaked back down the hall to make her excuses to her visitor.

Julian opened his eyes slowly, lest he aggravate the painful throbbing in his head that seemed such a part of him he could scarcely remember ever having been without it. The old crone with the keen, dark eyes was not in her customary chair he saw when he looked that way. Carefully he lifted his gaze and after a scan of the room found the crone and a maid just at the door talking.

The effort to examine the first young girl he had seen, caused the throb to increase to a pound. His eyes drifted closed of their own accord, but he did not doze off as usual.

For the first time Julian found he had some recollection of the origin of all his hurts—even now an ache in his shoulder began to vie for attention with the pain in his head. He did not recall the accident that must have overtaken him, but he did recall being on the box of that blasted carriage with rain lashing his face.

He'd been quite foxed, of course. A rather foggy image of a table with empty bottles on it came to his mind. Peregrine Alynwick had been there, across the table. Ah yes, they had been in Perry's study.

Only a little effort was necessary to recall why he had gone around to his friend's in the middle of the afternoon, a bottle or two under his belt even then. His father's aloof, aristocratic features swam into focus.

The duke had been very angry, which was not unusual. "You are a disgrace to the Montcrief name!" he'd said as he had done often enough before. "Another duel! And that though Prinny himself spoke to you on the subject. Why I am shocked, I cannot conceive. You have never possessed the least notion of discretion or comportment."

Chandley had paused then, clenching his fists in an effort to control his emotions. The memory appealed to Julian, even on his bed of pain. As far as he knew, he was the only person who could cause his rigidly correct father to lose his composure.

Nor had the duke entirely succeeded at mastering himself. A flush had colored his pale cheeks as he glared down his nose at the man who lounged with seeming unconcern before him. Then, teeth clenched, he'd exclaimed, "I have had enough! Hear me and hear me well, Julian. You may be my heir and as such entitled to Kereford Castle and my title, but nothing else is entailed, and I shall not sit by and see the estate our ancestors amassed with prudence and good judgment pass to a wastrel who is good for nothing but bedding other men's wives! Every cent I possess I shall leave to the your cousin, Bertram— unless you can prove to me you are worthy of my fortune. Why I give you another opportunity to redeem yourself, I can scarce say, except that you are . . . my son.''

The pause had been infinitesimal, but a light so mocking had blazed to life in Julian's eyes, the duke wheeled about abruptly to help himself to a glass of brandy from a heavy decanter that stood on a tray to the side of his desk. He did not offer any to Julian, but took his portion in one swallow before he turned back. Julian had not moved, except that a single eyebrow was lifted as he waited to hear how his father would have him prove himself.

"My test is this: you will go to Suffolk to take over James's estate, Wynchley Abbey. The place has come to me as he, in his typical fashion, made no will. From what I can make out, no one has seen to the place in an age, and I do not doubt it is in the worst state. You will have one year from today to have everything from the books to the fields to every inch of the house in order. Succeed and you'll have earned my wealth. Fail, for any reason, and you'll be obliged to keep up your ducal seat with what wealth can be gotten from selling the kitchen garden vegetables.''

On his bed, Julian winced, though of course he had not so revealed himself at the time. No, before his father, he had, as usual, assumed the ironical smile that had the power to further incense his parent. "A test, Your Grace. How amusing.'' He had risen and made an elegant leg, he recalled, "I feel very like a knight of the round table off to seek the grail. Until I've got it, I bid you adieu, sir.''

The briefest wideningof his eyes had betrayed the Duke of Chandley. He had anticipated a furious argument, and in truth Julian had been quite as angry as his father had expected he would be—perhaps angrier. His revenge was to outdo his father on the very thing Chandley prided himself upon most: restraint.

After rousting out Perry and downing a goodly portion of his good friend's cellar, Julian had reeled off in an angry haze to Suffolk, though why he had risen to the duke's bait so rapidly he could not say.

He would need his father's wealth to live in any style at all, it was true, but he'd not disliked army life. He'd not have starved at least as he proceeded from one of His Majesty's wars to the next. Of course Kereford would have fallen to rack and ruin, and perhaps that was the rub. It seemed he'd a surprising amount of feeling for the old castle.

The effort of thinking what he was about and why made Julian restless. He opened his eyes again to find the young woman had come to sit in the crone's chair. She was rolling bandages, but despite the menial task, he realized she was not the servant he had thought. Her dress, though out of style by a bit, was of fine merino wool.

Julian struggled to recall what Perry had told him of the neighborhood as they had drunk to his future. Alynwick had on occasion visited another friend, a Francis Basham, who lived close to Wynchley Abbey, but it was no good. Julian had not listened closely, and whatever he had heard had been lost in a pool of claret.

Examining the young woman with a practiced eye, Julian determined she was no startling beauty, though she was not homely either. Pleasant enough, he decided, would be the judgment of the *ton*. Her skin looked to have more color than was fashionable, but it did not seem to be blemished, and her face had a quite nice, oval shape. Her features, if undistinguished, were even, while her mouth had a rather inviting, soft look to it.

As she was seated, he could tell little of her figure, but that her bosom was less than generous. A fond mama would tout her as slender, but though potential suitors might concede the point, they would not fall into raptures over her. Voluptuousness was all the rage—and for good reason, Julian thought, one corner of his mouth lifting as he recalled the lush curves of his last mistress.

From the edge of his vision, Julian saw the girl glance toward him. He moved his head slightly and found himself gazing into a pair of wide, clear eyes. Though they were fringed by long, heavy lashes he could see they were an unusual shade. Hazel, he imagined, they would be called, but in truth he was not certain. Their deep, mossy green flecked with gold was a color he had not see before.

The girl's steady regard held no hint of flirtation, a strange experience for Julian. He'd only a half second or so to decide, but he thought she looked upon him with more compassion than aught else.

"If I am smiling like a fool, it is because I've awakened to find I'm in a fairy tale where the old crone turns into a pretty girl. In fact, my head hurts like the devil." Julian's voice was rougher and weaker than he had expected it to be, but he was not disappointed by the effect of his effort. The girl's smile illuminated her face and rendered her more than merely ordinary.

Putting aside her bandages, she came to put a cloth that had been dipped in some essence on his brow. "Cora said this would help," she told him in a voice Julian found soothingly low.

He sighed. "That is very nice, indeed," he reported softly, savoring the feeling. Then, when the effects of the cloth wore off a little, he looked up to add innocently, "But I don't doubt the touch of your delicate hand, my lady, would produce an even more powerful effect."

The girl chuckled, a sound Julian liked so well he smiled. It was a crooked attempt, because his effort to indulge in a flirtation had set his head throbbing again.

"You are gammoning me, now, sir."

Julian wanted to continue his play with the girl. He'd the impression the gold flecks in her eyes were sparkling. "Not I. I am not so unscrupulous."

As his eyelids drifted down, he heard her reply, "Ah, but I have it on the best authority that you are, my lord," and wondered who the accurate authority could be.

Isabella stood quite still, staring down at the marquess's sleeping face. His face was handsome in repose, as she had known. But when he was awake, it was another thing altogether. She had not been prepared for the effect of his eyes. They were a crystalline blue-green: aquamarine to be precise, the color of the sea, though not the sea off Suffolk. She had once seen in a book a representation of the sea in some tropical place or other, and that was the color of his eyes.

The tropical sea with the sun sparkling on it, she amended, recalling how alive and vital his eyes had been, though he undoubtedly had been in pain.

When the door opened behind her, she fairly leapt around. " 'E awakened, did 'e?'' Cora asked before Isabella could say anything.

She did not inquire how the old woman knew. She was afraid the answer might have to do with the heat she could feel in her cheeks. She could scarcely believe she had been staring in that way at a sleeping man.

"Yes, but not for long, Cora," Isabella said, making every effort to be her calmly dispassionate self. "I laid the compress on his forehead as you suggested, and he fell off again."

Isabella returned Cora's steady, perceptive gaze, though she was not entirely certain what it was the old woman read in her eyes. Abruptly Cora nodded. " 'Tis good, 'en," she said, and Isabella chose to believe she meant that her treatment had been the correct one.

Chapter 5

"By Jove! Julian Montcrief's the fellow's came a cropper, eh?"

Isabella thought she ought not to be amazed at this further proof of the Marquess of Roth's fame. The speaker, retired Admiral Manning, a confederate of her father's who had come for dinner with his daughter, Pru, had kept a close account of the war effort through his contacts at the War Office. Still, it did seem half the country knew the man. And to her surprise, given what Lady Prim had related, what the admiral knew of the marquess was entirely exemplary.

"The man was a real officer," Admiral Manning exclaimed. "Led his men brilliantly! Wasn't one of those well-born dandies who point to the objective and shoo their men out before them. Not Montcrief! Led the way himself!

"When our men were losing ground at Talaveras, he rallied them single-handedly, urging his mount forward into the enemy lines and turning the tide of the battle. Afterward Wellesley begged him to come onto his staff, but the lad refused. Said too little was accomplished at headquarters to keep him occupied! What could the old man do then, but clap him on the back and send him out again?"

When the squire remarked something to the effect that the "lad" would, therefore, be dead set against the Frenchies, the admiral, in loud tones, proclaimed that was only obvious.

Isabella did not pay much note. She was remarking how prejudice had let her astray. Though she had only seen the marquess in a darkened room and lying down, she had seen enough to realize, had she been more open-minded, that his was not the sort of build developed behind a desk at headquarters.

Still, there were two sides to the man, as she was reminded when the ladies withdrew from the table. In the drawing room,

Pru, without the constraint her father's presence had imposed, was eager to address the less noble aspects of the marquess's character.

"Think how cool-tempered he must be!" she exclaimed the instant the ladies had arranged themselves. No one needed to ask who "he" was. "They say he is almost offhanded when he duels, and yet he cannot but be reckless. After all, he's fought two duels in a year's time."

"Two duels?" Liza breathed excitedly. "You are certain, Pru? I had heard only of one!"

Pru nodded her curly head emphatically. "One last Season, Liza, but I heard from my friend Miss Johnstone only this morning, that stories are flying all over town about a second duel."

Isabella wondered if it was news of the second duel that had prompted the duke to send his errant son off to Suffolk, for she recalled vaguely that the coachman, Jennings, had mentioned his master's father had something to do with their journey. She did not voice the thought aloud, however, for it was only supposition. Nor, interestingly, did she divulge that she had actually had conversation with the infamous man. For whatever reason she found she did not care to have the few sentences they had exchanged subjected to the intense scrutiny she knew they would receive.

Turning her mind quite easily from contemplation of that reluctance, she found herself listening quite closely to the description the voluble Pru gave of the wife of the man who had challenged the marquess to his last duel. "A raving beauty, with masses of flowing auburn hair and a very generous figure, if you know what I mean. Her husband's reputation with pistols had kept the gentlemen at a distance until Lord Roth came along." Pru rolled her eyes. "What a devil of a man! I should be in alt to meet him, but no matter how handsome he is, I could not want him for my husband. Just think how mortifying it would be to have him make a conquest of every woman in sight!"

"But, my dear, it is entirely possible Roth would not stray once he were married." Lady Prim flushed slightly before the look of astonishment Pru gave her, but she did not retract her remark. "Truly," she insisted in her gentle way. "I have seen in my time more than one rake reform very nicely after marriage. It only depended upon the woman he wed."

Liza pronounced herself in agreement with Lady Prim. "If the man's wife is attractive, he would have no need to roam," she remarked with the assurance of a greatly admired young girl.

Pru, more realistic perhaps, disagreed, pointing out that a man such as the marquess never kept a mistress above six months, though mistresses were, almost by definition, quite the most beautiful creatures. "And if he does not stay with such a beauty, why would he stay with a wife?"

With that reasonable question, she looked to her friend, but Isabella would not take sides, professing herself without the least notion whether the institution of marriage could reform a rake. She thought it only fair to be so circumspect, though both Liza and Pru decried her refusal to enter an opinion. She did not know the man, she said, which was true, though to herself she did remark that she had little hope for the rake under discussion. After all, any man who could manage some flirtation even when he was racked with pain could not, she thought, be considered a candidate for constancy.

Weary of a sudden of the topic, she turned to smile at Pru. "Enough of a marquess who will very likely leave us before we've any chance to know him. Tell us, instead, dear Pru, about the Assembly you attended in Ipswich last week. Liza says you stood up twice with a certain gentleman."

"Liza, you are telling tales upon me!"

"Not so, Pru! You did stand up with Francis Basham twice. Ellie and I only reported what we could see."

Pru giggled, and Isabella could see she was not the least affronted. Quite the contrary, her eyes had taken on a particularly bright sparkle. "Mr. Basham was most attentive, I admit!"

"Do you think he intends to ask your father if he may pay his addresses?" Liza asked eagerly, and Pru significantly colored.

"I cannot say, of course." Her attempt to be demur did not last over half a second. "But he did ask me to ride out with him yesterday!" she added, quite obviously delighted.

Liza had a dozen more questions to ask, all of which Pru parried to one degree or another, but it was obvious from the blush in her cheeks, she was hopeful. For Isabella it was an odd moment, though she showed nothing of her ambivalence. Outwardly she demonstrated all the pleasure she felt for her friend. Only inwardly did she feel a certain heaviness overtake her. Pru's shining countenance was the very picture of what a young woman in love should look like, and the contrast with the quite contained look Isabella had worn during the time of her courtship could not but bite just a little; though Isabella did scold herself for so foolish a feeling.

"What an exciting spring this is!" Liza remarked, though Pru had admonished her not to exaggerate the importance of two dances and a ride. "There is the possibility," she grinned at Pru, "of something between you and Francis, and there is the certainty we shall all meet the Marquess of Roth."

"Will that be soon do you think, Bella?" Pru asked, for her interest in Francis Basham had not rendered her immune to a desire to meet the infamous marquess.

"Cora says only, ''E's doin' as well as can be expected," Isabella replied with a bit of smile. "I am not certain what that translates into, though I should think it would be over a week before he is out of bed."

Though the marquess did not, in fact, leave his bed for almost a week, a series of events were to lead Isabella to his bedside the next day.

Jack awakened feverish in the morning, and after Cora diagnosed influenza, Isabella had him moved to the attic nearer to Annie so that Cora might have an easier time nursing her two patients. Left with only Nell and Mrs. Hobbes for servants—Dobson and their gardener, a man of Dobson's age, did not count for much assistance—Isabella went along to the kitchens to discuss the pinch they were in, when Jepson overheard and offered with one of his broad smiles to help in any way he could.

Isabella had just seen him settled upon a stool in Mrs. Hobbes's kitchen and returned to her desk and her books, when quite suddenly the stable yard erupted in a fury of howls and barks and shouts.

The first sight that met her eye when she rushed out the kitchen door was a mild disaster. Over half the bed linens washed and hung out to dry earlier that morning by Nell lay strewn upon the ground, their pristine whiteness streaked with the dirt of the yard. She had time only to cry out at the sight before the baying of her father's hounds, intermixed with the cries of humans, and significantly a single, more piercing bark drew her to around the corner of the house.

"Catch 'em! There 'e goes now o'er by the chickens!" Jepson directed in a booming voice, while he struggled to lock the gate on the kennel where her father's hounds were kept.

They were baying as if a fox had gotten in their midst, but Nell heard her orders, and Isabella saw her run to the chicken coop, where the chickens had set up a wild, raucous squawking. Feathers flew, chickens made frantic, ungainly efforts to lift themselves from the ground, and Nell loudly berated the instigator of the chaos.

Isabella knew his identity from the shrill, entirely delirious barking he had set up, and in the next moment she actually caught sight of Mr. Buttons.

"No!" Nell wailed fruitlessly, as the small, energetic form darted between her legs and out of the coop. His black eyes gleaming with excitement, the little dog stood still, and taking stock before catching sight of Isabella, he dashed off in the opposite direction. Jepson, having secured the hounds, made a dive for him, but Mr. Buttons proved himself as agile as he was speedy. Easily evading the man ten times his size, he made for the dark of the stables.

Jepson dusted himself off, muttering a string of words that could only have been curses but were too low to hear distinctly, then set off in pursuit, with Nell puffing visibly behind him.

Isabella laughed as she looked about. It seemed the only appropriate response to the monstrous havoc so tiny a dog had managed to create. And then she began to gather the grimy bed linens from the ground, laying them across the line as she went. When Mrs. Hobbes trotted out into the yard, she was not so amused by the devastation and seeing only the image of a body behind the sheets, did not stop to confirm the identity of the person she addressed.

"Nell!" she cried impatiently. "Ye'll have to leave off with them sheets. Cora said the gentleman was to have his broth at half past, but the time's slipped away what with that scrap that ain't even a dog makin' such a mess . . . Miss Bella!''

Mortified to have been caught criticizing her mistress's guest, even if only by implying that the lady's dog was not worthy of the name, Mrs. Hobbes flushed painfully, but Isabella chuckled sympathetically. "I quite agree, Mrs. Hobbes. These sheets are bad enough, but if his escapade results in injury to Jepson, I shall not forgive him."

The thought of great Jepson bending low enough to catch the little dog one tenth his size made Mrs. Hobbes snort, her version of a laugh. "Belike Lady Sarah'd do a better job o' catchin' him," she reasoned.

Isabella nodded at once. "Of course! I'll fetch her—and take the marquess's tray up when I go."

"Nay, Miss Bella. 'Tis Nell's work!"

Isabella disregarded the good woman's dismay and taking her plump arm, ushered her into the kitchen. "This is it?" she asked, lifting a tray with a covered bowl and several slices of bread upon it. "See," she smiled at the cook, "it is no trouble to lift. And there is no one else to do it," she added realistically. "Jack and Annie are ill, you are preparing luncheon, and Jepson and Nell are giving chase."

Having fortuitously encountered Sarah upon the steps and dispatched the child on her mission of capture, Isabella was smiling as she nudged open the marquess's door with her foot.

"Eh! What's this Bella? Are you actin' the part of a servant?"

It was not the surprise of finding her father in Lord Roth's room that caused Isabella's heartbeat to accelerate suddenly. She had not exaggerated when she said Cora's reports as to the marquess's progress had been sketchy at best, and she was not at all prepared to find the man not only awake, but actually sitting up with the assistance of several pillows.

Steady, he is only a man, Isabella, she admonished herself as she sought out her father's familiar, rumpled figure, receiving only a blurred impression of a white smile. "Papa, I did not expect you here. I hope you have not been taxing our guest beyond his limits?"

" 'Course not!'' Her father exclaimed, as Isabella reminded

herself to put one foot in front of the other that she might advance into the room. "The lad was bored to tears with only the old crone to keep him company."

"I was glad to have the company, Miss Ramsey."

Now that he was alert, Isabella found the marquess's smile decidedly more powerful than it had been when she had first encountered it. Likely it was that his skin had lost its chalky color and regained a rather more bronzed tone than Isabella would have expected it to have, given the fairness of his hair. The contrast between his skin tone and his strong, white teeth made his smile flash with particular effect.

"I am glad to see you so much better, my lord," she said, and was relieved to hear that, although she addressed quite the handsomest man she had ever seen—a man who was besides a rake accustomed to beautiful and accomplished women—her voice sounded if not precisely normal, at least passably low.

"What was all that racket in the yard, Bella?" the squire would know. "Sounded as if all the hounds in the kennels had got loose."

The question had the happy effect of distracting Isabella as she settled the marquess's tray upon his lap and giving her reason to stand back quickly so that she might address her father.

"All that racket was the doing of Mr. Buttons, Papa. Somehow he escaped from Lady Prim and got out into the yard where one or two of your hounds, I suppose, mistook him for a rabbit and gave chase. They made short work of the bed linens Nell had only just hung out to dry, I'm sad to report, and it may be some time before the chickens are sufficiently calm to give us eggs."

The marquess, she saw when she looked, was enjoying the glass of claret Cora allowed him. At the same moment she realized he wore a sling. It was rather disconcerting to Isabella to realize she had not noted the quite obvious thing earlier.

"Your man Jepson, my lord, obligingly joined with Nell to give chase, and I do hope he does not come to regret his impulse, for I fear he shall have bruises to show for his efforts. The last I saw, the entire party had headed off in the direction of the stables."

"The stables!" Squire Ramsey billowed. "Good heavens,

he can get into the worst sort of mischief there. But wait! With any luck one of the horses will cuff the little devil so hard he's sent to kingdom come! You cannot imagine, Lord Roth, what a curst runt the thing is. Egad! He's too small for anything but sinkin' his teeth in an ankle! What you were about to let Lady Prim bring the creature here, Bella, I do not know.''

"You are quite right, Papa,'' Isabella admitted, a twinkle suddenly lighting her eye. "I am too soft a touch. But you are not. As master here you've every right to inform Lady Prim her dearest pet is a nuisance and have the carriage brought 'round for him.''

"The carriage!'' Squire Ramsey thumped the arm of his chair. "That is the problem with that pitiful excuse for a dog. Spoiled rotten, that's what he is!''

Isabella smiled outright at the way her father had taken the bait. "You must say so to Lady Prim, Papa. As you are an acknowledged authority on dogs, I am certain she will listen to you.''

"Hmpf!'' The squire rose ponderously from his seat. "Wouldn't ever hear the end of it, if I complained as I should,'' he groused. "Millie'd have a fit of the vapors, likely. Women!'' He glared fiercely down at the marquess. "They can be more trouble than they're worth, boy,'' he advised, forgetting momentarily the extensive knowledge of females the man he addressed was reputed to possess.

The marquess laughed, but Isabella had only the briefest moment to enjoy the fully amused sound before she took in what her father was about.

Even as she began to call out to him to stay him with some remark or other, anything, he waved amicably to the marquess. "I'll leave you to your luncheon, boy, and return betimes with a nip of brandy to see you through your aches.''

Chapter 6

"I find it little wonder you are out of patience, Miss Ramsey. Here we are alone together for a second time, and we have yet to be formally presented."

The amused remark went a great way toward restoring Isabella's sense of proportion. For just a moment, as she had watched her father's broad back disappear from sight, she had experienced something very like a sense of panic. She had never in her life been left alone with a strange gentleman, and this one was a notorious rake still in his bed.

Her mouth curving just a little, she gave him something of a curtsy. "I am Miss Isabella Ramsey, my lord."

He laughed aloud, and this time she was able to appreciate the rich sound as well as the way the marquess's eyes danced, when he was well and truly amused. "And I am Julian Montcrief. My friends call me Julian."

"As they are allowed to do, but I must address you as Lord Roth."

He responded to that prim remark with a lopsided smile she found very appealing. "At least you are smiling just a little, Miss Ramsey, which is more than I expected given the fact that your father mentioned you've living with you an elderly widow fresh from town who, as the squire put it, 'knows a thing or two' about me. Considering the sort of gossip I don't doubt you heard, I rather thought you might be looking upon me as Satan Incarnate."

The deliberate exaggeration disarmed Isabella so entirely she chuckled. "Lady Prim is most forgiving, actually, and only named you a thoroughgoing rake, my lord."

Julian made a wry face at that, though in the main he was enjoying watching his hostess. She'd a very lovely smile. "I am glad I got off so lightly, for I am going to ask a decided favor of you, Miss Ramsey. I cannot manage my spoon well with my right arm in this blasted sling, you see, and as Jepson is otherwise occupied, I hoped I might prevail upon you to help me.''

It took Isabella a full second to realize he wished her to feed him. To her dismay she felt her cheeks heat.

"Truly I shall be the model patient," he assured her with only the faintest twinkle in his eye to give her pause. "I did try drinking from the bowl last evening but only managed to spill half the contents over myself, a most frustrating experience, I assure you."

Isabella could see it might be. "I shall advise Mrs. Hobbes to serve your broth in a cup," she remarked perhaps a little stiffly as she went to take a seat by him.

Julian was very bad then, for he grinned as she perched herself gingerly just at the edge of his bed as if she held herself ready to spring. That most amused expression, informing her as it did that he had read her thoughts, caused Isabella to blush more deeply.

Annoyance overcame her awe. "Really, my lord, it is too bad of you to put me to the blush so. I am not accustomed to rakes at all. Or even gentlemen much for that matter," she added on a honest afterthought.

Julian's laugh was genuine. "I think you are rare, Miss Ramsey, for it is my experience women are eager to exaggerate their experience. But I see you do not care to be told how rare you are, and so in the interests of having my broth before it is stone cold, I shall leave off telling you what I think."

As what Julian thought included a distinct sense of appreciation for the softness of the rounded hip just touching his thigh through the bedclothes, it was as well he did fall silent. Isabella was having enough difficulty adjusting to how very intimate a thing it was to feed another person.

Sitting before Julian as she was now, she had an altogether different sense how wide his shoulders were than she had had when she was looking down on him from above. No, he'd not have done desk duty in the army.

"Did Papa tell you more than you care to know about the neighborhood, my lord?" she said rather hastily.

"Not at all. He only spoke a little of the neighborhood and some of your household. He informed me that your sister is soon to go to town for her come-out and that I am in possession of your brother's room, because he is away at school. But he did not get to you, Miss Ramsey. Do you go to London with your sister? She is the younger is she not?"

"Yes to the second question, but no to the first."

"Ah, you have had your come-out, then? It could not have been last year, or I'd have met you." He smiled. Her hand was close enough she could have traced with her finger the curve at the corners of his mouth. "And remembered."

Isabella put an end to such empty flattery by placing the spoon on his lips. "You think to turn me up sweet, my lord, but it won't do. I know from Lady Prim that Almack's would be deadly dull to a rake not interested in marriage."

Julian's mouth twitched. "You have well and truly caught me out, Miss Ramsey. I cannot imagine a deadlier place than Almack's. But if you do not go to town with your sister and had to rely on hearsay to know the truth of the hallowed Assembly rooms, then I take it you had a successful come-out locally and are engaged to a sober, young gentleman from Suffolk who watches you closely."

Julian observed the color rise in Isabella's cheeks, but had not long to wonder what had made her uncomfortable. His description of her betrothed could not have been further from the mark.

"Actually I did not have a come-out, my lord," she said quietly, avoiding his eyes as she continued to lift his spoon to him. "Shortly after I came out of mourning for my mother, I received an offer from the Viscount Wrexham. His estate marches with ours."

Julian had been accomplished since boyhood at hiding those emotions he did not care to reveal, and so he betrayed none of his surprise. He only said in a neutral voice, "I see," and accepted more broth.

Perhaps he had not been quite as emotionless as he'd thought. He found when he looked up that Miss Ramsey's wide, very clear hazel eyes studied him. She left off her scrutiny, however, when their eyes met and changed the subject, taking time to thank Julian for allowing them Jepson as a replacement for Jack.

He replied, evenly, that given the care he was receiving, the least he could do in return was to have Jepson appointed dogcatcher.

She smiled, and the subject of her betrothed no longer lay between them, though it did occupy Julian's mind for a bit. It was true he was little acquainted with Wrexham, but he did have a notion as to the man's age, and he knew with more certainty the man had a reputation for cool hauteur in public and rather excessive license even for Julian's tastes in the boudoir. An image of the two high flyers Wrexham had had on his arm at a certain masked ball came to mind.

And was mentally shrugged aside. Obviously it was a marriage of convenience, and he was cynical enough about his fellow man to observe to himself that Miss Ramsey must stand to gain in some way from the match, or she'd have refused the viscount.

"Tell me a little of the abbey, if you will, Miss Ramsey. Your father said my uncle did little to keep up the house."

"I do not know who is at fault," Isabella replied carefully. "But it is true the abbey has been neglected, which is a shame, for it is quite a fine house." She went on to tell some of its history. It had been one of the smaller abbeys before Henry had seized it and awarded it to a favorite, but it was a quite nice one and had been kept up exceedingly well by all its succeeding owners but for the last. "I am afraid now there is a great deal to be done, if you would restore it. The gardens are quite overgrown, of course, and five years of neglect have taken their toll. But if you wish to reclaim it, I believe you will be well rewarded. The cloister garden with its stone work is particularly lovely."

"And how long do you think it would take to restore the house, Miss Ramsey? Under a year?"

Julian had finished his broth, and she sat quietly thinking a minute. "Yes, I should think a year would do sufficient, if your effort is great. But if you think merely to instruct the land agent to see to it, the work will take longer."

"Your voice cooled distinctly upon mention of the land agent, Miss Ramsey. I believe your father gave his name as Jaspar Willis."

Isabella met the marquess's eyes and was surprised to see his regard had a keen edge now. "I do not like the man above half, my lord," she confessed. "But I had not thought to prejudice you, truly. And now is not the time to discuss him, for I must go."

"You intend to leave me just when you have whetted my curiosity?" Julian chided, only to add as he felt weariness rise in him, "But, devil it, I'm growing tired as a babe. I wish you will return later this afternoon to satisfy me on the subject of Mr. Willis, however."

"I would like to, my lord, believe me, but I've a meeting for the church bazaar to attend."

Julian smiled at her woeful expression. "I see I shall have to languish in boredom while you are martyred to a sense of duty."

"You cannot know how correct you are," Isabella replied, but spared him the details of how particularly officious Mrs. Smithby could be when she headed a planning meeting. "Still, you needn't suffer, my lord. If you are bored, you have only to call for Lady Prim. She would be in alt to sit with you."

"She is the gossiping widow? Your father's contemporary?"

Isabella smiled. Panic, fleeting perhaps but unmistakable nonetheless, had flitted across his handsome face. "Lady Prim will take her lead from you, my lord. If you do not care to gossip about yourself, she will forebear, and she does adore to play at cards. Truly, I think you will find her amusing. Or rather," she amended, realizing belatedly how different they were, "I would find her so. If you do not, you could always give the excuse that you are fatigued."

"Surely you are not suggesting I stoop to lying, Miss Ramsey?"

She grinned suddenly, her face lighting. "Positively decadent, am I not? Be warned, Lord Roth, or we shall ruin you down here in the country."

Julian laughed aloud. "Hope at last," he teased, and watched, amused, as her cheeks heated becomingly. "But why can I not have you, Miss Ramsey, after you have acquitted your charitable duties? I know we suit."

That last was the purest flattery Isabella told herself sternly, and the way her heart tripped only meant she was no match at all for him. "I've other duties, aside from the church bazaar and must see to them. But I'll not disappoint you on the subject of Jaspar Willis. Until later, my lord.''

Julian watched as she proceeded to the door, her rounded hips swaying gently, and waited until she was just there to call out, ''Enjoy your bazaar meeting, Miss Ramsey.''

A smile, entirely bright, though it came to him from across the room, met his sally. ''I imagine it will be rather more mundane than bizarre, but thank you, my lord. Enjoy your hour—or so—with Lady Prim.''

Chapter 7

As it happened, Isabella did return to the marquess's room that afternoon and only some two hours after she had left him. She went to say that Lady Prim was not available to sit with him, for the elderly lady had agreed to accompany Liza and two of her friends into nearby Arderby, a town a degree or two larger than Saxbourne village, to browse in that town's larger shops.

"I have brought you some books in her place, my lord."

To which Julian added, smiling, "And yours, Miss Ramsey."

Isabella had thought on Roth's smile quite a bit in the two hours she had been out of its sway. His smile and his grin were both quite powerful, and knowing that to a nicety, he used them to effect. Certainly they affected her. Even now her pulses had quickened in a way novel to her.

Nonetheless, she'd the sense the marquess had reined in his ability to charm. He played with her, true, but gently as a grown mastiff will with a pup.

She was, she told herself, relieved he did not find her so attractive he wished to sweep her off her feet. She was a betrothed woman, after all, and his lack of "that sort" of interest in her made for much easier relations between them.

"We've nothing half so contemporary in our library as either myself or Lady Prim," she informed with a half smile. "Here is a volume of poetry—everyone from Shakespeare to Gray is represented in it, I think. For a novel I brought you Goldsmith, and for something more serious there are two books on agriculture. Here is Charles Townshend, helpful but wordy, and another by Arthur Young."

"You wish to make a farmer of me, Miss Ramsey?"

Mr. Cummings's stolid, weathered countenance came to Isabella's mind. "I believe that would be rather beyond my powers, my lord," she returned, a twinkle in her eye. "I only brought the books along in the event that you are interested in general theory and good practice."

"And you do not think my land agent so excellent a man his methods would teach me good practice?"

"I admit I do not. Indeed, I believe quite the opposite. Jaspar Willis is more likely to deplete the land, if he sees he may reap a quick profit."

"But what is the harm there?" Julian asked, intrigued by the way Isabella's expression cooled at the mere mention of this Willis. "Surely he is entitled to some reward."

"I am certain Jaspar Willis would not have taken a position that was not properly salaried, my lord. Yet, though he was employed to husband the land, he plants wheat year after year in the same field simply for the immediate profit the army will pay him and not caring in the least that his practice leaches the soil. Eventually it will play out and be of little use of anyone for generations. By that time, however, Willis will have pocketed his gains and disappeared."

Isabella bit her lip, when Julian did not respond at once. She did not know much of the highest reaches of society, but she did know that even in her corner of Suffolk young ladies did not carry on about farming practices. "Forgive me, my lord. I did not mean to get on my high horse. You must think me quite a wonder to carry on so about mere soil."

"Fie on that, Miss Ramsey," Julian said readily. "We shall go on a great deal better if you remain in the habit of saying what you please to me. It makes, as in this instance, for far more interesting conversation than the usual chatter about weather or styles or the latest *on-dits*. If anyone were to hold themselves up to criticism, I should. I've never given the least thought to the soil, though it has supported me most luxuriously."

Isabella tipped her head, studying him, for no one of her acquaintance, but for Pru and Mr. Cummings, had ever cared to speak of agricultural practices, and she could scarce credit a notorious rake would.

He laughed. "You look quite amazed, Miss Ramsey."

"Oh, well, I did not mean to doubt you, sir!"

"But they seem unlikely sentiments for a rake?" He shrugged

lightly. "As it happens, I've reason just now to be interested in agriculture, Miss Ramsey. And, having played the truant when I was young, I know nothing whatsoever about it. Your interests and mine, as you must see, therefore, coincide very happily."

She was not certain she did see or even that he meant her to do so entirely, for his remarks had been rather elliptical in all, so she made no effort to resist his smile. "In that case, my lord, I shall leave you to agricultural theorists who know a great deal more than I."

Over the course of the following days. Julian was to learn a great deal about Miss Isabella Ramsey besides the fact that her interest in agriculture was not the least assumed. Lady Millicent Primley did knock gently upon his door the next morning and inquire with a rather charming mixture of graciousness and fluttery awe, if she might entertain him with a game of cards.

Julian paused the length of time it took to blink an eyelid, then smiled a welcome. He was bored, bored to tears, really, for he was an active man, and he could only hope the elderly gossip might divert him.

It seemed a likelier possibility, however, that the woman would be the deadliest bore imaginable and would grate far more on his nerves than his books and journals, hence the hesitation before he bade her enter.

It took only a little time for Julian to concede the point to Miss Ramsey. Lady Prim, as she begged him to address her, did indeed play a challenging hand of piquet, and possessed, happily, wit enough not to be deadly between hands. A gentle, gracious woman of good taste, she did gossip but never with malice, and restless as he was, Julian found himself listening with some interest to what she'd to say of the household in which he found himself.

From Lady Prim he learned, whether directly or not, that Miss Liza was a pretty flirt with something of a temper; that Peter Ramsey was a dreamy scholar without a care in the world but his books; and that Squire Ramsey was a most amiable fellow whose interests were confined to games of chance: his hounds, and his horses.

He learned as well that the whole lot relied upon the elder daughter to keep them afloat. The discovery took Julian aback, for he was not accustomed to young women managing even their own affairs, much less their family's. Indeed, he could not quite believe he had heard correctly when Lady Prim informed him why they would see nothing of Isabella that day. "She is with Mr. Cummings, a most helpful, trustworthy man. I imagine they are deciding something about the spring planting," she added rather absently as she studied the cards in her hand.

"The spring planting?" Julian echoed. It was one thing for a country-bred girl to have a passing acquaintance with agricultural theory, but quite another for her to be the implementer of those theories.

Called to account, Lady Prim looked suddenly anxious. "I forget, I fear, having resided here all these months, how, ah, unusual the household is in some respects. Isabella, you see, manages the estate."

Julian was, by then, on quite good terms with his companion. And, though he could see she was discomfited at where she had taken the conversation, she had piqued his interest. He cocked his head and smiled at her. "You may as well tell me the whole, my dear lady. You'd be cruel to leave me with no explanation for what, you must admit, is a startling announcement."

Lady Prim's cheek turned a bit rosy, though whether she was put to the blush at being called Roth's "very dear lady" or by his persuasive smile, or both, it was difficult to say. "It does startle, I cannot but allow. Isabella is young and a lady, but she's very capable. And you must not think too badly of William!" she begged, the very request implying some laxness on the squire's part. "Without Betsy by his side he became a trifle unsteady, and . . . well, I believe he was the first to agree that Isabella would do rather better with matters than he had done. I cannot speak highly enough of the child, really. She is quite, quite rare."

"You need not look so concerned, Lady Prim. I assure you that I shall not think badly of Miss Ramsey because she does not while away her days doing lamentable watercolors or stitching crooked samplers."

Lady Prim smiled, looking most relieved, and conceded he had read her thoughts aright. "I am glad. I should not want to give anyone a wrong impression of Isabella. Indeed, I believe she is a cut above most other young women of her age, and I am very pleased my nephew had the wisdom to choose her.''

Julian, to himself, did not argue her characterization or Wrexham's choice. Miss Ramsey was not at all in Julian's style, but she would, he imagined, make a worthy wife. And a quite acceptable mother of an heir, for he did not mistake the reason the viscount had chosen to become, after six years of freedom, leg-shackled again.

Julian could also understand why the squire would promote the match. His daughter would marry a title, and if she were in residence a good deal of the time in Suffolk, he would retain his estate manager.

That only left the girl's reason for accepting the viscount. The squire might be a self-centered man, but he did not appear to be the sort who would drag his daughter to the altar against her will.

Julian did not dwell on the puzzle. He had his cards to play, his books to read, journals to peruse, and Jepson to needle; but there were long, long hours to be passed, and he did, on occasion, find himself thinking of Miss Ramsey. He'd not have given her a second look in town, but then there would have been a host of other older, more experienced and more shapely woman on hand to distract him in London. And, besides, he was not thinking to bring the girl to his bed. She was merely on hand, and having the happy distinction of being different from the common run was a relief from his boredom.

It was some two days after she had dropped off the books that Julian actually saw Isabella again. When he did, he gained some further insight into the question of what she stood to gain by marriage to the Viscount Wrexham, though it was a while before he could credit the girl would give herself up to the man for such a reason.

Julian's first visitor that afternoon, after Lady Prim, was the squire. Normally loquacious and even amusing in his blustery way, Ramsey's manner was most abrupt that day, when he threw open the door. ''Pardon me, Lord Roth!'' he boomed rather perfunctorily before rounding upon Lady Prim with such a scowl her hand went to the pearls at her throat. ''By Jove, Millie, I cannot make heads nor tails of what Wrexham's chit tries to

say! She's bawlin' about Bella. Seems to think she's late and
that she's at the Prewitts? Is't true?''

Julian could not but wonder who the Prewitts were to merit
such thunderous disapproval, and he was further intrigued to
see Lady Prim look discomfited. ''Isabella did say she meant
to take a look in on several of your tenants who have contracted
the influenza, William, but as to the Prewitts, I, I cannot say.''

In her distraction Lady Prim forgot to hold to Mr. Buttons.
It was an error. Displeased to have been roused from a pleasant
doze, her dear companion leapt to the floor with a growl, and
before the squire could turn his thoughts from his daughter, the
tiny dog leapt high in the air to nip his enemy's fleshy thigh.

''Fiend!'' the squire roared. His attention quite captured, he
lashed out at his attacker with a booted foot. Lady Prim
attempted to intervene then, but Mr. Buttons had enjoyed his
taste of flesh too well. Yelping shrilly, he assaulted the other
thigh.

''What in the name of heaven goes on here?''

When Mr. Buttons flung himself out of the squire's orbit and
upon her, Isabella captured him but did not accord the little
fellow even a brief glance, though he licked her hand enthus-
iastically. ''Papa, I could hear you from the moment I entered
the house.''

Julian listened with only half an ear as Isabella remonstrated
with her parent. She had come to rescue him from an excess
of noise without taking the time to change from her riding dress.
By its style, Julian guessed it had belonged once to her mother,
and he was reminded of Lady Prim's hint that the squire had
not managed his finances well after his wife's death. Yet, though
the dress was not of fashion, its warm sable color brought out
the gold in her eyes, and its close fit displayed her waist. Long
and willowy, it looked to be the width of a hand span.

''That cur's the one at fault!'' the squire cried bitterly. ''Bit
me, Bella, and in my own house! You can't expect me to stand
by meekly and let him draw blood! And where were you, may
I ask? At the Prewitts?''

When Mr. Buttons was moved to growl menacingly in her
defense, Isabella gave him to his mistress. ''I think perhaps Mr.
Buttons needs some air, do you not, Lady Prim? Papa's voice
seems to send him into the boughs.''

"Oh, my dear, I cannot think why he makes such a to-do over your father!" Lady Prim looked most undone. "Truly, he was a dear all afternoon, and then . . ." She did not finish the sentence, but turned to give a flustered little nod in Julian's direction. "I shall return to finish our game tomorrow, Lord Roth. William . . ."

"Beast," the squire muttered under is breath, as the dog was carried by him, but he did not forget his grievance with Isabella and turned to her in the next breath. "Well, missy? Did you trespass?"

"Papa, I cannot think Lord Roth's room is the place to carry on like this."

Julian watched half amused as the squire turned quite red, for, though he could scarcely dispute that he had chosen an inappropriate place to take his daughter to task, he was not given to patience.

Afraid, perhaps, that her father might literally burst with impatience, Isabella conceded quietly, "I did go to the Prewitt's, Papa, but you needn't be concerned. I saw Willis, and we . . . came to an agreement."

"Willis agreed to your visit?"

Julian recognized his estate agent's name and frowned, though in the next moment his expression lightened. He knew evasion when he saw it, and Miss Ramsey's looking down to smooth the skirt of her dress, as she said, "Yes, Papa," was precisely that. The squire, less perceptive, grunted as if he were at a loss to know what to say.

And he was not given time to think, for the sound of light, running feet in the corridor announced another visitor. No sooner had the feet slowed than a slight child peeped into the room. Julian received little more than an impression of flaxen braids and a delicate face, before the girl catapulted forward to entwine her outstretched arms around Isabella's slender waist.

Julian scarcely noted the squire's subsequent departure. He was entirely absorbed by the sight of Isabella and the child he knew from Lady Prim must be Sarah Farley. In his circles mothers rarely bothered overmuch with their children. Indeed, too much attention was held to be quite deleterious.

It seemed Miss Ramsey did not subscribe to the prevailing theories, however, for she returned Lady Sarah's embrace without hesitation and certainly without thought for how her skirts were wrinkled in the process. After a moment she pulled back just enough to coax up the child's chin and gave her a quite special smile.

"I am sorry to be late, Sarah," Julian heard her say in a soft voice. "When I found myself near the Prewitt's, I could not but look in on them. I have told you what a brave boy I thought little Billy Prewitt, and I wished to see for myself he had not taken ill, but I wish I had not worried you."

Sarah sniffed mournfully, but she could not be unaffected by the warmth of the smile she received, and Julian was not surprised when her flaxen head moved in the merest nod. Isabella dropped a kiss on her head, then smoothed the tears from her cheeks. "That's better, poppet. Now then, you must know you look very pretty in your new pink dress, and as you are already in the marquess's room, perhaps you would like to meet him?"

Julian watched the child stiffen, as if she would pull away, but Isabella held firm. "He is a very nice man. Come, you'll see."

Smiling her encouragement, she took Sarah by the hand, and though the girl hung her head, Isabella, giving Julian an eloquently pleading look, made the presentation. "My lord, may I present Lady Sarah Farley? She is only six years of age, but already she can do her sums."

Emboldened by Isabella's praise, Sarah dared a swift, upward glance from beneath her lashes. Julian had the impression of surprisingly dark eyes that were very wide and far too anxious to belong to a young child.

"Good day to you, Lady Sarah." He imitated the quiet tones the older girl had used. "I must say I'm honored to encounter a young lady both lovely and quick-witted. Perhaps you will come to visit me in my sickbed from time to time, for I assure you, I become as bored with my own company as I once became with the pages of sums my old tutor used to assign me—to little avail I might add. I spent most of the time I ought to have been studying them on any and everything else."

Isabella thought, perhaps unfairly, that she could guess what the majority of "any and everything" had been, but Sarah was taken by the forthright admission of delinquency. A smile flitted over her features, and though she hid her head in Isabella's skirts, Julian, quite properly, felt triumph.

Isabella's smile seemed to indicate she, too, felt he had done very well. "Perhaps you will show Lord Roth your work, Sarah," she said, smoothing the girl's hair from her brow. "Who knows but that you may succeed at interesting him in your sums where his old tutor failed."

Brown eyes peeked quickly out at Julian, who nodded. "You may be my teacher as Miss Ramsey is yours," he said solemnly and was rewarded with a little sigh that he took to signify pleasure.

"Now, I think it time you make your curtsy to the marquess. We've lessons to do, and Lord Roth must yearn for the unaccustomed luxury of quiet."

Sarah did as she was bid, managing to Isabella's pride, a creditable curtsy, though she could not bring herself to speak and did rush off to wait outside the door.

"Thank you, my lord," Isabella said at once. "You were— quite wonderful." Julian found the smile turned on him luminous, indeed. It expressed far more feeling than any smile she had given him before and all on behalf of a child not even her own. "But I can see you are tired," she went on, before he could speak. "And little wonder after the several scenes we have put on for you. I apologize for us all, but particularly the commotion my father made. I cannot imagine that his shouting helped your head."

"My head may throb a bit now," Julian conceded with a smile that was, indeed, a trifle weary. "But I assure you I was highly entertained. They are rather a pair, your father and Mr. Buttons."

Isabella could not but chuckle. "Natural enemies, it would seem, but I shall endeavor to see in future that when they engage in combat, they do so at some remove from your bedside. Until later . . ."

"Before you go, Miss Ramsey, would you take some of these pillows away?"

Isabella complied at once. He could not sleep soundly sitting up, though with the facility of the convalescent, he seemed already to be drifting off. Preoccupied with her task, tugging gently at the last pillow for fear she would disturb him, Isabella bent close over Julian. Her face a few inches above his, she glanced at him—to find his eyes very much open. He gave her a slow, lazy white smile. "You smell good, Miss Ramsey," he said softly. "Like a wild rose."

Isabella's cheeks, when she went to collect Sarah, were still quite warm, though she knew very well that Roth had meant nothing at all by his words or by that smile beyond that he liked her scent, which was one of Cora's and was, in fact, the essence of wild roses.

Chapter 8

The Ramseys were to go that evening to an annual entertainment at the Bashams' at which the young ladies of the neighborhood, Liza among them, put their musical accomplishments on display for their elders. It was never a night of great anticipation for Isabella, for though she enjoyed her sister's playing and Pru's, she found almost all the other entertainers, despite their music masters' best efforts, more a trial than a pleasure.

She was, however, even less enthusiastic than usual that day, for what she'd found when she had visited the Prewitts on the purest impulse weighed heavily upon her.

Billy Prewitt had gained very little strength at all in the year since she had seen him. He was somewhat taller, perhaps, and his smile was still quite as gentle and sweet as it had been, but he was pitifully thin and pale besides.

It worried her greatly that he would contract the influenza. She could not see how he could escape the disease with his mother and brothers lying sick in the very next room, and she was glad she had delivered her basket of food and Cora's herbs, though her visit had brought her face-to-face with Jaspar Willis.

"And why are you trespassin' here, Miss Ramsey?" Willis had demanded, his dark little eyes narrowing upon her.

The land agent had been smartly dressed in a new coat and high leather boots, while directly behind him, stood the Prewitt's rough, dilapidated tenant's cottage. The contrast gave Isabella courage.

Throwing up her chin, she'd demanded in her turn, "Did you not know your new landlord, the Marquess of Roth is staying with us at Marsh House, Mr. Willis?"

When he blinked in astonishment, she realized her father had

told the truth. The man had been away and had not yet been
told of the marquess's arrival.

" 'Tis Mr. Montcrief's landlord here!''

"You are behind the times, Mr. Willis!'' With quite
uncharitable relish Isabella had related how the change of
ownership had come about. "And you may be certain that I
put the Prewitt's plight to him, Mr. Willis, and that he gave
me permission to come to them. Cora as well,'' she added on
an afterthought. "So do not think to threaten me again. I shall
come whenever I please.''

A smile of satisfaction curved Isabella's mouth only to fade
a moment later. However pleasing her rout of Willis might have
been, she'd now to face Lord Roth and admit she had lied
outright, using his name, to his land agent.

She was still preoccupied with how best to confess her sins,
when, dressed for the soiree and going along to consult with
Mrs. Hobbes, she nearly ran into Nell as the maid careened
around a corner just missing her by inches.

"I am that sorry, Miss Bella!'' the girl wailed. "Oh, but
everythin's gone wrong! I was just comin' to fetch ye. Miss
Liza took ever so long to dress, and the table's not set, and Mrs.
Hobbes needs helpin', but now Jepson can't take his lordship's
dinner up to him on account of he's burned his hand somethin'
awful . . .''

"It will be all right, Nell.'' Isabella patted the maid's rough
hand. "Calm down, please, or you shall fall ill from frenzy,
and we truly shall be in the suds. Cora is above with Jack and
Annie, is she not?'' The breathless maid could only nod. "Well,
I shall come and do what I can for Jepson, and then I shall take
Lord Roth's tray to him. You go and set the table, for we must
get on with dinner, if we are not to be late for the Bashams'
affair.''

Isabella was relieved to see that though the area where Jepson
had splashed boiling water was inflamed, it was not large. She
applied a salve, then wrapped it loosely in clean linen, and gave
the great man a goodly helping of her father's port before
sending him off to his bed for a rest. "We shall get your master
seen to, you needn't worry. Off to bed with you, Jepson. I know
that burn hurts like the devil.''

This time, when she entered Roth's room, his tray balanced upon her hip, Isabella cast him a brief, wary glance from under her lashes. She had not forgotten the way he had unnerved her just at the end of their previous encounter.

She was reassured at once, however, for there was nothing in his look to make her heart race—at least not as rapidly as it had that afternoon. As ever she was arrested, for the merest moment, by his looks. He did not wear the dark blue smoking jacket he had worn on the other occasions she had come. That night he wore only a fine, lawn shirt. Open at the throat, it did reveal perhaps a little more of his lightly bronzed skin than was strictly good for Isabella.

She removed her eyes from the sight to see that neither was his hair combed back from his forehead as it generally was. Several dark golden strands had fallen forward onto his brow, as if he had carelessly raked his hand through his hair in a fraught moment.

She discovered the reason both for his lawn shirt and his tousled hair, when after returning her greeting, he announced in a tone that reminded her of his coachman's reference to his temper, "I struggled to rouse myself from this bed, Miss Ramsey, only to find I am as weak as a kitten. My ribs protested the entire way, and though I only got as far as the fireplace. I am now as tired as if I had walked to town and back."

So much for fearing he would smile with lazy indulgence upon her and tell her she still smelled good.

"I suppose for a man with broken ribs, a separated shoulder, and a concussion you did the equivalent of walking . . . to Saxbourne village, at least." She smiled despite the stony, look he gave her. "And you are free of your sling, I see. Surely that is good news."

At that a twinkle came to life in his eye. "You could not be further off the mark there, Miss Ramsey. The only compensation I have had for all my injuries was the pleasure of having you feed me."

She made a dismissive sound as she settled his tray upon his lap, the memory of how it had affected her to feed him overtaking her. Recovered, she stood back and asked, obviously preparatory to leaving, "Will you need anything else, my lord?"

"What? You intend to leave me to dine all alone!" Julian demanded. "Oh come, Miss Ramsey, you cannot. I feel like a great stone toad with only myself for company."

Isabella laughed, though he looked cross as could be. Certainly, he did not look at all like a stone toad. Afraid her eyes might reflect what she did think he looked like, she busied herself with lifting the covers from his dishes. "Well, you are progressing nicely," she remarked upon finding Mrs. Hobbes had sent up roasted chicken, nicely cut up, and a ragout of asparagus and potatoes. "And, as I would not wish you to feel so terribly weighty as a stone toad, my lord, I will stay for a little."

Their eyes met. He was smiling his very white, strong smile, and she abruptly went to seat herself, wondering as she did so, if she was not a fool for accustoming herself to that smile and the marquess's company. His next remark, however, did a great deal to settle her.

"Now," he began rather briskly as he took up his fork with something of a flourish. "I wish you to indulge me by describing—in full—your encounter with my land agent today and your previous history with him, not excluding an explanation of who the devil the Prewitts are." Pausing, Julian arched his brow at Isabella in such a way she was reminded he was a marquess and would be a duke, and that he had had a command in the army. "And I warn you, Miss Ramsey, you will not fob me off as you did your father."

Reminded she had sins to confess, Isabella flushed slightly, and Julian seeing that telltale sign said before she could speak up, "Good Lord, it cannot be so bad as to put you to the blush, surely."

"I am ashamed to say, my lord, that I not only lied quite dreadfully to Mr. Willis today, but I even dragged your name into it!"

She looked so young and thoroughly anguished, Julian bit back a smile. "You do not strike me as the sort to lie capriciously, Miss Ramsey. Why do you not begin at the beginning?"

Quite taken aback by his display of unexpected tolerance, Isabella needed a moment to gather her thoughts. When she did, she told the whole, beginning with how she had driven Cora to his tenants' home at the end of the previous winter because the old woman would have found it difficult to walk in the mud. She described the Prewitts' two rooms; then told how Billy Prewitt's sweet spirit had impressed her so she had returned often to inquire after him. She did not need to add she had generally taken something for the family. Julian guessed it. She did say Billy had needed all Cora's skills and his own courage besides to fight off the fever that had afflicted him, and that he had not, even a year later, recovered much of his strength. Then she gave an abbreviated version of her unhappy encounters with Jaspar Willis, scrupulously describing the barefaced lie she had told him that very day.

When she was done, Julian considered her story for some minutes in silence, then, catching her completely off guard asked, "Are you often told you are exceptional, Miss Ramsey?"

"Oh, I cannot think . . ."

"If you are not you ought to be," he broke in with a half-amused smile. "There are not many who would bother themselves about a poor tenant's child."

"But he is very valiant, my lord," she replied, her great hazel eyes quite earnest.

"Hmmm," was all Julian said. Isabella was not certain what to make of the noncommittal reply, particularly as she could not read his expression. There did seem to be some amusement in it, but there was something else besides. Unable to fathom he might be regarding her with admiration, she was still at a loss when Julian turned the subject to Willis, himself.

"And this Willis gave you no explanation at all, when he forbade you to bring Cora to Wynchley?"

Isabella's eyes flashed suddenly, the evidence of strong feeling half taking Julian by surprise. "He told me I was a busybody, when I have never concerned myself with his affairs, and he told Cora she was a witch. Absurd man! Had she been a witch, she'd have cast a spell, and we'd have been spared any more of him!"

Julian's laugh was so spontaneous, Isabella could not but smile at her own indignation. Then, as he sobered, she inquired cautiously, "But you do not appear to be angry that I used your name as I did, my lord?"

"I am not, Miss Ramsey. Far from it, I applaud how neatly you outfaced the man."

Isabella could only hope the burst of pleasure she experienced was not obvious. "But Mr. Willis may be disaffected . . ."

"It is what I think that matters in this instance, Miss Ramsey, and I think Mr. Willis's behavior most curious. I cannot believe it is in the estate's best interest to deny the tenants Cora's abilities. Do you intend to go again to these Prewitts?"

"Yes, I wish to take Cora tomorrow, if you've no objection. With Mrs. Prewitt ill, there are only two young girls to care for the sick ones, you see."

Julian wondered what she would do, if he did object. Go along anyway, he suspected. But of course, he did not object, and he added he desired her to take Jepson with her. "I think it advisable . . ."

"Thank you, my lord!" Isabella exclaimed, so grateful she did not wait for him to finish. "I should be in alt to encounter Mr. Willis with Jepson by me."

Her relish was so great he laughed again. "I think the pair of you will rout him."

"Oh not I!" Isabella said and in the unguarded moment her expression revealed what her earlier words had not. Her encounters with Jaspar Willis had not only been unpleasant, but frightening.

Julian did not examine the resolution he made on the instant. He did not need to. It was intolerable to think he would employ a man who bullied young women. If the depth of his feeling was a little strong; if, in fact, he'd a sudden, quite unrealistic desire to confront Willis on the spot, he ignored it. The girl had very expressive eyes that could have persuaded anyone to a desire to protect her.

Which brought Julian to the squire, and he asked, before he could stop himself, "What of your father, Miss Ramsey? Did you not ask him to speak to the man about his manners?"

That the question made her uneasy, he saw at once. She allowed her gaze to slip away from his. "Papa believes Mr. Willis had the right to keep people off Wynchley. You do understand his edict did not apply only to Cora and me? He'd not have anyone cross the estate's boundaries. He even made the annual repairs to the dikes that protect Wynchley from the marshes—if he made them at all—with only his tenants' help. Normally, because it is such a large project, additional men are taken on for the work. I'd not be surprised, though, if it wasn't merely to pocket the leftover monies that he made do with fewer men.''

"You are saying Willis is a thief as well as a tyrant?''

Isabella looked a little rueful at having been so outspoken, but she did not retract her words. "Not very charitable, am I? And I must say I've no proof at all, my lord. I only find it suggestive that Mr. Willis looks very prosperous, when his tenants are the poorest in the neighborhood, and the abbey itself is a shambles.''

Julian, after swallowing a bite of chicken, agreed he found those circumstances suggestive. Only to himself did he remark he also found it interesting that she had veered quickly away from a discussion of her father's relations to Willis. She was sitting very straight with her hand clasped tightly, and he found he did not care to press her on the matter. Again, he was behaving somewhat out of character, but not so greatly he needed to account to himself. He was a guest in the girl's home, after all.

"Enough for now of Wynchley's puzzles, Miss Ramsey,'' he said and watched her shoulders relax fractionally. "My fatigued body can endure no further heavy contemplation. Tell me instead what Suffolk's busy social round holds for you tonight. I have not told you, but you look very nice indeed in that dress.''

Julian's eyes echoed the approval of his words as he took in the gold satin gown she wore. The dress displayed only a trifling amount of ornamentation. There was a border of fine needlework at the hem and around the neck, but the color looked very well on Isabella, while the high-waisted style with its tiny bodice made the most of her assets. Indeed, the low neckline revealed that if she did not have a great deal of swelling bosom, what she did have looked as if it would be satiny smooth to the touch.

Isabella stood. She could not keep from it. Though she knew that his look was likely tepid in comparison to the sort of looks he would have given his mistress—the voluptuous one with the auburn hair—Isabella had never been the object of a male's slow perusal. To her considerable dismay she could feel her skin tingle just at the edge of her scooped neckline where his appreciative gaze had come to rest.

"You are right, sir, about the evening," she remarked whisking away his empty tray without a by-your-leave. "And I must be off, or we shall be late for the performances of Ellie Bashams's friends." When she was a safe two steps back from his bed, an impish light suddenly lit her eyes. "I am so sorry you, my lord, cannot attend. I've no question at all that you would be positively riveted by Letty Smithby's voice, and that is not to mention Ellie Bashams's efforts on the harp."

"And I can tell when you are lying through your teeth, Miss Isabella Ramsey." Julian smiled at her. "But why not cry off, if the thing will be so deadly? Come, instead, and spend the evening in a rousing game of cards with me."

She ignored the spurt of interest the entirely teasing suggestion aroused. "If I did, I should spend all tomorrow in a rousing row with Liza. She has been practicing for weeks."

"And you, Miss Ramsey? What will you play?"

Isabella's laugh was sincerely amused. "To the relief of all attending, I shall play absolutely nothing. As my neighbors, who all know me well, know, I've no accomplishments in the realm of music."

"If they know you so well, then they must know you've the largest heart among them and value you for it."

"Oh! My lord!" She was quite thrown off her stride by this, to her, very high praise indeed. "You have put me to the blush!" was all she could think to say.

Quite unrepentant, he grinned, "And a very pretty blush it is. Enjoy your evening, Miss Ramsey."

"Thank you, my lord."

Chapter 9

"Well do look!"

"What are you doing here?"

Isabella smiled as did Julian. "Ladies first, Miss Ramsey." She inclined her head as she crossed to the chair where he sat. "I was only remarking your progress, my lord. It is the first time I've seen you in a chair, you know."

"I hope I do not disappoint."

As if you could, Isabella said quite under her breath. Flicking her gaze from shoulders broad enough to obscure the chair, to his clothing, she registered that he wore the lawn shirt again and a pair of buff trousers and over them a green smoking jacket. Nothing extraordinary, and he wore the clothes carelessly, as if he had thrown them on. His jacket, for example was not even belted. It did not matter. He'd have been compelling in a farmer's rough clothing.

Aloud she said, "You look quite regal upright." He grinned at that, then she added, frowning, "But perhaps you are too upright. I've a chaise in my room. Shall I have Jepson bring it to you?"

"I should be grateful, if it won't put you out. The chair is a little stiff."

"Do you wish to take your luncheon here, then? Or is this too uncomfortable?"

"The alternative being the bed I have come to know far too well, I shall be pleased to dine in regal pose."

He smiled as she put his tray down, and they discovered together that he had been given cold cuts, bread, beef broth—in a cup—and an aspic salad. "Now back to my question, Miss Ramsey. What the devil are you doing here? I thought Jepson had been commandeered to drive you ladies to a picnic."

The faintest creaking of the door as it opened very slowly interrupted them. "Ah, here she is," Isabella said as if she had been expecting someone, and Julian looked up to see Sarah enter, carrying a large vase of bright daffodils before her. "We went for a picnic of our own this morning," Isabella explained. "And these flowers are the result."

"A very happy result," Julian said, watching little Sarah progress toward him. When she ducked her head out from behind the flowers, he smiled at her, and instantly her delicate features were warmed by a smile that lingered at the corners of her mouth.

There was a moment's hesitation when the child reached him, for she would be quite exposed without her flowers before her, and Isabella prompted gently, "I think the marquess will want to hold his gift, poppet."

Her chin tucked in, Sarah held them out.

Julian accepted the flowers with a most formal inclination of his head. "Thank you, Sarah."

For a long moment, the little girl kept her head bashfully averted and worked a fold of her dress with nervous fingers. Just before Isabella could intervene to rescue her, she slanted a sly glance at Julian.

"I, it is m-my h-honor, my l-lord."

Julian experienced a quite unexpected burst of pleasure when Sarah spoke to him. "The honor is mine, Sarah. But do you know what young ladies in town sometimes do with flowers?"

A quick shake of her head was Sarah's answer.

"They wear them in their hair. Come and I'll show you."

The readiness with which Sarah stepped forward said a great deal, in Isabella's estimation, about the Marquess of Roth's ability to charm.

When he had tucked one of the daffodils behind Sarah's ear, Julian smiled. "Now, go and look in the pier glass there and see if you approve the effect." A dash to the glass was followed by a little giggle. "Well?" he asked.

Sarah turned, her eyes shining, to nod. "Th-thank you."

Then, perhaps from an excess of ecstasy, she dropped a curtsy and fled the room.

Isabella's eyes met Julian's, but he did not allow her to voice her obvious gratitude. "You needn't say you are grateful, Miss

Ramsey. Sarah is entirely charming, and I feel absurdly swelled with pride that she brought herself to speak to me. But why is she so shy? It is not usual for a child of her age, I think?"

"No, it is not at all. She lost her mother when she was born, you see."

"Did she not have a governess?"

"Yes, but a governess is not the same as a mother, or at least Miss Bargon was not. As I understand it from the servants at the Hall, the woman believed Sarah's stammer to be deliberate. She was very harsh in her discipline with the result that Sarah became very nearly mute."

"But what of Wrexham?" Julian demanded, outraged by the harm done the fragile little girl. He had had his difficulties with his father, but, and he acknowledged it, even Chandley would never have thought to abandon him to a governess who would render him too shy for normal speech.

"I, ah, cannot say, my lord." Isabella averted her eyes, but not before Julian saw a sudden bleakness veil their depths from him.

"Miss Ramsey . . ."

He was not certain what he intended to say, to apologize for upsetting her perhaps, but Isabella did not allow him to get so far. "I think it is undeniable mistakes have been made with Sarah, but she is doing much better now, and I intend to see that she continues to progress."

Her cool, contained tone informed him clearly that she did not wish to discuss the subject further, and Julian could not but respect her wishes. It was not his affair. Certainly he'd no right to demand if it was for the sake of Sarah that she had agreed to give herself to a cold roué whose very name caused her eyes to darken. And what if he did ask, and she did admit as much, though even then he found it hard to believe she could have such a motive? Would he call her exceedingly foolish or absurdly noble?

He did know only that Sarah had come on a bit of luck, and he said so. "You will stand the stories about wicked stepmamas on their ends, Miss Ramsey."

Isabella accepted the compliment and the change of topic with a smile that did not quite lift the shadows from her eyes. "Thank you, my lord, and now I must leave you to your luncheon. I've a deal of work to do before I meet with Mr. Cummings.''

And she was gone before Julian could coax her into a laugh that might banish those shadows altogether. He'd also not gotten a direct answer to why it was she had gone on a picnic with Sarah, but not the grander affair Lady Prim and her younger sister attended. Then he realized that her final remark had been something of an answer. She had work to do that nice spring afternoon.

Julian did not seen Isabella until the next day, but though he had had to wait longer than he wished, he did think of the issue. Jepson had only just carted in her chaise, when Isabella came in with the *London Journal* in her hand.

''Oh that is good, Jepson! Now your master may have a comfortable goal to attain.''

To Julian's amusement, Miss Ramsey's luminous smile had the effect of causing the normally quite imperturbable Jepson to beam happily. ''Aye, Miss Bella. 'Tis better'n the chair, and 'tis good of ye ta give it.''

Julian marked the familiar address Jepson was allowed. ''And may I say, I second the sentiment?'' He was not disappointed, Isabella's smile had not dimmed when she looked to him.

''I wish you great pleasure of it, sir. And to amuse you, while you languish upon it, I have brought you Papa's *Journal.* Having already had his nap under it, he will have no need of it again today.''

Julian chuckled. ''Not a bad use for a rag that is three parts tittle-tattle to one part information.''

''Well, after you have enjoyed your own satisfying nap, my lord, I hope you will feel so grateful for its restorative effect that you will indulge me in a favor.''

''It would be my greatest pleasure to indulge you, Miss Ramsey.''

Isabella was not prepared for the amused tenderness in Julian's tone. Flustered by it, she busied herself for a moment with laying the *Journal* upon a small, rosewood table that Jepson had placed by the chaise. When she had reminded herself that a practiced rake would inevitably speak so, she looked back at Julian to find his regard quite as indulgent as his tone.

''You may regret your impulse to generosity,'' she said quickly, before she could think very long on how much she liked the light warming his eyes. "I had it in mind to ask you whether you would mind terribly if Lady Prim brought my sister, Liza, to meet you." Isabella saw at once that her request had taken Julian aback, and surmising he did not wish to bother himself with an eighteen-year-old child, she rushed on, "It would only be for a very little time, I assure you, and Liza has been quite looking forward to meeting you."

Summoning to mind Lady Prim's discreet but not entirely favorable portrait of Miss Liza Ramsey, Julian rightly understood that last to mean the young girl had thrown a tantrum at being the last in the house to meet him.

"I assure you I was sincere when I said I would be pleased to grant any request you might make, Miss Ramsey. If I looked startled, it is only that young girls are more often than not kept from company."

"I hope you do not think us too forward!" Isabella exclaimed, dismayed by the sudden thought that he might think they were pushing Liza at him.

Julian laughed at her misunderstanding. "It is I who am generally thought too forward, Miss Ramsey."

"Well, I have not found you so." Their gazes locked, and Isabella could only be grateful when Jepson, who was yet occupied with his master's clothing, made a movement that intruded into her awareness. She had spoken too urgently, as if she would defend Julian, a grown man quite up to defending himself, and he, arrested by the evidence he'd a champion, had looked rather too deeply into her eyes.

She did not make the mistake of becoming trapped by his sea-green gaze again. A loose thread on the sleeve of her dress provided some distraction as she added, as offhandedly as possible, "I cannot think you the sort of man to compromise a young girl with her life ahead of her." Thinking of Liza's immediate future brought Isabella's head up. "And her Season, as well, my lord. Truly, I think it would do her some good to have a little of your polish rub off on her before she goes to town. She has been indulged here, I fear, and I've a notion she might at times seem a trifle forward, though in truth she is not."

"A nanny," Julian remarked with a soft laugh, his eyes never having left Isabella. Had it been anyone else requesting him to subdue her sister, he'd have dismissed the request as an obvious matchmaking ploy. Rake he might be, but marquess he was and also wealthy, so long as his father did not disinherit him. He knew Miss Ramsey well enough to know she was not up to subtle stratagems. He knew as well, for he had seen it in her eyes, that she did trust him. It was a rather rare moment for him. And he only knew he was glad.

She smiled at his characterization of his role. "Something like that, I suppose. Surely as an officer in the army you played nursemaid to some of your men."

"Good Lord, where did you hear of my army career?"

"Papa's good friend is a retired admiral who keeps close track of the war effort. He's a prodigious admirer of yours and regaled us for quite some time over dinner one night with your heroics at the battle of Talaveras."

Julian's response, a noncommittal grunt, had the effect of causing a slow smile to light Isabella's face. "I do believe you are embarrassed by honest praise, my lord."

She received confirmation of her theory from Jepson, who broke in as no servant ought, to agree. "Aye, ye've the right o' that, Miss Bella." Jepson was not put off when his master frowned dampeningly. "Ne'er will 'ear talk o' 'is deeds, though they fair got 'im killed."

"Enough. You ought to know, none better, Jepson, that battles are ugly, wretched blurs. I only acted as I did because retreat is more wearisome than plunging on."

Isabella was entirely taken with this new side of Julian Montcrief. She had not suspected he could be so diffident, and her expression revealed her feelings quite clearly. He glared, started to say something, but she laughed before he could. "You may as well save your breath, my lord. I can accept that battling one's fellow man is not as glorious as we at home are led to believe. It only stands to reason that what issues forth from the War Office is in the main hyperbole. Still, I do not believe you can persuade me to the notion that retreat requires as much daring as plunging on."

"You, Miss Ramsey, are a stubborn case, if an endearing one."

Julian was not displeased to see Isabella cast into immediate confusion. She looked very fetching when her cheeks went hot with color. "I think you are trying to have the last word," she accused when she could think to do so.

He did not deny the accusation with words, only a lazy grin. She colored further then and left in rather a whirl, which further pleased him, for Julian did not think Isabella Ramsey had received enough flattery in her life. It was only later that afternoon, when her sister, Liza, was chattering—prettily enough—about the picnic she'd attended, that he was reminded he had wished to inquire of Isabella why she had not gone. He made a mental note to do so in future and turned his attention, after a time, to delicately informing the younger Miss Ramsey a crimson habit would not do for the Park.

Chapter 10

Liza went into raptures over Lord Roth. She exclaimed at length upon how handsome he was, what address he had, and how charming he could be. She also informed her family over dinner that he had advised her the better sort of young men in town would not look with favor upon a girl who could not restrain herself. ''Lord Roth says one must be quite contained, if one is to appear well brought up,'' she related as if she informed her companions of something they did not know.

Isabella glanced over to see Lady Prim watching her, a twinkle in her eyes. They exchanged the merest of satisfied nods before Liza broke into speech again.

''He invited me to visit him again tomorrow, which means I shall have seen him twice before I go the bazaar on Thursday. And I shall see what Wilfred Jameson thinks of that!''

Rather relieved in all to hear Liza was not so overcome by Lord Roth that she had forgotten all her flirts, for it would not do for her to fall head over heels for the marquess, Isabella agreed that Wilfred Jameson, who it seemed had neglected Liza at the Southlands' picnic, would be quite overcome.

With so much to look forward to, then, Liza ought to have been in quite the best mood on the day of Saxbourne village's church bazaar. It was a clear day, the second in a row after a week of, to Isabella, blessed rain. The grounds at the vicarage would be green but not soaking wet, and after the bazaar, all the Ramsey ladies were to go directly to a supper dance at the Arbuthnots', friends who lived nearer to Ardsley than Saxbourne village.

It promised to be an exciting affair in part because it would be the first of the spring season, and perhaps it was the excess of exciting events that made Liza more snappish than usual that day. And she was generally demanding when she was preparing for an entertainment. Annie, who most often helped her dress, knew how to soothe her, but the maid was not yet well enough for the task, and poor Nell was made clumsy by Liza's sharp tongue.

She dropped a bottle of Liza's favorite perfume and managed, somehow, to wrinkle the very sash the girl wished to wear that day. If that were not enough, she pulled Liza's hair not once but three times as she was taking it down from its wrappers. The final time, Liza shrieked loudly and hit Nell, whereupon the maid burst into tears.

Isabella, having dressed with Lady Prim's help, went along to smooth matters over, and after sending Nell off to Lady Prim, combed out Liza's hair herself.

Liza was not entirely satisfied with the results of her sister's efforts. She thought the ribbon and curls made her look a little girl. "But I suppose there isn't time to change! Anyway I shall get Ellie Basham's maid to do my hair for tonight. She will create something elegant."

Isabella scarcely heard the muttering. Her eyes had been caught by the dress Nell had laid out to pack for Liza, the distance to the Arbuthnots' being such they would save mussing their gowns by changing there. It was a new gown, a pretty white net dress with white satin slip. At the bottom was a deep flounce of lace, and Isabella might have, had she looked, admired the work of Mrs. Enoch, the village seamstress. The good woman had faithfully copied the plate Liza had shown her with one exception. And it was at that exception Isabella was staring.

Liza had had the bodice cut lower than in the plate. Isabella, mindful of her sister's mood, thought to approach the matter tactfully. "Nell has not yet got out the fichu you wish to wear tonight, Liza. Tell me which one it is, and I shall find it."

"Don't be gothic, Bella!" Liza cried, the slight uncertainty she had entertained about her daring neckline making her quite scornful. "Fichus are for old ladies or children, and I am certainly not a child. And besides, Lady Prim approved the dress."

Aware her sister took liberty with the truth at times, Isabella gave her a close look. "Lady Prim has seen this dress?"

Lady Prim had approved the plate not the dress, as Liza knew very well, and perhaps it was that Isabella had seen through her ploy that made her so very angry. "You cannot tell me what to do, though you are forever trying, Bella!" she cried suddenly and jerking the dress from her bed, she whirled to the door, throwing it open so vigorously it banged against the wall. As the thud reverberated throughout the room, she spun back to fling at her sister, "You are not my mother! And besides, you have no notion at all of the latest style! Just look at that old thing you are wearing! You look a perfect ape-leader. I shall ask one who knows if this dress is unexceptional, and then you'll see!"

It was only when Isabella realized Liza had stalked off toward Lord Roth's room, not Lady Prim's, that she followed. Otherwise, she'd have played least in sight, the wisest thing to do when Liza had gotten to the stage of saying things she would repent later.

At least, Isabella thought, flicking a wry look down at the afternoon dress Mrs. Enoch had refreshed for her a year before, she hoped Liza did not truly think she looked an ape-leader. When she arrived at the marquess's room, she found Liza had surprised Lord Roth while he reclined upon the chaise, reading a book Isabella noted distractedly was Townshend's advice on agriculture.

She also saw with some relief Jepson was in the room. At least Liza had not barged in upon Lord Roth while he was quite alone. It was one thing for a betrothed woman to attend to him while they were rendered short of servants by the epidemic of influenza, but quite another for an unmarried girl to do so, a point Lady Prim had impressed upon Liza only with an effort.

Those thoughts were entertained and dismissed in some half second, for Isabella heard Liza say her name and then, " . . . she thinks I am a babe, but you must tell her you think this dress is just the thing!"

Mortified to have the marquess drawn into their sisterly squabble, Isabella opened her mouth to say she knew not quite what, anything that would smooth the matter over, but Julian spoke first.

"This dress is perfectly acceptable, Liza," he began and the younger girl rounded upon her sister with a great shout of triumph. Before she could do more than open her mouth, however, Julian continued in the same, steady tone, " . . . if you are angling to enter the world of the demirep. Were a girl of your age to be seen in it in town, you would be considered either too green to know what you were about or too fast to care."

Liza rocked back on her heels, twin spots of color rising on her cheeks. But Julian had not done with her. "That is not all I have to say, Liza, and you will indulge me as you burst in upon me without a by-your-leave—and that after we had a discussion on the importance of restraint. I could not but hear how and what you screamed at your sister, for you must have been standing in the hallway when you carried on so. What you said was not only unforgivably rude, it was quite off the mark. You would be well-advised to take your sister's advice, my dear, in the matter of your clothing. She possesses a considerable sense of style. That is, you see, quite different from keeping to the fashion of the moment and turning yourself out as everyone else does. Your sister, no matter that what she wears may or may not be in the height of fashion, always looks somehow right, and I might add, exceedingly pleasing to the eye."

Isabella felt sorry for her Liza then. She thought Lord Roth had gone rather far, holding her up as such an example. She did not believe that he meant a word of what he said, only that he intended to teach Liza some manners.

"After you have begged your sister's pardon," he continued, immune to the pitiful sight Liza made with her head drooping forlornly, "you may be excused. Then, if you wish, you may return to show me the dress you will wear tonight. I would be pleased to see it. I am certain it will be quite nice, and you will look lovely in it, for you are an exceedingly pretty girl, Liza, so long as you are not throwing a tantrum worthy of a child."

That sent Liza's hand flying to her mouth as tears flowed down her cheeks. To have received the compliment of her dreams at the same time she had received the scold of her life and all from Lord Roth! She spun about and almost fell into Isabella's arms, mumbling through her tears, "I am sorry, Bella.

I never meant it. You must know that. Oh, Bella! I only wanted to look very well tonight. Wilfred Jameson will be there, and . . .''

Liza sobbed much of the way down the hall, but by the time they reached her room and she had heard half a dozen times she was forgiven, she straightened. Sniffing, she stood back to study her sister a moment and recognized the muslin Isabella wore as one of their mother's. But she had, in the end, to concede Bella looked remarkably fine in the old thing. The rich apricot color brought out the warm tones of her skin and set off her nice, if not striking, soft brown hair.

"You know you do really look very nice, Bella," she said, and the wonder in her tone caused Isabella to laugh aloud.

Julian heard the sound only distantly, for they had closed Liza's door, but he smiled a little. And he had Jepson bring him paper and pen.

His note to Isabella read, "I meant every word I said. Lord Roth." That was all. He gave it to Jepson with the instruction to ask Isabella if she'd the time to see him before she left, and if not, to give her the note.

As it happened, Isabella did not have time to see Julian. There was still Sarah to dress, and as the child was a little unnerved about attending a gathering with so many people, Isabella spent all the time before they departed in the nursery.

She remembered the note Jepson had given her only after she and Sarah had seated themselves in the carriage and Lady Prim was coming down the steps, Liza just behind. Unfolding it and holding it at arm's length, for she did not have her spectacles, Isabella read it and greeted the latecomers, when Jepson assisted them into the carriage, with such a bright smile, Lady Prim remarked upon it.

"I must say you look quite lovely, Bella. The prospect of all these activities before us seems to agree with you, and I must say I am very glad, for you know I think you too seldom amuse yourself."

Isabella made some fitting response, but hugged to herself the truth of the sparkle in her eyes: that she was in alt because Julian Montcrief had just proven he was her friend.

Though she still could scarcely credit Julian truly did mean his flattery, the fact that he had understood her well enough to know she would doubt him, and that he had taken the time to assure her, all combined to make her want to laugh for the sheer joy of it.

They found a great crowd of people milling about on the wide, rolling vicarage lawn for the annual bazaar. Liza had waved to three friends before they even descended from the carriage, but she did not go at once to join them. In part to make amends with Isabella, but also because Sarah was indeed appealing, she took the child by the hand and made for the table upon which the spin-wheel game had been erected. There she made a great show of demonstrating just how to give the wheel's handle a proper heave before she lifted Sarah up to take a turn. A little shy at being the object of some attention, for several passersby had joined Isabella and Lady Prim to cheer her on, Sarah blushed profusely—but she had incentive. The prizes, cloth dolls that were Pru Manning's contribution to the bazaar, sat in plain sight on a shelf behind the wheel. Using two hands, she pushed as hard as she could, sending the arrow spinning around and around, fast at first, then slower and slower until it came to rest at last upon one of the two spaces decorated with a doll's face.

Wilfred Jameson came up as they were admiring Sarah's winnings, and Isabella, pleased for Liza's sake, though she knew her sister had no abiding interest in the boy, readily approved when he asked if he might escort Liza about. They looked very young and happy as they drifted away, Lady Prim in discreet accomplishment. Mr. Jameson smiled down at Liza, and the younger girl, her head tipped, giggled up at him.

They seemed very young, all their futures ahead of them. Futures filled with possibilities, Isabella thought, and then pushed the thought aside, for it seemed to dim the day slightly.

''Isabella!''

It was Pru, waving to them from a long table arrayed with old books, chipped china and all those items families in the parish no longer desired, but which Mrs. Smithby insisted their neighbors would part with a shilling or two to own.

Isabella noted Pru's brighter-than-ever-smile and the excited sparkle in her eyes, but had not long to wonder at the cause for her enthused manner. When the young man just beyond Pru turned, she saw it was Francis Basham.

A tall, thin young man with twinkling brown eyes, he greeted Isabella with the familiarity of an old playmate, who, though he had not seen much of her in recent years, recalled very well several forbidden and therefore highly prized forays into the marshes with her.

"And who is this young lady with you, my dear Bella?" He smiled down at Sarah, who was holding very tightly to Isabella's hand. "Can it be the prettiest young lady at the bazaar— excepting one or two, of course?" he added with a grin for Pru.

Pru turned a very pleased shade of pink when their eyes met, and it was a moment before Francis recalled he had asked a question of Isabella. When Francis and Pru did break off gazing at one another, Isabella presented Sarah, who curtsied very nicely, though she could not quite bring herself to look up until Pru exclaimed over the doll she had made, and Sarah had won.

"But I am so pleased, Sarah, that you've the prettiest of the lot! Do you know I even thought of you when I made her? Look she's pretty golden hair, just like yours."

Sarah then gave Pru a smile so full of wonder and pleasure, Francis was prompted to invite all three of the ladies to the sweet table that he might obtain a refreshment for them. The alacrity with which shy Sarah accepted the invitation was cause for some amusement among her elders.

"How is Lord Roth progressing, Bella?" Francis asked as they strolled along. "I do hope he'll be up and about soon, for I fear, if he is not, Mother and Ellie will collapse from the pernicious ailment known as hysterical anticipation."

Isabella chuckled at that, then reported Lord Roth was up and should soon be about. Pru did not say much, certainly not as she had when Francis was not by her, only remarking that she was looking forward to meeting the marquess.

At the sweet table, Isabella and Sarah made their choices rather quickly, the small apple tarts their own Mrs. Hobbes had produced being irresistible. Pru took longer, and Isabella standing by her, heard her say with a giggle in her voice, "The tarts do look delicious, sir, but I believe you promised me an almond cake especially made by your mother's chef."

Francis leaned forward to say in a whisper that could be heard plainly, "If I was in my right mind, Miss Manning, I am certain I promised you the moon."

Pru giggled; Francis grinned, and they stood gazing raptly at one another, the rest of the world quite, quite forgotten. Isabella slid away. She had already thanked Francis for his treat, and she did not think she and Sarah would be missed.

They were not. Only a few moments later she saw Pru and Francis, their almond cakes in hand, seeking what little privacy the broad vicarage lawn could afford. They leaned into one another as they walked, whispering.

Abruptly Isabella turned about, seeking Sarah. The child had asked if she might select some treats to take home to Lord Roth and had wandered a little away. But, though she had a mission, she stood still a moment, battling her own feelings, for they dismayed her. She thought it unworthy of herself that her friends' quite wonderful pleasure in each other could prick her even a little. It appalled her that she, who had been so happy, now felt oppressed and strangely restless.

Thrusting aside an image of the Marquess of Roth—it only dismayed her further that she would think of him just then— she applied herself to looking for Sarah's flaxen head among the crowd. She even became a little worried until she caught sight of the child standing at the end of the tables near the roadway studying the plates of ginger candy and chocolate drops.

At the same moment her gaze strayed to the road where she saw a horseman proceeding down the village's main and only thoroughfare and absently identified him as Jaspar Willis.

Isabella never held her distractedness to blame for what occurred next, for in truth the incident happened so quickly, there was nothing she could have done even had she been by Sarah. One moment the child was absorbed by the display of sweets, and the next, she was jerking around so abruptly, she took both Willis and his mount by surprise. The horse reared. Terrified, Sarah gave a piercing scream and after scrambling backward, her doll falling from her nerveless fingers, she fled off down the road as fast as her feet would carry her.

For Isabella the next moments were some of the longest of her life. She called to Sarah but to no avail, and running after her, saw the child swerve out of sight behind a house. Another wild scream sounded in the next instant, followed by utter silence, though Isabella cried out Sarah's name several times.

Her heart in her throat, Isabella rounded the corner and saw Sarah instantly. The child had tripped over a large tree root and gone tumbling forward. By her small head was a large rock. Isabella's heart was beating so heavily, she could scarcely force air into her lungs, though when she knelt down by the child, she found voice to cry, "Sarah!" again with the sharpness that comes from fear.

Isabella, herself, almost cried when she saw Sarah open her eyes, then seeing who it was beside her, promptly burst into tears. The poor child trembled pitifully as Isabella examined her to find she'd scraped her knee rather badly and torn her dress. She could not speak at all, only sob and cling tightly to Isabella, who thought Jepson's large figure to be quite the best sight she'd ever beheld, when he appeared seemingly from nowhere. In a trice he had them in the carriage and on their way home.

When they drew up before Marsh House, Sarah still held fiercely to Isabella and would not go to Jepson, though they had become odd, but fast friends, when the batman valet had brought her a splendid osprey feather one day. After he had helped them from the carriage, Isabella bade him return to the bazaar to explain to Lady Prim and Liza what had occurred and to transport them and the squire on to the Arbuthnots' as planned. She had lost all interest in a gay evening and said she would stay with Sarah, who still trembled; whether from fear or shock, Isabella did not know.

Fortunately Cora disdained social gatherings such as church bazaars and was on hand to mix up a posset to give the overwrought child. The other servants had been given the afternoon off, for they did not share Cora's attitude. Isabella managed a bath for Sarah, then tucked her into bed.

Despite the soothing drink and bath, however, Sarah did not fall sound asleep at once. She would doze fitfully then wake with a start as if she thought someone meant her harm.

Isabella attempted to learn what Sarah feared, but the child began to shiver so when questioned, it seemed cruel to persist. In the end she only sang softly to her and held her hand and dozed herself, until after what seemed like hours, Sarah succumbed to a deep, healing sleep.

Feeling quite drained and adrift, Isabella made her way to the one room in the house she knew would have a fire. It was the sort of day that is warm in the sun, but cool in the shade, and she knew her father, who had gone late to the bazaar, would have had one burning in his study.

The embers still glowed hot and red, and after she threw a log on and poked at it, she had a nice blaze. The bright flames were as cheerful as they were warm, and Isabella sank down in her father's chair before it, feeling she needed that cheer after what had turned out to be a very, very different day from the one she had expected.

Chapter 11

When Julian entered the squire's study, he had to look twice to be certain it was, indeed, Isabella sitting in the squire's chair, her forehead resting on her knees. He had not heard her return, as he had slept away a deal of the late afternoon, and, of course, expected she would be at the supper dance.

"What has happened?" he asked at once.

Isabella gave a little cry. "Oh! Lord Roth!" The exclamation registered a great deal of surprise, for if he had not expected to find her there, she certainly had not thought to see Julian standing in the doorway. "You managed the stairs."

His smile was full of boyish pleasure. "With an effort, I fear, but I needed the exertion. I was growing fat sitting day after day."

Isabella was powerless to keep her gaze from slipping downward. It was the first time she had ever seen the marquess fully dressed, that is to say in buckskins, boots, and a lawn shirt—and standing.

Grown fat, he had not. Not at all. Nor was he thin. The marquess was lean, another thing entirely. His close-fitting shirt revealed a solid, muscular torso, wide shoulders, and an enviably narrow waist. His legs were, she could plainly see, because his buckskins were more a second skin than a concealing garment, long and very, very satisfactorily shaped.

"I hope you approve of me now that I am not supine."

Color heated Isabella's cheeks, as her eyes flew upward. The marquess was tall, taller than she had guessed as she learned when she was obliged to tip her chin to see that his eyes were twinkling at the way she had gawked. "I, I am sorry. I did not mean to stare. I was only surprised . . ."

She left what had surprised her open to interpretation in the hopes that Julian would assume it was his show of regained strength at which she marveled.

If Julian had any notion otherwise, he gave no hint of it. "When I confided to your father that I intended to negotiate the stairs while no one was about to laugh at my feebleness, he was so good as to inform me a full decanter of brandy would await me in his study. It was a most effective incentive."

Isabella smiled a little at that. "It is there, my lord, on th tray by his chair."

Julian did not go to the tray, but came to frown down at her. "What has happened, Miss Ramsey? You look, if you'll forgive me for saying it, rather done in."

Isabella's sigh held no displeasure, only acknowledgment. "I do not doubt it. Sarah had a terrible fright at the bazaar, when Jaspar Willis's mount reared in front of her." Isabella went on to relate all that had happened, then shook her head. "She ran so frantically, it was almost as if she thought Willis meant to hunt her down and harm her, but I cannot think that she ever met the man before. Miss Bargon rarely took her on outings from the Hall, and Willis would have had no reason to go there. Perhaps she was merely afraid of the horse. I cannot say, but the sound of her scream was truly dreadful and then to see her lying there so still . . . I thought for the awfulest moment she might be dead."

"Oh, my dear, girl." Isabella smiled rather tremulously as Julian took her hand, and finding it cold, chafed it. "I think a brandy is in order for both of us."

Quite needing the comfort of Julian's attention, Isabella did not reject the glass he tucked into her hand, though she had not cared for the one sip she had had previously of her father's favorite drink.

"I hope you find the brandy's effect better than the taste, Miss Ramsey," Julian said, when she grimaced as her first swallow slid down her throat to pool in her stomach.

"Well, it is warm at least."

Julian chuckled at the faint praise. "I am glad to report some of your color is returning." Almost absently he outlined the edge of the faint flush of her cheek with his finger. The warmth that followed his touch made Isabella's thick eyelashes part very wide, but Julian seemed unaware of her start. "I did not like to see you so pale. Nor so despondent. Is it that you feel responsible in some part for Sarah's fright, Miss Ramsey?''

"How did you know?" Isabella was so amazed that the tall, handsome, thoroughly sophisticated man standing over her could touch her thoughts as he had her cheek, she looked at him in wonder. "I do, you see. It was on my account Sarah went at all today. She had never been in such a crowd before and was quite reluctant to go until I urged her. I ought to have listened to her.''

Julian nodded as if he had thought as much then bent down so that his eyes were almost on a level with hers to pronounce quietly but emphatically, "That is the purest balderdash, my very dear Miss Ramsey. You cannot spare Sarah all fear. If you tried, you'd be obliged to wrap her in cotton wool which would be the greatest shame of all. She cannot experience the joys of the world without encountering some difficulties, and she will do splendidly in the end, as long as you are somewhere nearby to soothe away her tears, which you do very well. You are very good with her, you know.''

"Truly you do not think I was wrong to urge her?''

Julian was very certain. "No, I do not. And I would wager until this quite chance thing with Willis occurred, she was enjoying herself.''

"She was, in fact," Isabella allowed slowly. "She was quite proud, for Liza helped her to win a cloth doll at the spin wheel.'' Mention of her sister reminded Isabella of the scene Liza had put on before the bazaar. Then she recalled Julian's note.

Feeling unaccountably shy of a sudden, she averted her gaze and only heard Julian say, "I am glad to hear Liza was in a better temper.''

"I wish to thank you for how you managed her, my lord,'' Isabella said softly, keenly aware Julian had seated himself on the arm of the chair just by hers, and with his long legs stretched out to the fire, watched her. "It was a quite horrid scene to inflict upon you, yet you handled it very well.''

"And did you get my note, Miss Ramsey?''

She flicked him the merest glance. "I did, my lord, and thank you for it as well.''

Julian's amused laugh brought her head around. "But you still do not countenance a word I said, do you?''

Isabella flushed. But it was not the accuracy of his perception that heated her cheeks. It was the warmth of Julian's gaze. His eyes had never reflected quite the light they did just then, and her breath seemed to come late.

"And now here you are at home, as usual I might add, well away from all the young men who would inevitably shower you with so much flattery you would, overwhelmed, know I spoke only the truth."

It was impossible not to respond. His white smile was very strong. She smiled. "You are an optimist, my lord."

"A realist, Miss Ramsey," he protested. "The first young gentleman who danced with you would prove me right."

She gave an unsteady laugh at that. "The poor unfortunate would be far too busy nursing wounded feet, if I danced with him to shower me with praise. I've little notion how to dance."

"Why not?"

Slightly taken aback by the sharpness of his tone, Isabella shrugged. "Well, I suppose there wasn't time to learn. I did have a lesson or two—we shared a dance master with the Bashams—but then Mother fell ill."

"And what of balls, learning on the floor as it was?"

Isabella had been to only one ball. Mrs. Basham had given it that she and Wrexham might announce their betrothal to the neighborhood. "I am not a quick study it would seem," she said, biting her lip as she recalled how the viscount had informed her succinctly, though not cruelly, that she needed practice.

Julian did not consider why he found Isabella's expression unacceptable. Some memory had taken all the light from her lovely eyes, and he thought only to banish it, whatever it was, from her mind.

He set his empty glass upon the table between them and rising, held out his hand. "Come, Miss Ramsey. Even now I hear the musicians striking up a waltz, and though you've not been approved by Almack's patronesses, I think they cannot frown upon what they do not see."

She looked from his hand to his eyes, and he smiled. "I am not mad. Come, you'll hear the music, too, and it is quite a simple dance, really, particularly as we shall have to move infinitely slowly out of respect for my ribs."

The invitation was entirely preposterous. Isabella ought not even to have been in the room alone with Julian, for though he had left the door open, she did not know how many, if any, of the servants had yet returned to the house, and, of course, all of her family was away.

She had not before, nor did she then, once give thought to their isolation, however. She had grown accustomed to being alone with Julian, and though the circumstances were very different now he was up and about, she had been too distraught at the first, thinking of Sarah, to sort out the difference.

Now, when she was not so distressed, she still did not bethink herself of decorum. Perhaps the tumult of emotions she had experienced that long day had left her too drained to think clearly. Perhaps it was the strange melancholic feeling that had settled over her when she had watched Francis and Pru—almost as if she stood on the outside of a pastry shop with her nose pressed against the window never to be allowed inside—that clouded her mind.

Whatever, she was prompted to place her empty glass beside Julian's and slip her slender hand into his.

It was a little awkward at first as they arranged themselves. Isabella did not know where to put her hands, and they had also to consider Julian's various injuries. But in the end she managed to fit well enough in his arms.

Julian counted their steps at the first, and Isabella listened, though she could not but register a series of quite separate impressions as they began their dance. He had not thought to don a coat to descend the stairs of an empty house, and the fine shirt he wore was both very soft and thin. Beneath her fingertips she could feel the play of his strong shoulder muscles. Encircled by his arms, she becames aware by degrees of the warmth of his body. And of the pool of heat at her waist, where his hand held her.

He smelled good, too. She detected the faintest suggestion of sandalwood as they wove slowly around and around and about her father's chairs and tables.

"One and two and three and four . . ."

Miraculously Isabella did not stumble over Julian or herself. Inhaling deeply, almost sighing, she relaxed into the seductive rhythm of the melody he had begun to hum softly in her ear as her feet followed his.

"Hmmm. That's it."

Isabella felt as graceful and light as a feather on air as Julian's low, soft voice reverberated around and through her before curling at last into her ear as the merest whisper.

It was an enchanting moment, the fullest, certainly of Isabella's life until then. And its like would never, ever come again.

She shut her eyes hard, for of a sudden, all the melancholy, all the wistfulness, all the sad, strange yearning, she had felt before seemed to surge up inside her in the form of hot, scalding tears. She bit her lip, trying hard to push them back, to regain the magic that had been hers so very briefly and in the effort, missed her step, causing Julian to stumble.

When she heard him catch his breath as his ribs protested the unexpected movement, she flung up her head to apologize.

She had forgotten, in her concern, her tears. Julian stopped still at the sight of them. And did not need to ask what had made her so sad. He knew. He knew with the heaviest feeling of sadness he had experienced since he was a child that it was her future, loveless and long, stretching out before her, that had brought her to tears.

And he could not bear them. "Isabella, Isabella. Lovely, lovely girl."

Through her tears Isabella could see the gentleness in Julian's blue-green eyes, and when his hands came up to cup her cheeks that he might brush away with his thumbs the tears spilling from her eyes, she made no protest.

She stood quite still, as if her feet were rooted to the floor. Even when she knew with certainty he meant to kiss her, she did not move, only watched his eyes drop slowly from hers to her lips.

Then his mouth became the sum total of her world. It looked so very beautiful as she watched it descend to hers. Masculinely beautiful, she might have added, had coherent thought been hers just then. Strong, finely cut, sensuous, and very, very desirable.

The taste and feel of his lips on hers was like nothing Isabella had ever imagined. All her senses quickened. Her lips parted as her hands lifted on their own accord to his shoulders, and a shudder went through her as the intensity of Julian's kiss deepened in response to her touch.

They seemed to spin around and around, though in truth they stood quite still, until Julian, his hands encircling her waist, drew her closer to him.

It was the feeling that spiraled through Isabella when her breasts encountered the hard wall of Julian's chest that shocked her into a realization of what she did. The feeling was so intense, she took fright.

"Oh!" Breathing hard, panting almost, she pulled her head away to stare up at Julian as one stunned. He did not flinch from her look, nor did he relax his hold on her, indeed his hands tightened where they rested on her reed-slender waist.

"I would give you this, Isabella."

"No, no!"

Though she did not know the exact particulars, she knew "this" included more than the kiss that was itself infinitely more than she ought to have allowed, and her denial was harsh. Julian shook her. Later she would recall that his breathing came almost as heavily as hers, but just then she registered only the impatience that flashed in his eyes. "There is nothing wrong in what we do. At this moment Wrexham is in bed . . ."

"No! Oh, don't!" Squeezing her eyes shut against the power of his eyes, Isabella heaved heavily against him. She needn't have used such force. Julian had never held a woman against her will.

He released her so suddenly, she stumbled backward and half fell against the table where their glasses stood. Their rattling went unheeded.

Isabella had her wish. She'd not been aware she made it as she watched Pru and Francis earlier, but some small corner of her mind had beseeched the powers that be in the merest whisper to give her just once a moment in which a man looked at her as if he were oblivious of all else in the world. But, as often happens when dreams are fulfilled, the fulfillment had a most unexpected and undesired twist.

Julian's handsome face was not softened with some dreamy expression of love. Quite the contrary, his expression was so intent as to be fierce.

"Why not, Isabella?" he demanded, his voice husky. "Can you say you truly wish to know nothing more than the touch of a man who saw fit to abandon you only days after your betrothal? You must know his interest in you—in any wife—is limited to the begetting of a son.''

"Stop! Oh, stop!" Isabella put her hands to her ears to block out the hateful words. "It does not matter!" She realized she was shouting and bit her lip. Lowering her hands, she strove for calm when she had never felt in greater tumult. "It does not matter what Wrexham is." Her voice was not steady but she went on. "I gave my word . . . in effect that I would be . . . that I am . . . unused.''

The horrid word choked her. In the next minute she knew she would cry out in anguish and that if she did she would end up back in Julian's arms, for even then she could scarcely keep from throwing herself into them.

Had Julian had the least inkling Isabella meant to run, he'd have caught her in time. Unprepared, he was too late, and though he pursued her, his injuries slowed him. The front door slammed shut behind her before he was halfway down the hall.

What would he have done had he caught her? Persist in his seduction? Perhaps. Or perhaps only have ended the wretched scene in some other way. As it was, he felt furious enough to strangle someone.

She had looked so very sad. He'd only thought to kiss away her tears.

Truly, at first that was all. A light kiss upon that soft mouth, after she had felt so very good in his arms while they danced. But she had opened at his touch like a flower. Her mouth had trembled with its eagerness to yield him its sweetness. He could yet taste her on his tongue.

One of their empty glasses found its way into his hand, and after staring at it a long moment, Julian flung it as hard as his ribs would allow into the fireplace.

Damn! Of all the things he had not meant to do, he had not meant to make her cry again. Oh yes, he had seen the tears he'd brought to her eyes and seen her hand clasp over her trembling mouth. How far all that was from the pleasure he had thought to bring her—to both of them.

"Devil take her," he growled aloud, anger surging to the fore now. Why had she remained alone with him when the house was empty, if what she wished was to remain so blessedly pure? Any woman with the least grain of sense would have seen the danger. She had almost floated into his arms when he'd asked her to dance, of all dances, a waltz, brandy still on her lips, though he suspected she drank brandy in the middle of the day as often as pigs flew.

She'd known his reputation. From the first.

How could she know you? You taught the innocent to trust you.

More fool she then! Julian silenced the voice taking Isabella's part with a savage snarl. But the voice was no weakling to be so easily routed, and it took all the squire's bottle of brandy— and two others Julian roused out, besides—before he slept that night.

Chapter 12

"Isabella, my dear girl, you look perfectly dreadful! I hope you've not contracted the influenza as half the neighborhood seems to have done. Rest, that is what you need! You needn't worry over Letty and me. Though Dobson was nowhere about, we did encounter Lady Primley. She was most gracious when I asked, and has gone up to announce us to Lord Roth."

"Ah." It was all Isabella could say. She had come in from riding and stumbled upon Mrs. Smithby in the hallway, amazingly rigged out in a purple silk dress dripping with so many beads it would have dazzled the guests at Carlton House. Beside her mother, Letty looked the drabbest sparrow in a pretty jaconet muslin of light blue.

Mrs. Smithby nodded sharply, as if Isabella had made a most insightful remark. "You can imagine how delighted I was to hear of the marquess's progress from Liza yesterday—she did say she had visited twice with him, you know—and as I knew you would not wish to be accused of hoarding your guest," Mrs. Smithby interrupted herself with a braying laugh of mercifully short duration, "I brought Letty directly along that we might welcome him to Mr. Smithby's parish."

Letty tittered rather shrilly but seemed unable to speak. No matter. Mrs. Smithby, after efficiently tweaking one of the curls adorning her daughter's forehead into a new position, spoke for her. "She has been simply pining to meet Lord Roth, and I believe her young spirits will do the marquess enormous good, or, of course, I would not have indulged her. Ah, look! There is Lady Primley now. I do hope Lady Sarah is feeling more the thing today. The child is skittish, Isabella. Be firm with her. The child is skittish, Isabella. Be firm with her. And do not forget your rest!"

Any other time Isabella would have attempted to confound Mrs. Smithby's intent to swoop down upon Lord Roth, even had the woman already got as far as directing Lady Prim to announce her—as if Lady Prim were no more than an underling.

Isabella was not up to such heroics that day. She felt far worse than she looked, and she knew from her pier glass she looked quite as wretched as Mrs. Smithby had so unequivocally proclaimed.

She had not slept. She had made an effort to get into her bed, when she had crept back to her room hours after she had fled the house. Quiet as could be for fear the marquess would hear her, she had bolted her door behind her, an unnecessary precaution. Julian had not come. There had been no sound at all until Liza and Lady Prim returned. Then she had heard Jepson's heavy tread a time or two, followed much later by her father's.

When the eventual silence had oppressed her so she could not bear it, she took herself to her window seat to hug her knees to chest and scan the darkness for some magical balm.

She had been warned by everyone in a dozen different ways. Yet, she had remained quite alone with the man she knew to be a rake, though the house was, as they had both been aware, to all intents and purposes deserted. She had tossed off a glass of brandy; she had slipped into his arms for a waltz.

Of course he had read only one thing into her actions. Of course! Because he had had only one thing on his mind. How could she have been so . . . stupid! He had spent a lifetime charming women to one end only. She had known that. She had known, and yet she had thought . . . what exactly?

That he could not be interested in a plain country girl with no sophistication at all? Fool! He had needed a diversion, any diversion. Confined to his sickbed, the marquess had been obliged to take what was at hand. He had even been obliged to take the time to earn her trust. How tedious for him. How he must have wished she were already married! How much easier to persuade an experienced woman, bored with her life perhaps—and safely shackled to another—to pleasure him.

And be pleasured in return. Shame flooded Isabella at the memory of her response to his merest kiss. No, that was not fair. It was no "mere" kiss. Roth was thoroughly practiced. But still! to have reacted with such abandon.

Had she moaned aloud? The fear that she might have betrayed herself with so telling a sound made her hide her head in her hands.

At least he had not been unmoved! Her chin lifted as she recalled Julian's labored breathing. At least she had that thought to which to cling. Though she had been only the latest conquest in a long line, and likely, she knew with a wretched pang of regret, the plainest, he had desired her.

As she had desired him. How would she ever face him?

She could not. The thought of meeting him, perhaps, at breakfast—he was mobile now, after all—galvanized her into action in the early hours of the morning. Leaping up, she dragged out a riding habit, and after she'd thrown it on, took the time only to run up to Sarah's room to see if the child was awake and fully recovered from her fright.

Sarah was not only awake and entirely recovered but happily occupied decorating the cloth doll Jepson had been thoughtful enough to search out for her. She wished to give it to Lord Roth because, she told Isabella gravely, she thought he needed a friend to sleep with him as she had her doll and one old bear.

Isabella's responding smile had been thin, but Sarah did not notice, nor did she see that Isabella took the servants stairs just to be sure she did not meet any others of her family on the off chance that lightning had struck the house, and they had been roused from their beds at seven in the morning.

Scooping up a roll on her way through the kitchen, she waved with every appearance of cheerfulness at Mrs. Hobbes, but did not give the good cook time to observe the circles beneath her eyes, she flew so quickly out of the house and down to the stables. Once mounted, she rode long and hard, and with, for perhaps the first time in her life, no thought for even one of the responsibilities that lay on her shoulders. She did not think of Sarah's lessons; she did not remind herself of the letter she owed Peter; nor even did she spare a thought for the tenants and servants ill with the influenza.

Her thoughts were all for the Marquess of Roth, and after a time in the brisk spring air, she came to some clarity.

She could, nay she would, face Lord Roth with dignity. She had desired him. It was true. He was handsome, very handsome and very charming. She was . . . a normal young woman.

She recalled how she had felt watching Pru and Francis and added to that she was a susceptible young woman. Her betrothal to Wrexham was not the betrothal of her dreams. She had known that but had not known how, in a weak moment, the gap between her dreams and reality could leave her vulnerable to a man like Julian Montcrief.

She did now. She knew a great deal more today of men and of herself, and with little cost—if one did not count a lost night's sleep. What had Ju . . . Lord Roth said? She could not wrap Sarah in cotton wool. Life must be experienced.

So, she had had her experience. And had come to some understanding of it. And had even forgiven herself, at least somewhat. It was certainly not the greatest mistake ever made, and if she suspected her final response to Lord Roth might have been very different had he spoken of love and not of Wrexham, she thrust the thought aside.

The marquess had not spoken of love. Certainly he had not spoken of marriage. And she had done the only thing she could aside from dealing his face a slap, a course of action that would have been unfair in the extreme, given that she had stood so very still while his mouth came down to hers.

But she would not think of that! She would do what she must. She would put her transgression behind her and behave with as much dignity as she could summon.

Thus resolved, Isabella returned to Marsh House only to find she was not so strengthened as she had thought.

Almost when the vicar's wife had announced she meant to drag Letty before the eligible marquess, she had cried out, "But, Mrs. Smithby, the child is not married or betrothed! Get her at least pledged to another—only then will he take notice."

Absurd, stupid tears welled up in her eyes then, and the effort it took to hold them back left her too weak to do more than watch in silence as Mrs. Smithby sailed up the stairs, her bosom billowing out before her and Letty trailing along in her wake. Roth would have to deal with the vicar's wife. Isabella did not doubt he had dealt with encroaching mamas before.

She went to her study. It was time to resume her customary habits. She would bury herself in her ledgers.

When it came, Isabella realized she had been waiting for the knock on her door. She had heard, distantly, Mrs. Smithby and Letty depart. After Liza and Lady Prim had bid the pair farewell, silence had fallen, and she had returned to her books.

She had not heard the footsteps coming to her door, but, still, the single knock did not surprise her. She called out. The door opened, and she blushed fiery red, then her color leaving, her face went pale as a ghost.

She had not expected Lord Roth to come to her. She had thought it would be Jepson with a note, or Nell. She had planned her excuse. She had decided not to face him until later, whenever that was.

Isabella sat staring at Julian a full half minute, giving him the opportunity to take in the half spectacles he had never seen before. She looked very prim with them perched on her nose. Delightfully so. How deceiving. She had proven herself a warm-blooded, if quite innocent, woman in his arms the day before. And a woman of swift revenge today.

It only dawned slowly on Isabella that Julian was furiously angry. She was at first distracted by his looks. She had not seen him in a cravat before. Perhaps it was in honor of his visitors, he had gone to the trouble of tying it at his throat. The knot was simple but looked elegant in an offhand way.

His coat was of blue superfine and superbly cut. Isabella had seen other coats of like quality—on Wrexham, for one—but she had never seen a coat displayed to such advantage. The marquess's strong, lean build must have been his tailor's greatest wish come true. Any gentleman seeing the garment would want the name of Roth's man.

But the tailor—Weston she felt certain—would seldom come by such raw material as Lord Roth presented him. The hopeful gentleman would be doomed to disappointment. Perhaps even to gloom, Isabella added to herself, as she flicked her eyes over the skintight buckskins that disappeared into his boots.

But he had not come for her to admire him. Abruptly swinging away from her stunned countenance, he sent the door to her study slamming shut with the toe of his boot.

The violence of his movement startled. He had not come to beg her pardon, it seemed. She rose from her seat, intending to attempt an equal footing with him. She had forgotten her little spectacles. Jarred, they slipped off her nose, and she only just managed to catch them before they clattered onto the desk.

Oddly, in that moment she was given, when she had excuse to look away from Julian and rescue her glasses, the explanation for the angry tightness of his mouth came to her.

She looked at him directly and spoke before he could. "I did not send Mrs. Smithby to you."

"If you did not promote Mrs. Smithby's visitation, you did nothing to stop her."

"That is true," Isabella admitted, her voice a little high. "But Mrs. Smithby is a formidable woman when she has set her mind upon something, and . . ."

"You know damnably well you could have prevented her from inflicting herself and that idiotic daughter upon me had you wished!"

Such anger blazed in Julian's eyes that Isabella clutched her spectacles tightly. "I could have. You are right. But I was not in any frame of mind . . ."

Whatever Isabella's frame of mind, Julian's was beyond reason. "You wanted me to endure that encroaching, fawning, shrill harridan! And her simpering chit of a daughter besides. Well, count yourself avenged, Miss Ramsey. I never spent a worse morning!"

"Nor did I."

Isabella clenched her fist. She had not meant to say it, had even, after she realized he had come to rail at her over Mrs. Smithby, entertained the craven hope that she could end the interview before they got around to "the other." But he had made her angry, railing at her over a half hour spent with Mrs. Smithby, when she had lost an evening, a night, and a morning on his account.

What little composure she thought she had possessed dissolved then, and Isabella felt tears prick the back of her eyelids. There seemed nothing to do but carefully lay aside the spectacles she still held and hope her tears would recede before he could see them.

If the one tightly uttered phrase about what could only have been a wretched morning for her had not doused the flame of Julian's anger, the sight of Isabella arranging her spectacles upon her desk as carefully as if they were the Magna Carta, certainly did.

Despite the several bottles of brandy he had enlisted in his effort to plunge himself into an untroubled sleep, he had not slept long at all. And had come awake to a raging headache, the only lasting effect of the brandy.

His head throbbing, his mind groggy, he had lain a long while in his bed considering his next course of action. Several possibilities had occurred. Among them even, when he had entertained a vision of Isabella sliding into Wrexham's sheets prior to having the viscount's pale, bejeweled hands caress her, had been the thought that he might offer himself up as her groom in the viscount's place.

But Julian had, not without reason, a quite abiding distaste for the state of matrimony. He could yet recall, and vividly, the moment when he, a rather tender ten, had learned from a jealous schoolmate that the Duchess of Chandley was notorious for her infidelities and the identity of Julian's own father was open to question. For pride's sake he had bloodied the boy's nose, but too much about Chandley's attitude toward him was explained for Julian not to realize he had heard the truth. With a youth's fierceness he had vowed then that he would never allow any woman to betray him and hold him up to public ridicule as his mother had her husband.

It was a vow he had not once questioned since, and so almost as quickly as the notion had arisen, he discarded it.

Which left him in the end as foggy as to his immediate future course as his head felt. The indecision had not sweetened his mood, already corroded by the blistering headache, and it had only needed the officious vicar's wife, got up in a hideous dress of blinding purple, to send him in a rage to Isabella.

Mrs. Smithby was a blessing in disguise. He almost laughed. Almost. At least he was no longer furiously angry, and he could see far more clearly what it was he wanted.

She stood before him, her head bowed, still working on the proper placement for her glasses. "Isabella . . ."

He got no further. His sudden soft tone, his use of her name, the step he'd taken closer to her desk, all were quite unbearable to Isabella. "My lord," she said swiftly, too swiftly, and in a high, shaky voice. "I did not think to use Mrs. Smithby against you. Truly."

She was clutching her glasses now so tightly her knuckles had gone white. Julian said carefully, "Had I stopped to think even a little I'd have known that before I raged in here. I am sorry I stormed at you, Isabella. I've a temper at times, and today it was only waiting to be ignited. Mrs. Smithby, I fear, was a more than adequate spark."

He was addressing the top of her head. A mass of soft brown curls caught into a knot, it was not an unpleasant sight, but he wanted her eyes.

"May I sit? I am weaker than I thought."

Her head flew up. She had managed to blink back most of her tears, but there was still a suspicious shine at the corners of her eyes.

It took Isabella a moment to realize Julian meant he was obliged to stand so long as she did. She had not intended to tax him, of course, only to face him as an equal. Still, for the merest second, she hesitated. If he was tired, would not the inevitably painful interview be ended the sooner?

"Isabella we cannot pretend that nothing has occurred between us."

Color surged into her cheeks. "No, no." She looked desperately around at the chairs in the room, her gaze not settling on any particular one but successfully avoiding him. She thought Julian's eyes had never looked quite so blue-green and penetrating as they did just then. "Please," she made a vague gesture that included any and all of the chairs.

Julian did not move. "If we are agreed on a discussion, then you must bring yourself to look at me." He watched her bite her lip, but she did not turn her gaze to his. "I do not think I, alone, am to blame for the . . . for yesterday, Isabella." Softly, without accusation, he continued, "You did stay to drink and dance with me."

He saw her wince, but she still did not face him, only said

so softly he had to strain to hear, "I thought you were my friend."

She studied the wall by the door where there hung a portrait of her mother's mother, a woman of modest expression who would never have found herself in Isabella's predicament. She heard Julian make an impatient sound, then suddenly he stood in her line of vision, his broad shoulders quite blotting her grandmother from her sight.

"Isabella, Isabella, I am not your enemy. You cannot believe I meant to force you against your will?"

"No. I do not believe you had it in mind to force me to anything."

Julian studied her pale face a long moment, raking a hand through his hair and disordering it so a waving strand of dark gold fell onto his forehead. Then abruptly he turned away. For the space of a heartbeat Isabella thought he meant to fling out of the room and could not determine if the sudden pang she experienced was disappointment or relief.

The question was rendered moot when Julian continued by the door, and she realized he was only making a restless circuit of the room. At the end he stood before her again.

Close before her, so that she caught the faintest whiff of sandalwood. She squeezed her hands into tight, tight balls and succeeded at stifling the cry that rose in her throat.

"Isabella." He came a step closer that she could not but be aware of every tall, well-made inch of him.

And be aware how intense was the look in his eyes. Again there was nothing soft or lover-like about Julian's expression. Grave but for the intensely compelling light in his eye, he looked prepared to prevail over her by sheer force of will.

"If it is that you believe I have been no friend to you because I have somehow misled you, Isabella, then I shall be clear. I did not have it in mind to seduce you yesterday." She caught her breath at the plain speaking, but Julian was not diverted. "I knew you to be kind and amusing. I knew you to be capable of warmth, but not I thought, yet, passionate. I was quite wrong. You are passionate now and warm as the sun. I would make love to you, Isabella. I would love you as you will not be loved in Wrexham's cold marital bed."

Isabella let out a shaky, pent-up breath. Her legs felt weak enough that she put one hand to her desk to steady her.

Dear God. Had he said anything but that last! He'd not even have had to say he loved her—a far different thing, and she knew it, from saying he would make love to her—he need only have said he had affection for her, then, she was appalled to realize, she truly could not say how she'd have replied.

She still felt his attraction, when he had offered her nothing more than a slip on the shoulder!

Isabella began to tremble in earnest then, as a red haze of anger rose in her. She had never, ever been so angry. Engulfed by the emotion, she could not or would not stop to analyze it: to consider that she might be the source of her own fury as much as was he.

All she could think was that he, who had been so thoughtful and gentle and kind, and who was more handsome than any man had a right to be—he had, in the end, treated her as little better than a trollop.

The gold flecks in her eyes blazing to angry life, she was not prepared to examine closely the source of her anger, only to fling it in the Marquess of Roth's very handsome face.

"My congratulations on a well-said line, my lord! Practice, no doubt, has polished it."

Isabella jerked her chin higher, when her sarcasm provoked a dangerous flash in Julian's eyes, but she was not subdued. Her blood fairly singing in her veins, she bit out, "Again, it seems, I must ask you not to revile Lord Wrexham. He is my husband-to-be, and whatever else he has done, he has done me the honor of offering me his name, something you have not." A muscle worked in Julian's jaw, but he did not argue the truth of Isabella's statement, though, despite her best intentions, she did pause. "As to what you do offer me," she continued, and there was the faintest tinge of bitterness in her voice, "a brief, pleasurable, I do not doubt that, affair. There is only one rub. And if you knew me as well as you claim, I would not have to tell you of it. You would know that if I were to become your mistress, I would betray myself. I've no doubt in your rarefied circles, it is quite out of fashion to say so, but for me honor, loyalty, and trust are not merely hollow principles to be invoked at my convenience. Before you ever left me, Lord Roth, as you would eventually do—having bestowed upon me, as is customary I am told, a pretty bauble to make the parting easier—I would feel an empty, fickle, shallow, even treacherous woman of little or no worth at all, and I can call no one friend who would endeavor to persuade me to come to that pass!''

Isabella had the satisfaction of seeing Julian had gone very pale and that the muscle worked again in his jaw.

He said, "I see." His voice was utterly toneless, a stranger's. "You have indeed spoken plainly, Miss Ramsey, and your eloquence has made it abundantly clear that my continued presence at Marsh House can only be a source of discomfort to you. As I would not repay you so poorly for the generous care you have provided me, I shall bid you adieu and continue on to my destination. Farewell, and may your worthy principles bring you comfort."

After inclining his head formally, Julian turned on his heel and departed the room.

Chapter 13

"Ah yes, Willis." Julian looked up from his ledger. It was the second time he'd met his estate agent, and he found the man's fox-like face no more appealing because it was familiar. "Have a seat there, in the blue chair. It should hold you as it seems by some miracle to have escaped the rot."

"Ha! Ha!" Willis's laugh did not touch his narrow, little eyes. "Your uncle, the late Mr. Montcrief, God rest his soul, cared not a whit for the house, your lordship. Never said to spend a penny on it, an' we respected his wishes. I know it must be a trial . . ."

"Yes, it is, Mr. Willis." Julian tipped the ledger away from his lap so that it lay open on his desk and watched as the estate agent was unable to keep from darting a sharp look at it. "Which brings us to the subject of servants."

"I'm doin' my best in that regard, your lordship." Willis bobbed his head. "But these locals are a superstitious lot. They believe the abbey's haunted. The only person who needed the work more than she feared the place was old Mabel Jenkins who's come to cook."

"No doubt Mrs. Jenkins was confident she could use the rubbish she turns out to repel restless spirits."

"Ha, ha! 'Tis a fine jokester you are, m'lord. Mabel does her best, though I'm sure it don't come close to what you're used to. She's never cooked for a lord before, you see. But now you've come and seen what's what, there's no need of you stayin' on here. It's not a fit place for the likes of you, Lord Roth. Only tell me what it is you want done, and I'll see it through."

When Julian steepled his fingers and subjected Willis to a long look over the top of them, the estate agent shifted uneasily.

"'You may as well leave off the theme of my leaving, Willis,'' Julian advised softly at last. "I've every intention of supervising the restoration of Wynchley Abbey personally. Is that quite understood?''

For the merest instant Willis's eyes hardened, then he recovered. "Oh, aye, m'lord. You'll be stayin'.''

"I wished to see you this morning Willis, because I've some questions for you.'' He gestured toward the open ledger, and the agent craned his neck in a vain attempt to see it. "The books show that money was drawn from the estate for upkeep on the house. I am at a loss to imagine where you might have spent it.''

"Eh, well, there's a deal to be done just to keep the place from fallin' down. An' Mr. Montcrief never said as how he would live here.''

"I do not imagine he said he'd a desire to grow moss on the walls of his home, however.'' A flush mounted on Willis's angular cheeks, but Julian was not done. "It was your duty as land agent to keep the house up to the minimum degree required at least for safety, Willis. If any accident should befall me, any of my staff, or any guests I may have, I shall hold you personally accountable.''

"Me?'' Willis blustered. "An' what d'you mean by that, ah, m'lord?''

Julian marked the slip in diction with some pleasure. "I mean, Willis, that as I was walking to the stable yard yesterday one of the gargoyles adorning the roof of this pile came tumbling down. I have reflexes honed by several years of battle to thank for escaping with an intact skull. Now,'' Julian held up his hand as Willis started to protest his innocence, "stonework may be easily assessed and repaired. You, Willis, are directly responsible for having neglected to carry out the duty. As land agent, it was your place. I have posted a letter to that effect to my man of business in London. Should any more masonry happen to fall but not, shall we say, miss the mark, you will be brought before the authorities. Do I make myself clear?''

The man of good humor had quite disappeared. "Aye, m'lord. You're clear enough.''

"Good.'' Julian held Willis's eyes until the land agent looked away. "Tell me how it is, Willis, that you came to do the books at all. There was a secretary at one time, I believe.''

"Smithson," Willis half grunted. "But he left an' Mr. Montcrief said naught as to replacin' him."

"And so you took over the books. I see. Tell me, Willis, why is it the estate has not shown a profit for five years?"

The answer came easily, too easily. "Bad luck, that's what m'lord. We've had troubles an' not the least of 'em's this long drought." He made a vague gesture that seemed to imply bad conditions for all the previous five years, possibly more.

"And, therefore you did not wish to raise the tenants' rents even once, I suppose?"

Willis drew himself up righteously. "Couldn't do that to 'em, m'lord. They're all good men. I culled out the bad ones when I first came."

"They are pleased with their situation and work hard as a result?"

"You'll not hear 'em complain, m'lord," Willis replied, not quite addressing the question put to him.

"Did you ever think to try a crop other than wheat?" Julian asked, recalling how Isabella Ramsey had decried Willis's practice of planting only one crop year after year.

" 'Tis wheat the army wants, naught else, m'lord. Another crop'd not bring the same money."

"And yet, the books show you made no profit the last few years."

"I'm not in charge o' the rain, m'lord!"

"No, that you are not," Julian answered. "But you are in charge of the dikes," he went on, the same conversation with Isabella prompting him. "They are in good order, I trust. The books show large sums were withdrawn to pay for repairs."

"There's nothin' wrong with the dikes! Who says there is?"

"Perhaps you did not hear me, Willis," Julian chided with silky patience. "I only asked if you made the repairs with the money you withdrew."

"Well, as to that," Willis muttered sullenly. "I did the inspections and the repairs as was needed, m'lord."

"Good, good. Then all will be in order when I ride out to inspect them. But," Julian appeared to consider a moment. "Yes, I think it is important, as the dikes are our defense against the ever-encroaching sea, that we make a special effort there. I shall relieve you of all your other duties as land agent, Mr.

Willis, in order that you may concentrate upon the dikes. Take some men out and, beginning with the dikes that border the Ramsey estate, institute the repairs that are needed. I shall expect a report daily. You may give it to my man, Jepson, if I am not available. Thank you, Willis. That will be all.''

Willis's face had gone red in ugly, angry blotches, as he groped for some response to his demotion—for that was what had been handed him as offhandedly as if he were no better than a cur.

But there was something in the Marquess of Roth's eyes that held him mute, and when his employer said very softly but quite distinctly, ''Good day, Willis,'' the estate agent lurched to his feet. He rocked onto his toes, his jaw working, then turned sharply and careened out of the room.

Silence reigned a long moment after his departure, and then Julian said, ''Well, what do you think?''

There was a fumbling behind one of the curtains before Jepson finally emerged. He worked his shoulders as he came forward, for the window seat had been far smaller than his considerable bulk.

''The bloke's a rogue, m'lord. I'll be bound 'e never made a repair to anything.'' Jepson's eyes narrowed. ''An' 'e knew something about that bit o' fancy stonework nearly took your 'ead off.''

''Yes, he did not seem pleased with the notice that he would be held accountable for future accidents. You could not see it, but mention of the authorities turned Jaspar Willis quite green.'' Julian frowned. ''And that only adds to the question, why should he so brazenly attempt to put me out of the way? He's no fool. He must know there would be an inquest were I to turn up dead suddenly, and I'll wager he'd not care for that.''

''Mayhap 'e only thought to encourage ye like to leave, the rot 'ere 'avin' failed an' all. Might not 'a been aimin' directly fer yer 'ead.''

''Yes,'' Julian nodded slowly. ''That explanation does make more sense. He does not seem to care who owns the place, only that the owner reside anywhere but here.''

'' 'Im an' the squire.''

Julian shot Jepson, who now dwarfed the chair Willis had vacated, a keen glance. ''The squire?'' he repeated.

His batman nodded. "Ramsey were fair put out you'd a notion all of a sudden like to leave 'is bed and board. Near pulled ye off yer mount, 'e fought so ta keep ye at Marsh 'ouse."

"But he was right to say the abbey is scarcely fit for habitation," Julian observed. "I dread to think what will happen when it rains. It is bad enough now with mildew like a thick scourge everywhere, rotted boards to make walking an adventure, and half the furniture past saving. That bed I'm in may hold up another night, or it may not. The matter hangs in a most delicate balance."

"Aye, puts me in mind o' Spain, it fair does. Why I remember one night . . ."

"Spare me the sentimental pap, Jepson. Wynchley Abbey is scarcely habitable and the food prepared by that hag in the kitchen is dangerous. Ramsey was right to say the conditions here are unfit for civilized people. Lady Prim went on in much the same vein, as did Liza Ramsey."

"But no Miss Bella," Jepson remarked, slanting his master a sudden, searching glance. "Strange it was, she weren't on 'an' ta wave ye off."

"She had made her adieus earlier." Julian's brusque reply precluded further inquiry. "As to the squire. Was his dismay at my departure greater than that of the others?"

"Nay." Jepson shook his great head. "That bit o' fluff, Lady Prim, was ever' bit as bad. 'Tis only that, while she strikes me as the kind to go on an' on over another body's comfort, the squire don't seem that sort. Might say a word or two, but then, seein' ye were set on yer course, I'd 'ave thought 'e'd send ye off with a bottle o' his best brandy."

Julian's smile was sudden and dazzling. "That sort of reasoning, my good Jepson, is why I keep you on. Not," he inclined his head when Jepson assumed an attitude of affront, "that you do not keep my cravats starched and my boots gleaming, but I do value your opinion. It so often coincides with mine, you see."

Jepson's face split into a wide grin. "Which makes us both bloomin' idiots, m'lord, or . . ."

"Underrated geniuses," Julian finished dryly.

Jepson gave his master a token bow. "But what d'ye make o' this business, then?"

"I don't know what to make of it, in truth," Julian admitted with a wry look. "These books tell little. At first glance, they seem very neat, but upon closer inspection one finds odd inconsistencies such as debits with no explanation and transposed figures that yet manage to balance.

"Then there's Willis's distinct reluctance to have outsiders come onto the estate. He plainly does not want us here, and he has kept the locals off, including Miss Ramsey and Cora Geddes, though they only came to offer what healing skills they possess. That seems an odd thing for a land agent in need of able-bodied men to do. And there's the possibility he has neglected repairs to the abbey and the dikes, not merely because he pockets the expenses, but because he would be obliged to supplement his handpicked tenants with men from the neighborhood.

"Finally, there is the question of Squire Ramsey. Though there is no public connection between them, his interest in keeping us, and others, away does seem to coincide with Willis's. As you say, Jepson, he was almost frantic to keep us at Marsh House, and I was witness once to an exchange between him and the eldest daughter in which he was quite angry to hear she had defied Willis to visit the Prewitts."

Julian frowned thoughtfully. "I wonder how it is the squire is able to finance Liza's come-out, when by Lady Prim's account, he rendered his own purse rather short of coin."

"That Mrs. 'obbes said something one day 'bout a bit o' blunt that come in last summer like. It were the savin' o' them, she said. There were debts o' the squire's to pay, and the doin's for the young miss to bring off, and school for the squire's boy."

Julian nodded. "Remiss of me to forget the absent Peter, as I made myself at home in his room. So, substantial funds came in some time last summer. I wonder if it is coincidence that Isabella became betrothed to Wrexham then. Perhaps he made a settlement upon her at their betrothal. Possible, only I seem to recall rumors going about last Season to the effect that Wrexham, himself, suffered losses at the gaming tables. I'll write to Perry. He'll know. A settlement would explain her decision to marry him."

Jepson had no need to ask who "she" was, nor did he see cause to remark aloud how Miss Ramsey had become Isabella in the course of his master's musings. But he did have a thought on Miss Isabella's decision to wed herself to a man not one of the servants at Marsh House favored.

"Mayhap Miss Bella was thinkin' o' the child, when she said yes to the father?"

Julian winced at the mention of Sarah Farley. The little girl's brown eyes had filled with tears when he had gone up to bid her farewell. Like the adults at Marsh House, she had been unable to understand his sudden decision. All at once, though, she had brightened and run to a large table that was situated by her nursery window to return with a rather raggedy cloth doll. Ducking her head from shyness, she had confided she wished him to have the doll she had won. "She'll be y-your friend. If y-you are l-lonely at the abbey, y-you may sl-sleep with h-her."

"Yes, I think it likely Lady Sarah figured into Miss Ramsey's considerations," Julian said abruptly. "And I may be imagining there is something odd afoot. Willis and Ramsey may only have my best interest at heart."

"Mayhap," Jepson agreed, following Julian's gaze toward the ceiling that was festooned with a profusion of cobwebs and dangling pieces of plaster. "But that was a bit 'o nonsense Willis spewed about the village folk fearin' the abbey's ghosts. 'Tis Willis, himself, they fear, or so they told me when I went along ta see who'd work 'ere. To their minds, ye'll stay at the abbey only a bit. 'Tis Willis they think'll stay on, an' they don't want 'im as their master, not a one."

"Except for Mabel Jenkins, God rest her cooking."

"The widow Jenkins be the grandmother of Willis's child."

"Willis is married?" Julian asked, surprised.

"Nay. 'E didn't go to the bother."

"Ah."

"Now!" Jepson protested his master's knowing tones. "Ye canna blame the man fer takin' a wench to 'is bed. 'Tis what ever' man tries ta do after all." The blandest of looks accompanied the remark, but a muscle clenched in Julian's jaw. Jepson went on to other matters. " 'Ave ye thought 'ow ye'll run the place when ye've not got Willis's 'elp? Do ye mean to be yer own steward?"

His master's look had not warmed since the rather pointed

remark about what all men tried to do. "I shall, if you've no objection, that is."

A quite unruffled smile split Jepson's untidy countenance. "Not I, m'lord."

"I am relieved." Abruptly Julian raked his hand through his hair, and his manner changed. "I must act as my own steward in fact. Those were the terms of my father's—challenge. Within a year, I must have the situation here in hand. He did not say anything against an adviser, though, and that is what I'm in sore need of. You could write down all I know about agriculture on your thumbnail.

"The Bashams come to mind, of course. I know them at least a little, but the father is a close acquaintance of Chandley's, and I'll be damned if I'll have my father kept informed of every question I ask and every mistake I make. There'll be too many."

"Tha' Cummings man over't Ramseys," Jepson said thoughtfully. " 'E seemed a level sort an' all." Suddenly the large man slapped his knee with a meaty paw. "That does gi' me a notion 'ow ye might get servants."

"Oh?"

Jepson nodded forcefully. "What ye need is a person the local folk set a deal o' store by, an' that's Miss Bella. She's a rare fine lass, and they'll believe 'er if she tells 'em ye'll not leave 'em to Willis. Nay, they'll come right along to air out the bed sheets an' fix up 'em grinnin' 'eads on the roof."

"Miss Ramsey has matters other than Wynchley Abbey, its linens and its charming gargoyles, with which to concern herself. We shall have to make do without her."

Jepson seemed inclined to argue. He even opened his mouth, but Julian arched an eyebrow. "Give it up, Jepson."

It was an order Jepson could not but obey and take note that his master looked suddenly weary. "Ye're tired as the devil, m'lord and ought ta be in yer bed even if't does reek a bit. Come along." He bullied Julian, who was, indeed, weary up the creaking stairs to the huge, musty room that was the master bedroom.

Julian looked very grim all the while, and after a time, Jepson, a twinkle in his eye, sought to lighten his master's mood. "I've another notion who'll 'elp ye, m'lord. The vicar's wife'd be ever so willin'."

"Bring that woman in, my good fellow, and you'll be sacked without references," Julian warned darkly only to smile when Jepson guffawed. "Egad, was she not the outside of enough? Even now in my nightmares I see that corseted bosom bearing down on me, and I wake up in a sweat."

" 'Twas my fear she'd never let go o' your 'and. 'Eld it for 'alf the visit—after shakin' it up and down like a pump 'andle. Ye were lucky it weren't yer bad side."

"As far as Mrs. Smithby goes, I do not have a good side," Julian announced. "And I am not at home to her, if she should come to call."

Chapter 14

"But he cannot be out riding, man!" Julian came to an abrupt halt. Mrs. Smithby's strident tones, issuing from the direction of his front hallway, were unmistakable. "You mistook your master's remark! Why, only a few days ago the marquess had scarcely recovered enough to walk! He will be about. Do go and fetch him! He will be most pleased to learn Letty and I have come to offer our assistance. We shall await him in the library. It is along here, if I remember correctly."

Julian measured the distance to the far corner of the hallway with his eye. He would never reach it before Mrs. Smithby appeared at her end. Cool under pressure, Julian slipped into the very room that was her destination and without a glance at its dusty shelves, made for the French windows. He did not panic when the first door did not budge, though Mrs. Smithby's voice came ever closer. He went at once to the next, then the next.

Finally a handle gave, and when Mrs. Smithby entered, Julian was slipping through the cloister garden to shorten the distance to the stables. It was no mean feat to saddle a mount, but Julian had only to summon an image of the vicar's wife to spur himself on. Mounted at last he felt quite smug, if tired, and struck out down a small lane leading away from the stables.

The first sight of fallow fields sobered him, reminding him as it did of all the work there was to be done. Work he had not the slightest notion how to carry out properly.

The estate's tenants would not be a source of guidance, he knew, for despite his painful ribs, he had ridden out to visit many of them over the course of the last two days and had found them to be so guarded with him as to be virtually mute. He suspected Willis had warned them against him and marked it as one more sin for which the agent would account when Julian had solved the mystery of what he had been about on the estate.

He could not, however, hold Willis responsible for his ignorance of land stewardship. Chandley had set out lessons on the subject for him, but for many reasons—not the least of which was they'd equally strong wills and had clashed from the moment of Julian's birth—Julian had long made it a point of honor to never to make the least push to please the duke. Indeed, proud to a fault and rebellious to boot, he had more often than not taken a perverse satisfaction in doing the very opposite of what his father wished.

Until now. Now, when the task was almost beyond him, he was bent on proving himself more capable than Chandley believed. And he intended to succeed. He only needed a counselor.

Still considering who he might approach, Julian ambled along his narrow lane to its end where a dike rose up before him. It was a great mound of earth, running as far as he could see to his left toward the Ramseys' and to his right, curving out of sight very soon. Idly scanning the somewhat larger lane that ran parallel to the dike, he frowned suddenly. There were great ruts in the road only very heavy loads could have made. Julian could not think what the estate produced that would weigh so much, for the ruts were exceptionally deep, then noted an even more curious thing. The ruts did not mar the lane in both directions. They began—or ended, he could not say which—only a little way behind him. Why should someone wish to transport heavy burdens either to or from this place, where there were naught but dike and fields? On the other side of the dike was only marsh.

Julian followed the ruts until they turned off onto a lesser-used lane similar to the one that had brought him to the dike. His geography of the estate was still sketchy, but he'd the notion the lane skirted close to the abbey and came out at the main road that ran from Saxbourne village to Ipswich and thence to London.

On impulse Julian tethered his mount to a tree in the woods and scaled the dike to look out over the marsh. Low-lying reed beds dotted here and there by taller clumps of weedy, arching willows stretched out to meet in the distance the gray, shimmering line of the sea. There was movement aplenty. All sorts of ducks bobbed in the water below him and at least twenty wading birds darted busily along the bank of the dike, while overhead gulls and terns and, even higher, a single osprey floated on the wind watching for dinner, but nowhere could he see any human activity.

The sound of a horse's hooves returned Julian's attention to the road behind him just as a trap, being driven at a sprightly pace by someone who had had business on Wynchley, appeared from around the corner. A fluffy dog he knew very well sat perched beside the young woman who drove. He could not see her face for it was obscured by a wide-brim chip bonnet that tied beneath her chin, but he knew without needing to look that the dark green of the pelisse she wore would deepen the green of her eyes.

The dog by her, Mr. Buttons, must have caught sight of the man standing atop the dike, for suddenly, barking furiously, he strained urgently at the lead Isabella had secured to the trap. She tried to calm him, but even as she slowed the trap that she might reach out to stroke him, the lead, unused to such taxing, snapped in two, and Mr. Buttons hurtled away to freedom.

Isabella had only to think what the scamp would do when he caught sight of the abundant waterfowl in the marsh to make short work of pulling up her pony, Dan, and scrambling down from the trap to give chase. She had gotten almost to the top, when the quality of Mr. Buttons's bark changed. She knew it as the ecstatic one he gave in greeting.

Isabella did not need to tip her head and look out from beneath her wide-brimmed bonnet to identify the man about whose polished black boots Mr. Buttons scrambled in such delirium. Even as she stared at the little dog, as if he were the only creature present, Julian went down on one knee to ruffle his fur in greeting and to seize what was left of his lead.

Had a stranger been watching the meeting, he'd have thought it an odd one indeed. Even when the gentleman did turn at last to glance up at the lady, he spoke no word of greeting, nor even smiled. The young lady was no more amiable. She stared in silence, and the only evidence she gave that she was even aware of the gentleman was that the color in her cheeks receded as quickly as it had risen, leaving them very pale.

"I trust this fellow's presence does not indicate his mistress is ill."

Isabella watched Mr. Buttons lick Julian's fine-boned hand. "Lady Prim has the headache, no more. I thought to give her a rest and him an outing." *And I will never be so kind to the wretched ingrate again.*

"And the Prewitts? I take it you have been to visit them."

A quick thrust of concern for the family she had indeed visited, prompted Isabella to slant Julian a glance from beneath her bonnet. And to look away again as quickly.

It was almost as if she had never seen him before, though he had invaded her thoughts constantly for days. But those thoughts, most of them harsh, had altered Julian's image in her mind so that she was taken aback to see no sign of a debauched, arrogant libertine, only a very handsome man with sun-streaked hair and eyes an impossibly brilliant aquamarine.

She gazed unseeing at a heron in the distance and reflected on the strain she had also recognized on his face. The thought that Julian might find their meeting as difficult as she, oddly, helped a little. She found her voice, for the family was his responsibility now. "I did take Cora to the Prewitts' and found their situation mixed. Mrs. Prewitt has recovered, and the two boys are much improved, but one of the daughters has taken ill, while Billy has developed a cough." Isabella met Julian's eyes with an effort. "Cora thought to spend at least one night, if you've no objection?"

"Of course not." His voice sounded harsh to Isabella's ears, and she dropped her gaze to Mr. Buttons. Panting contentedly, he seemed utterly at home by Julian's knee. "I visited them yesterday and thought the youngest boy looked weak as a kitten."

Isabella's eyes flew wide. She had not heard mention of Lord Roth's visit, but she had spoken only with Billy and his sister, both of whom had been entirely absorbed by the funny dog she'd brought to play with them.

"I see you are surprised to learn I did what is expected of any landlord, Miss Ramsey."

Their gazes held and clashed, and Isabella lifted her chin. She would not apologize for believing the condition of the abbey would overwhelm any interest he might have in the estate.

"I'll keep you no longer, Lord Roth. Thank you for apprehending Mr. Buttons. I should have hated to face Lady Prim had he plunged into the marsh." Isabella held out her arms, expecting Julian to rise and return the dog that they might end their unfortunate encounter.

He eyed her outstretched arms a moment, then gave her a grim smile. "For the sin of trespassing, albeit in a good cause, I shall detain you a few minutes, Miss Ramsey. I've something to ask of you."

"And if I do not care to be detained?"

"I've no intention of endeavoring to force you into a betrayal of yourself, Miss Ramsey, if that is your concern." Having coolly delivered that assurance, Julian left Isabella to stand with her cheeks awash in color while he led Mr. Buttons further along the dike. The little dog, in an excess of energy, executed a high leap and managed to lick his benefactor's cheek. Julian chuckled. The amused sound contrasted mightily with the tense silence he had left behind. "You will find your thanks premature, you bit of energetic fluff. I intend to tether you to this bush."

Julian suited his actions to his words and soon Mr. Buttons, though not as free as he'd have liked, was at least able to sniff urgently at the ground and bark excitedly at anything that moved below.

Long ago large stones had been hauled in to strengthen the marsh side of the dike. Julian, when he turned back to Isabella, all trace of the amiability he had displayed toward Mr. Buttons quite gone, gestured toward the nearest of the boulders. "Would you care to have a seat, Miss Ramsey?"

Isabella did not care to be seated at all. The atmosphere between them had gone from tense to hostile, and she wanted nothing more than to stomp off down the dike. She could not, however, quite bring herself to bolt. The man before her, the one with the sardonic look in his eye, the one she did but did not know, might very well restrain her. She did not believe he would hurt her, but he would touch her.

"My request has to do with Wynchley."

He said that evenly enough, but Isabella could sense that his temper—with which she was acquainted—was becoming strained. She took the sop to her pride and inclined her head.

He gestured again to the boulders, and she seated herself upon a large, flat rock that jutted out over its brothers while he chose a seat some five feet away. Isabella noted and appreciated the distance.

From the corner of her eye she saw Julian gather a fist-sized rock from the ground and send it high over the marshes. They watched it arch into the air, then fall among the reeds without a sound.

A silence followed. Isabella could not but find it fraught with a good many memories she would rather not consider.

"Your ribs seem greatly improved," she said still gazing out over the reed beds below them.

"They are mending nicely, thank you."

How very cool he sounded, and he had been the one to demand an interview. Vexed but unable to still her tongue, for silence had fallen again, she asked in rather rapid succession, "Did you ride here? I should think riding would jar them."

"It does," he conceded. "But the alternative was much worse."

"What do you mean?"

"I exaggerate, Miss Ramsey," Julian said, his voice softening slightly, and she realized with some dismay that she had leaned forward in concern. Instantly she pulled herself up straight. "The alternative to a ride was a likely lengthy visit with Mrs. Smithby. When she descended upon the abbey with no advance warning, I sought the nearest avenue of escape I could find."

Isabella could not, then, find any humor in an image of the hero of Talaveras skulking off to his stables. Acutely uncomfortable associations revolved around the vicar's wife, and she demanded abruptly, "You wished to ask something of me, my lord?"

"Yes." He expelled a long breath, as if he did not find the prospect of saying what he must easy. Isabella cast him a look through her lashes and thought Julian looked very grim. "Yes, you see, I need assistance with administering Wynchley." Another rock was flung rather more violently over the marsh. "I'm in the devil of a pickle, in fact, for I must have Wynchley on a sound footing in a year's time."

That so took Isabella aback she forgot what lay between them

for a moment and exclaimed aloud. Julian gave her a thin smile.
"Not much time is it?"

"But why?"

Julian sent a handful of pebbles tumbling down the rocks,
then dusted off his hands before, at last, he turned to address
her directly. "My father and I have always found our relations
to be . . . difficult," he began, holding her gaze steadily, though
she'd the sense he was finding the conversation difficult indeed.
"It is a long story, one I will not bore you with, but the result
is that my father doubts I will be capable of administering his
admittedly complex estate when it comes to me. As a result,
he has made my inheriting that portion of his estate that is not
entailed conditional. I must rectify the damage that neglect and
mismanagement have wrought here . . ." Julian did look away
then to wave at the land behind him, but Isabella did not follow
his gesture. She watched him catch his lip between his teeth.
In the next instant, when he looked back at her, he was once
more the cool, daring Corinthian up to any rig, but she had
witnessed that one revealing gesture and knew Julian Montcrief
was more anxious than he cared for anyone to know, ". . . In
a year's time."

"You need your father's entire estate?"

"If I am not to be the first Duke of Chandley without a ducal
seat and the first Montcrief without Kereford Castle, then I do
need it, yes. There is not much land in the entail, only the title
and my home."

My home. He held the place dear, Isabella realized with some
surprise, for she'd come to think he did not value a great deal.

"What is it you want of me?" she asked, fighting to contain
a rise of her sympathies by reminding herself he was adept at
playing on her emotions.

"I should like your permission to ask Mr. Cummings to come
to me on a regular basis that I may have his counsel."

It was not what she had expected but she thought it was
perfectly reasonable. "You have turned Willis off, then?"

"No." Julian gave her a grim look. "I have kept Willis on
in a diminished capacity, but you needn't fear I've a soft spot
for the fellow. I suspect he's as villainous as you believe, and
I want him close at hand until I've full proof of all his
misdeeds."

She absorbed that news slowly, then nodded. Whatever else she could say about Julian Montcrief, he was not a fool to be wound around Willis's sly finger. She did not let herself think of her father. "I see. Well, as to Mr. Cummings, if he is willing, I've no objection, my lord. He's years of experience to draw upon and is honest."

"I shall need him a great deal."

Honest of him to admit that, Isabella remarked quite to herself and a trifle sharply. "Yes, of course, you will have a great deal to do," she said aloud. "But we've matters fairly well in hand at home."

Isabella turned to look off to the marshes, seeking some inspiration in them to help her as she wrestled with her tongue. She knew from Mrs. Hobbes and Nell that no one from the village had been hired on at the abbey, and from her own experience she knew how sorely the house needed a full regiment of industrious servants. Abruptly conceding victory to her curiosity—not anything else, for she refused to feel the least bit responsible that he had wound up at the abbey before it could be rendered even moderately fit for residence—she asked, "Have you a housekeeper, my lord?"

"No." Though the reply had not been unexpected, Isabella was still surprised. "I have not found any servants."

"But how can you live there?"

Julian did not say, as she steeled herself to hear, that he had had little choice. "Tenuously, I assure you." He gave a dry, unamused laugh. "What is not rotted is covered with dust or mildew, depending upon the state of the ceiling above. But the local people refused to come in answer to Jepson's summons. Depending upon who is giving the opinion, they are either afraid of Willis or of ghosts."

"Willis," Isabella remarked, almost absently. "There are no local tales of the abbey being haunted. But who does your cooking then? Jepson?"

Julian shook his head. "A Mrs. Jenkins. Willis found her."

"Mabel Jenkins?" Isabella could not mask her astonishment or her revulsion. The woman was a slattern whose unkempt house and numerous offspring, all of dubious parentage, were well-known in the neighborhood. Enlightenment of a sort dawned as she thought of Mrs. Jenkins's children. Nell had once hinted that one of the daughters had had a child by Willis.

It occurred to her to wonder if the unscrupulous land agent had not hoped to poison the employer who had appeared so inconveniently, but she dismissed the notion as too gothic. Likely Willis had hoped only that Mrs. Jenkins's cooking would run Julian off.

Who did or did not serve the Marquess of Roth was none of her affair, and Isabella had every reason to keep her distance from the man, but Mrs. Hobbes's sister, Mrs. Goodbody, had visited Marsh House only a few days before with a most unhappy tale. It seemed the house where she had served as housekeeper in Ipswich had burned to the ground in the night. The owner had died in the blaze, and as there were no heirs, all the servants including Mrs. Goodbody had lost their positions.

The bustling, efficient-looking woman had been most distraught, for she would not soon find another position where she would be allowed to keep her several children, "all good workers," with her, a necessity as her husband was deceased.

Isabella had been casting about for some way to take on the tribe at Marsh House, but there were simply not the funds. "I, ah, have no wish to interfere in your affairs, my lord," she said as a loose thread on her glove caught her eye. "Should you have no wish for a suggestion, you have only to say so."

"If all that thinking was to the purpose of recalling who in Saxbourne village is presently in need of employment, Miss Ramsey, then, please be assured that I would welcome your suggestion."

Isabella successfully resisted the slight tug Julian's wry, perhaps even amused, tone exerted upon her and succinctly told him of the tragedy in Ipswich. "I can vouch for Mrs. Hobbes's sister. Mrs. Goodbody . . ."

"I beg pardon?"

There was no question he was amused now, and as Isabella had found Mrs. Goodbody's name irresistible, she was particularly hard put to keep her mouth from curving. But she reminded herself where sharing his lordship's humor had led her.

"Yes, Mrs. Goodbody," she repeated rather crisply. "She quite lives up to her name, for she's a good worker, and she comes complete with a family of children to work beside her. She is staying in the village just now with her mother, and I shall be happy to send her to you tomorrow, if you like.''

There was a moment's silence, but as Isabella did not look to Julian, she could not guess his thoughts, and when he did speak up to agree to the arrangement, it was in a voice as neutral as hers.

She then stood, and he went to fetch Mr. Buttons to her before standing aside to allow her to precede him down the hill. There was only one awkward moment after that. When Isabella made to climb onto the seat of her trap, Julian, without asking permission, placed his hands about her waist and lifted her onto her seat. Her mumbled thanks were very stiff, but Julian turned away even before she got them out, giving her to understand that touching her was nothing at all to him.

As she flicked Dan's reins, she reminded herself that, even without such evidence, she had known well enough the marquess's interest in her would be ephemeral.

Chapter 15

"I quite agree, Mrs. Smithby, such chaos as you describe must be most distracting, indeed." Lady Prim smiled uncertainly. "Yet, surely, it is inevitable, given the scale of the restoration being undertaken?"

The several rows of jet beads adorning the bodice of Mrs. Smithby's dress shook as her bosom swelled. "I cannot agree that chaos is ever inevitable, Lady Primley. One need only be orderly. I would not have had the marquess so discomfited, had I charge of the restoration. One room at a time would have been quite the better plan of attack. I cannot imagine what it was prompted you to suggest that Goodbody woman to the marquess, Isabella."

Distracted by the militant swing of her guest's jet beads, Isabella only knew a question was being put to her when her name was said. But her blank look went unremarked, for the squire, having remained in Mrs. Smithby's company only to hear what she had to say of her second and most recent visit to the abbey, saw an opportunity to needle the vicar's wife and seized it.

"Why, the woman, Mrs. Goodperson or whatever her name, had charge of some baron's household over by Ipswich! Isn't that so, Bella?" He waggled his remarkable eyebrows at his daughter, received a decorous nod, and then rounded on Mrs. Smithby. "I'd say that's reference enough! And I don't doubt she knows her business, Mrs. Smithby. Can't make a pudding without breakin' eggs, so I've been told. But if the lad's surroundings are truly in such an uproar, I've a mind to invite him to Marsh House for the night. Likely he's in need of a peaceful rest. By damn! Beggin' your pardon, Mrs. Smithby, I believe I'll go right over and put the question to him."

Isabella watched her father's departure with a rather wistful expression. Everyone in the neighborhood, and most particularly Mrs. Smithby, seemed beside themselves at the thought that the Marquess of Roth actually intended to remain in their midst. Dozens of questions were pondered, though, to be sure, one received the greatest share of consideration. What, everyone asked, could there be in Suffolk to interest a man of the marquess's tastes?

When the question had arisen earlier in that very afternoon, Mrs. Smithby had given it as her weighty opinion that Roth stayed among them because he was overcome by the beauty of their low, marshy countryside. The squire, with relish, had objected and mused aloud that there must be some toothsome widow—he had intended to say stray wife, but had accorded the vicar's wife some consideration—of whom they had not yet heard.

As Isabella did not feel at liberty to divulge the answer, she bit her lip and listened in silence to the ceaseless flow of speculation. Nor was she any more interested when, after the squire departed, Mrs. Smithby launched into an exactingly detailed account of the repairs being undertaken at the abbey. Liza and Lady Prim listened attentively, but Isabella heard almost daily from Mr. Cummings and found his laconic remarks far more interesting than all Mrs. Smithby's rattling.

She had been, she admitted, exceedingly curious to hear how Mr. Cummings's first meeting with the marquess had gone, and had not been above a little prodding when the countryman did not at once launch into an account.

"And your meeting yesterday with Lord Roth, Mr. Cummings?" she had asked. "I hope it went well?"

He had nodded thoughtfully. "I'll confess to ye, Miss Bella, I did question how it would be with the gentleman, him bein' a lord an' all. But he's none too high in the instep to listen, when he's the need, nor too proud to ask what he's ignorant of, neither." Another day Mr. Cummings had added "Lord Roth don't forget what he's told. Thinks on it, he does. Mayhap he'll have his own notion, too, but if he does he puts it forth with courtesy. A true gentleman, his lordship."

Isabella also learned what crops the marquess and Mr. Cummings had decided between them to plant and why, and a myriad of other details. Mr. Cummings had been particularly impressed by the speed with which Lord Roth had had a drainage ditch cleared. ''I had only to tell him how the fields thereabouts would flood at the next rain were the thing not cleaned out, and he called his tenants together that afternoon. Worked alongside them, he did, and a right good thing, too. You'll remember we had rain that night, Miss Bella.''

Mr. Cummings's expression had revealed some wonder at the thought of a nobleman condescending to work in his fields, and it was a feeling Isabella could not but share. She tried to picture the scene but got only as far as the marquess's shirt stretched tight across his wide, muscular shoulders and thought better of the exercise.

She had the opportunity to see for herself how or if Roth's labor had changed him the next night, for her father's notion to invite the marquess for dinner had not been, as she had thought, merely an excuse to escape Mrs. Smithby. Indeed, to Isabella's astonishment, the squire had gone so far as to insist their neighbor stay the night at Marsh House. Her father was not generally so solicitous of another man's comfort, but she decided it was simply one more example of Roth's effect on people.

Earnest labor, as far as Isabella could see when old Dobson showed him into the drawing room, had done nothing at all to harm Julian's appearance. He was dressed rather formally, in trousers of kerseymere and a coat of midnight blue, against which his snowy white cravat, though casually tied, looked very elegant.

He seemed a trifle leaner, perhaps, as he kissed Lady Prim's hand and put a rosy glow in her cheeks with a fond smile. But Isabella was relieved to see, as he turned to Liza with a slightly broader smile and remarked flatteringly upon her new dress, that his ribs did not seem to bother him at all. She had been afraid his work might aggravate his condition.

It was her turn then to be greeted, Isabella realized, with an unsettling little rush of feeling. She fought it successfully. Her greeting was polite but lacked the warmth of either Lady Prim's or Liza's. She bade the marquess welcome, and he, after a rather bland glance down at her, bowed over her hand, but did not touch it with his lips. Nor did he tease or flatter her as he had the others, merely remarked he was pleased to have been included for dinner at her table. Sarah came then, surprising everyone but Isabella, with whom she had plotted her entrance, and gave Julian reason to turn away without another word.

Isabella endeavored to be pleased that she had what she wanted. She reminded herself that she was susceptible to Roth's smiles, and that it was for the very best that, if he did not precisely ignore her throughout the dinner, he only grazed her lightly with his smiling regard before he turned to smile fully upon Liza or Lady Prim or even the squire.

He was an unscrupulous rake, she reminded herself, who would have seen her dishonor herself without a qualm. Her resolve strengthened as she repeated the litany, she managed to quell successfully each and every impulse to tell some amusing story and see his smile flash white and strong at her.

She even resisted the urge to question him about the abbey, though she acknowledged she was not put to much test there. Liza, Lady Prim, and the squire could do little else.

Julian gave a somewhat exaggerated and quite hilarious account of the efforts undertaken by his legion of good bodies. His glance did stray to Isabella as he said that, but she was studying the veal in Madeira sauce that Mrs. Hobbes had outdone herself to prepare and did not see.

"I have yet to decide if the matron of the tribe is a real person or some fantastical genie out of eastern lore," he said with a chuckle. "I do not believe I have ever seen her still. She is always whirling around and around, mops and dust cloths and brooms and pails flying out at all angles, and, I am delighted to say, leaving blissfully clean sparkles in her wake."

"I am glad for your sake she is efficient, Roth, but I do think living with such a whirlwind would be almost as impossible as Mrs. Smithby says." Liza wrinkled her nose only to brighten in the next moment. "But, do think! If the Goodbodys are as industrious as you say, you'll soon be able to replace all that dreary old furniture with new pieces!"

Julian did not look vastly diverted by the prospect. "I suppose in time I shall have to think of replacing the furniture, but just now I've enough to do to see the drive is cleared and that the roof overhead is solid."

"But you must put your mind to the style you shall wish to

adopt!'' Liza protested. ''You have only to go along to Mrs. Basham's to see the possibilities. I vow you will be struck dumb by her new drawing room!''

''Jove!'' This from the squire. ''You'd be struck dumb with horror to see that pharaoh's room, lad. Why, Hortensia would have a man take his rest on a backless couch! Can you countenance it? And she's chairs with feet carved in the manner of claws and the backs done as serpents' heads! Blast! Gave me a nightmare to look at 'em.''

''The Oriental style is all the rage, Papa! Prinny himself has endorsed it, has he not, Lord Roth?''

Before Julian was forced to take sides with one or the other glaring Ramsey, Lady Prim cleared her throat. ''The Prince of Wales has many, many interests, Liza. But, when one has a house the size of the abbey to attend to, I imagine one would want to begin simply. Later, perhaps certain, ah, refinements might be instituted.''

''You make excellent good sense, Millie!'' the squire nodded sagely at Lady Prim who turned a pleased pink. ''I don't doubt you know a thing or two about furniture, either. Bound to have redone a room in your time.''

''Well, yes,'' Lady Prim allowed. ''Of course one is expected to keep one's house refurbished.''

The squire, an idea taking him suddenly, waved his fork at Julian. ''It's the very thing, lad. Get Millie, here, to advise you on the furniture you'll need and the paper for the walls and,'' he waved his fork more vigorously, ''all that nonsense. She'll think of your comfort as well as the current mode, I'll wager.''

''Oh, William!'' Lady Prim cried, mortified to be thrust upon the marquess.

Julian, however, knew an excellent notion when he heard it and smiled warmly at the blushing lady. ''I think the squire is absolutely right, Lady Prim, and I do hope I can persuade you to take pity on me. Surely it will not surprise you greatly to learn that I've had deuced little experience at the cabinetmakers and even less at the drapers.''

Everyone, including Isabella, laughed. It was not even possible to picture Julian Montcrief in a deep study over wallpaper samples.

''Well . . .'' Isabella half smiled to see the arrested look in

Lady Prim's blue eyes. The honor of having a hand in the
redoing of a house as venerable as Wynchley Abbey was clearly
enticing. "I suppose I do have some knowledge that might be
of use to you, Lord Roth. I could narrow the choices for you,
saving you the trouble of poring over sample books yourself."

"Dear heaven!" Julian's anguished groan at the mere thought
of sample books inspired more laughter.

" 'Tis woman's work, indeed!" the squire commiserated,
which thought caused him to address his daughters next. "And
it wouldn't hurt both you misses to go along with Millie. You
never know, Liza, but you might take in town and have some
house of your own to redo shortly."

Liza tossed her glossy head at her father's teasing. "For once
I think Papa is at least close to the mark, Lady Prim, and I am
certain I should find consulting with you most amusing."

If Lady Prim was uncertain whether she wished to amuse
young Liza, she did not by either word or gesture indicate as
much. She only murmured, "Very good, my dear," before
turning to Isabella. "Say you will come, too, Bella, for Liza
will soon go off to town, and I shall be quite overwhelmed if
I've no one with whom to discuss my notions."

"Oh! I, ah, really know very little on the subject of furnishings
and such, Lady Prim," Isabella demurred. Whether or not she'd
have liked to share an opinion or two on her old haunt, she knew
it would be a great deal better for her if she were to see less
not more of the marquess and become less not more involved
in his life. "I am certain Lord Roth has other more knowledg-
able people to call upon to assist you."

She could not but glance at Julian then and found him
regarding her with an inscrutable, but on the whole, rather cool
expression. "Actually, I have no one else in mind to call upon,
Miss Ramsey," he said in such a way that Isabella could not
tell if he was put out or not. When he looked to Lady Prim,
however, his expression did lighten. "Do say you shall not be
deterred, Lady Prim. You will be entirely up to the task, I know,
and you are not so occupied as Miss Ramsey."

"In very truth, I should be in alt to help you, Roth," Lady
Prim confessed with a little laugh. Though she was too modest
to proclaim it, she had redone her husband's entire home in

town, and her efforts had received considerable acclaim. To think what she could do with the Montcrief resources behind her made her almost giddy. And such a house as the abbey! Why, there were over a hundred rooms there!

That thought gave Lady Prim immediate pause. It had been twenty years since she had undertaken such work, and even then she had occasionally found it, though exhilarating, exhausting. She looked rather anxiously back to Isabella.

"Truly, Bella, I do wish you would reconsider! Only think, my dear, before you protest again—and I know it is only your modesty that makes you hang back—you shall have the redoing of the Hall after your marriage to Wrexham, for I cannot imagine that my nephew will have his wife live in a house that has had few if any improvements made to it in over a century. We Farleys are very proud of our traditions, I grant, but it is time the Hall was rendered at least comfortable. Working with me at the abbey will be very good experience for you, my dear, as well as a service to me."

Isabella did not share Lady Prim's belief that her betrothed meant to put her in charge of refurbishing his ancestral home. He had never said a word on the subject, and she'd the sense that the viscount would not care for any change he did not instigate himself. That last thought, contrasted with Lord Roth's easy acceptance of his limitations, made her want to have done with the whole subject. Slowly, aware that Julian watched her with a quite impassive expression, she nodded affirmatively to Lady Prim.

Lady Prim was most eager to go to the abbey to "make a survey" as she put it, and it was decided she and Isabella would visit the very next afternoon, despite the fact that Julian could not be present to guide them. Isabella immediately leapt to the conclusion he meant to avoid her, only to be forced to acknowledge herself oversensitive when Julian explained with something of a grin that he had been accorded the singular honor of being invited to accompany Mr. Cummings into Ipswich to purchase seed.

Isabella did not sleep well that night. It disturbed her, though she wished it did not, to have Lord Roth under her roof again.

Every time she fell off to sleep, she seemed to dream of aquamarine eyes or strong, warm arms, and sometimes a sensual mouth.

All the more remarkable then, that as she tossed fitfully in her bed, she never heard the least sound of movement in the house. Julian and Jepson both slipped down the servants' stairs and departed Marsh House well after midnight to go separate ways: Julian to the high ground, where he could watch the bay below Wrexham Hall, and Jepson to the woods, where he could observe the road with the deep ruts.

Later, when they met again in Peter Ramsey's room just before the first light of dawn, only Jepson had success to report. " 'Twere five carts in all with a driver fer each one, an' Willis overseein' the whole. Aye, my lord, 'e was there. Punts come out o' the marsh. I dunno 'ow many, I couldn't see from the woods, but ye was right: they'd kegs on 'em. 'Twas work to roll 'em up the dike, though they'd levers, but 'twas naught all to roll 'em down an' onto the carts before they covered 'em with straw. Quiet they worked an' well, an' soon the carts moved away. I followed 'em 'til they turned on the road for London."

"Good work, Jepson." Julian clapped his valet on the back. "We know with certainty now why the squire was so set on our staying the night away from the abbey. He's in league with Willis to smuggle." Julian shook his head. "They must have been in a panic to get their contraband by the abbey before the servants' quarters are rendered fit for all our Goodbodys. Ten pairs of ears are not so easy to remove for a night as only two. The question now is, do they intend to continue their operation after the abbey is filled with people who are not under Willis's thumb and who may report the odd sound of carts rumbling by in the dead of night?"

Jepson waited in silence while his master considered the matter, but when Julian looked to him, he gave a firm nod. "Aye. A taste for easy blunt's no simple thing ta lay aside. Mayhap they'll bring the kegs 'cross the squire's land, or on another path further along from the abbey. But do ye think those two are the leaders o' the thing, m'lord?"

"No." Julian's answer was immediate and unequivocal. "The squire's no schemer. He'd never have thought of smuggling until someone came to him with the suggestion. And though Willis would think of smuggling in a trice, his mind is not subtle enough to have concocted this particular scheme. He'd have brought his brandy directly ashore in the bay and carted it off the same night, making noise and raising questions. No, someone sly and clever thought to keep the contraband hidden in the marshes until all was very quiet, and then to bring it to by routes only a few marsh men would know, to an estate at the very back of the marshes; an estate open to only a very few people. My guess is our leader also had the foresight to order that the smuggling vessel, the one from France, make its way into his bay only on the night of the new moon, which is why I did not see it tonight."

"So, 'tis the viscount, ye believe?"

"I do. I've had Perry's reply. The Viscount Wrexham was so heavily in debt only last summer that there were some who refused to play with him, for fear he'd not be able to make good his wagers." Jepson let out a low whistle, and Julian nodded. "Yes, a heavy blow for a man like Wrexham, but then, quite suddenly, he was flush again and all was right as rain . . . and Perry, who knows him better than I, says he's not the sort who would be above putting money in Boney's hands, though doing so would mean the death of Englishmen. We'll play along awhile yet, to be certain how the thing is carried out, then we'll see what is to be done."

Chapter 16

The abbey was truly the hive of activity Mrs. Smithby had proclaimed. Gardeners and masons and bricklayers and carpenters, all were hard at work, and everywhere young maids could be seen energetically wielding their mops and brooms and dusters.

"I see you are getting on very well, indeed, Mrs. Goodbody," Lady Prim remarked, when the housekeeper bustled up to welcome them.

"Aye," Mrs. Goodbody nodded briskly. " 'Tis in a grand hurry his lordship is to have his house set to rights, but little wonder, too. How he could live in it a day as it was, I shall never know."

With a good deal of head shaking and clucking, Mrs. Goodbody then escorted her visitors about the house, and though the renovation of the abbey had begun and most vigorously, it was entirely apparent a massive amount of work was still to be done. Rather overcome, Lady Prim was most relieved at the end of the tour to find at least one sitting room was free of dust. Heavily paneled in dark wood, its white plaster ceiling blessedly intact, it was off the marquess's own bedroom, but Mrs. Goodbody hastened to assure her guests that his lordship had left specific instructions that the ladies from Marsh House were to be served tea there. "This was the first room after his lordship's own bedroom that we put our hands to, and 'tis in better condition than any downstairs," she exclaimed. "Only wait a half minute, your ladyship, and I'll have a tray brought up to restore you."

Mrs. Goodbody was as good as her word, returning before Isabella's gaze could stray more than half a dozen times to the marquess's bedroom door with their tea tray and something more.

A workman accompanied her, carrying a small, ornate, gilt frame. "Just see what Luke, here, found in one of the rooms below. It had fallen down behind a cabinet. Could it be his lordship's mother, Lady Primley?"

Isabella could see at once why Mrs. Goodbody would ask. The woman in the picture had both Lord Roth's thick, dark gold hair and his aquamarine eyes. "Yes, it is a likeness of Lady Chandley," Lady Prim confirmed as the workman, Luke, propped the portrait against a settee. Isabella saw him dart it a look of masculine approval before he departed, but she did not fault him. Lord Roth's mother was undoubtedly beautiful.

And seductive. Though it was an uncomfortable opinion to form of someone else's mother, Isabella could not but think so as she took in the languid tilt to Lady Chandley's glorious head and the rather provocative smile that turned up the corners of her faintly pouting mouth.

"When she was young, it was the common wisdom that no man was immune to Caroline's smile."

Isabella glanced up in almost guilty surprise, but her companion had not read her thoughts. Lady Prim had merely voiced her own as she studied the likeness of Lord Roth's mother.

Though the portrait was not a formal one—it was too small for that—Lady Chandley was dressed regally in a splendid silk gown cut low enough over her bosom to cause Isabella's eyes to widen. The décolletage of Liza's gown was nothing by comparison, and Isabella was rather glad her sister had had a previous engagement at the Bashams'. Otherwise she might well have taken it into her head there could be nothing wrong with following a duchess's example.

"I wonder why Lady Chandley's portrait should be here?" she mused aloud.

There was silence a long moment, then Lady Primley sighed. "It is possible James painted it. He had some talent in that direction."

"You were acquainted with him then?" Isabella exclaimed, recalling that she had suspected as much.

Lady Prim smiled a little, looking from the portrait to Isabella. "My dear, every girl then knew James Montcrief. He was a merry rascal who would rise, I fear, to any challenge."

Lady Prim's eyes shifted, almost against her will it seemed, to Caroline Montcrief's portrait, and Isabelle exclaimed faintly, "You do not mean . . . !"

A slow, reluctant nod was the answer. "It was commonly believed at the time that it was on Caroline's account that James left England so abruptly." Isabella gasped, but Lady Prim did not seem to hear. "Caroline was very beautiful then, irresistible in a way, really, for she'd an air all her own. She still has, in fact, and still has men aplenty." This time Lady Prim did hear Isabella's sharply drawn breath and gave her a wise look. "I fear I have shocked you, my dear, but in town, if a woman is discreet, she is allowed more latitude than here in the country.

"Only with James did Caroline go rather farther than raising a few eyebrows. Younger then, she had not yet learned discretion, and there was a great deal of talk about her obvious interest in her husband's brother. And James . . . well, it would have been quite a feat had he not been interested in her. As you can see she was a rare beauty, but before anything could be known for certain, James left the country altogether. With his departure, the gossip might have been laid to rest, for their is nothing less interesting than a stale *on-dit,* but all too soon it became obvious Caroline was in an interesting condition, and only eight months after James's departure, she was delivered of a boy."

Isabella's eyes flew to Lady Prim. "Yes, my dear," the elder lady said sadly. 'He was Lord Roth. The boy's parentage has ever been a matter of intense question. Unhappily for him, his looks did nothing to decide the issue. As you can see he took after Caroline, and his tendency toward recklessness has seemed to many to owe more to James's gay spirit than to Chandley's contained manner."

Isabella could scarcely take in what she was being told and asked the first thing that came to mind. "Then Lord Roth may not be the duke's heir?"

"That is the one issue not in doubt," Lady Prim replied firmly. "James Montcrief's child would have been the next in line after Richard Montcrief and James, himself.

"But I must tell you I am not one of those who ever believed Lord Roth to be James's child." A wistful smile lit Lady Prim's blue eyes. "I knew James Montcrief rather well once," she admitted, and did not need to add that she had had a tendre for him. "He was a gay buck, true, but he was not a rogue. He'd never have betrayed his brother. It was not in him to do." Suddenly Lady Prim chuckled. "And there is another thing, though only a few have remarked it: for all the ways Lord Roth differs from his father, he can be Chandley to the inch when he desires. James never could have looked so forbiddingly arrogant as Lord Roth did that day when Mrs. Smithby inflicted herself upon him."

Isabella smiled vaguely at the thought but was preoccupied with debating upon whether Julian knew there was question as to the identity of his father, then realized she was being naive in the extreme. Of course the gossip would have reached his ears in one way or another.

His reaction to it had been predictable. There would be no shrinking back from curious eyes for Julian Montcrief. Snapping his fingers in the *ton's* collective face, he had behaved as recklessly as he pleased, giving the *ton* double the amount to gossip over. And in the end he had so dazzled his peers, the questions surrounding his origins were either forgotten or dismissed as irrelevant.

Only a few of the older generation remembered and Lord Roth, himself, of course. Little wonder he'd little enthusiasm for the married state. To learn his own mother was such a one that he could not even be certain of his own father . . .

"Caroline's behavior over the years cannot but have affected the man," Lady Prim said, as if she had read Isabella's thoughts. "How could he not imagine all women to be equally as faithless as she, and with such looks as his to tempt them," Lady Prim shook her head at the inevitability of it all, "they soon were. Still, I have found Lord Roth to be a far better man than either of his parents deserve. He is not James's son, but he did inherit his uncle's sweetness. It lurks there beneath all his gay-blade manner, just as it did with James. I do hope that Lord Roth will be luckier than his uncle and find a woman who would call forth that side of him. He will make a good husband, if he does. I truly believe he will."

Isabella stirred uncomfortably. She had caught a glimpse of

that side of Julian Montcrief when he had dealt with Sarah, but it was not the side he had shown to her. With her he had been the same man he was with every other woman—a less than satisfying thought, but not one she cared to contemplate at all, and she could only be relieved that her restless movement had the effect of recalling Lady Prim to the present.

"Oh, my dear, I do apologize! I have been going on, and this old history can be of little interest to you." She rose, but could not seem to leave off looking at Julian's mother. Slowly, shaking out her skirts, she said, "Isabella, my dear, would you object if I directed Mrs. Goodbody to take Caroline's portrait to the attic, at least for the time being? Its presence here in James's home cannot but raise unpleasant questions I should like to spare Lord Roth, if possible."

"I would not object at all, Lady Prim. I think the attic a very satisfactory place for it," then she added, putting Lady Prim to the blush, "and I think you a good friend."

That evening Lady Prim unearthed several books of wall coverings and paint samples that she had brought with her from town, for she had thought to amuse herself with them in a purely idle way at the Hall, and the very next day Jack, who with Annie had quite recovered from the influenza, loaded them into the Ramsey carriage along with Isabella, Liza, and Lady Prim.

At the last minute Sarah ran out to beg that she be taken along as well, delighting Isabella, who thought, among other things, the more people the better on this day when Julian would likely be at home.

He was, and strolled up to greet them soon after they arrived. Rather as if she were watching a play, Isabella observed him charm her three very different companions. Nor were his smiles insincere. He seemed truly fond of Lady Prim, genuinely amused by Liza, and quite devoted to shy, little Sarah. Only after he had greeted them each in turn did he nod in Isabella's direction and say quite cordially, "Miss Ramsey."

"Have you come to take us on the grand tour, Lord Roth?" Liza cried, batting her eyes outlandishly.

He was moved only to smile. "I fear it is Mrs. Goodbody who will have to take up where she left off yesterday. I shall meet you later for tea, but just now I've books to pore over."

"Oh!" Liza made a play of hitting at him with her parasol. "You are quite as bad as Isabella, Lord Roth!"

Isabella felt the faintest line of heat rise in her cheeks even before she felt more than saw Julian flick his gaze to her. She prepared herself for mockery, and got, "You flatter me, Liza. I am not half so good as your sister. Shall I meet you in the sitting room for tea in an hour?" he then asked Lady Prim before Isabella could decide if he had, in fact, derided her.

"Two hours would be more reasonable, I think, Lord Roth," Lady Prim replied. "There is so much to do!"

She looked as eager as a girl, and Isabella smiled even as Julian gave a chuckle. "Two it is, then."

Isabella got no further that day than the first room Lady Prim chose to consider. It was the library, her favorite. While Sarah drifted off in the direction of the stables where Julian had informed her there was a mother cat with a litter of kittens, and Lady Prim and Liza held samples of wall coverings up to the wall, taking care to view them in the full light of the French windows before recording their observations on the small note cards Lady Prim had brought for that purpose, Isabella wandered away to revisit old friends.

She found, to her delight, that most of the leather-bound volumes were in surprisingly good repair, the glass encasing the heavy bookcases having warded off the damp, and she was sitting atop a feature of the library that she had particularly loved as a child—a mahogany ladder with little wheels on the bottom—reading, when Lady Prim and Liza were ready to depart. Liza scolded her for having forgotten their purpose, but Lady Prim waved her hand. "We shall be in one or another of the rooms on this floor, when you are done with your reading, my dear, but don't hurry yourself. You look very comfortable up there."

Isabella was entirely too delightfully occupied to take issue with Lady Prim, and an entire hour passed before the first twinge of duty assailed her. Then she decided she really must go and make herself of some use to Lady Prim as she had promised she would.

She was just closing a slender volume of poetry she had come across, when the library door burst open, and Julian strode into the room, an opened ledger balanced on one arm. He crossed directly to a tall, heavy desk carved out in the gothic style to rifle through several pieces of paper scattered upon it. "Where the deuce can it have got to?" he muttered crossly.

From her perspective Isabella could plainly see a piece of paper lying beneath a nearby chair, and when she heard, "Damnation!" far more irritably, she took pity.

"My lord . . ."

"Good God!" Julian whirled about. "Miss Ramsey! You nearly scared the life out of me. What in the name of heaven are you doing up there?"

It was an effort to bite back a laugh. He looked cross as a bear to have been taken by surprise. Isabella gestured to the book in her lap. "Lady Prim gave me leave to stay behind and enjoy, ah, this for a time."

"This?" Julian echoed, Isabella's effort to evade too obvious not to intrigue.

He was rewarded with something of a blush. "Yes. I think I made mention once that I was accustomed to borrowing from the library here."

More evasion and equally transparent. "And what particular author did you find to hold your interest today, Miss Ramsey?"

There was a split-second pause, and then, as her mind had gone utterly blank and not one other name in the entire history of literature came to her mind, she said, "Ben Jonson."

Isabella was too far from Julian to see his eyes, but she could well imagine the sudden glint that must surely have sprung to life in them. The very phrase. "Gather ye rosebuds while ye may," seemed to fairly dance in the air between them, and so she added far too quickly, "The print is large."

"Ah." Julian bent down to flick a speck of dust from his breeches, then, his sudden grin mastered, he straightened. And found Isabella, her back to him, descending the ladder. Had she been listening very carefully, Isabella might have heard him mutter under his breath, "You blasted little innocent," in a less than admiring tone, but even had she, she'd not have understood Julian's vexation, for she did not have the slightest notion what a tempting view her soft, rounded, thoroughly feminine bottom was at eye level.

Happily innocent, but still having her own reasons for not
meeting his eye—she was not certain he believed she had been
reading Ben Jonson's scandalous advice only because the
volume's print was very large—she crossed to a heavy, leather
reading chair, knelt down, and came up with a piece of vel-
lum.

"Were you looking for this?"

Julian frowned intently at the paper upon which a rather
disorderly series of figures had been scrawled, all other matters
forgotten. "Yes," he said half to himself. "These are the notes.
Still, the figures do not balance by some six thousand, and I
cannot say whether it is through my ineptitude or Willis's
villainy that the sum has been lost."

For just a moment, as she had held out the paper, the faintest
scent of sandalwood had drifted to Isabella and caused her heart
to trip almost painfully.

But the mention of a puzzle, and it must be confessed, the
suggestion that Willis might escape being held accountable for
something, piqued her interest to such a degree that without
thought—or permission—she lifted the ledger Julian held
balanced upon his arm.

Frowning, she held the book almost an arm's length away
and tilted it toward the light of the French windows. Watching
her, Julian was reminded of the little half spectacles she needed,
and he recalled how she had looked with them perched on her
slim nose. So very prim she had been but for her soft mouth.
Her lower lip, particularly, was lush. Bee-stung some would
call it. By purest coincidence, as she concentrated upon the
ledger, Isabella lazily and entirely absently moistened her lip
with the tip of her tongue as she sometimes did when she was
distracted.

"I confess I've some difficulty without my spectacles, my
lord . . ." Isabella looked around blankly when she realized
Julian no longer stood beside her. "Oh," she said rather
uncertainly when she found him the length of the desk away,
his expression closed, unreadable. She flushed brightly and held
out the ledger. "I am sorry, my lord. I did not mean to
commandeer your ledger. You must think me . . ."

But he surprised her by holding up his hand. "Please, Miss

Ramsey. Nothing of the sort. I should be most grateful to hear your opinion.''

Isabella searched Julian's eyes but unable to detect any insincerity there, decided it was possible his odd expression was a result of the strain he felt over Wynchley's chaotic state. ''Well, I can see enough to say anyone would be hard put to account for the missing sum. Very few of the entries have any notations to explain them, and look here,'' she laid the ledger on the desk between them, ''Willlis has carried this sum over but incorrectly. Perhaps he only inadvertently transposed the numbers, but his error leaves three thousand pounds unaccounted for.''

''I did not even see that,'' Julian admitted, making a most impatient noise as he lifted the ledger to study it. ''Yes, I see. And he goes right on. Damn, but I shall be forever with this mess.''

It was time to give some vague encouragement and then to leave. ''I could take the ledger with me to study,'' Isabella heard herself say instead. ''I've more experience with accounts, and I do love puzzles. Perhaps I can find the missing sum.''

Julian looked up slowly from his perusal of the ledger. When his eyes met hers, Isabella felt her cheeks heat at the searching look he gave her. ''You would do that?''

Isabella had not stopped to consider all the ramifications of her offer, prolonged contact with Julian being only one, but she felt she'd seem the veriest idiot if she reconsidered. She smiled to cover her uncertainty. ''I would see all Willis's sins uncovered.''

Perhaps Julian read her sudden doubts or perhaps he entertained some of his own, for he did not immediately reply, but did continue to study Isabella closely. She could not but regret having made the offer and was just on the point of informing him so, when Liza's voice sounded from the hallway. ''Bella! Are you not done yet with those musty books?''

''I would be very grateful for your help, Miss Ramsey,'' Julian said, just as Liza whirled through the open door.

With her sister looking on, it was not possible for Isabella to say, well I am sorry, I have decided you may not have it after all. Instead she inclined her head and extended her hand for the ledger. "I shall return it with any notes I may have tomorrow," she said crisply, then added just to be certain they understood each other, "by Mr. Cummings."

Chapter 17

Julian grinned down at the eager stable boy who had come to him, as had most all the servants, through Mrs. Goodbody's offices. "An extra ration of oats for Sampson this morning, Tim," he directed, dismounting. "He'd the devil of a workout."

When a blur of movement by the stable door caught his eye, he looked to see Sarah's flaxen head peep out and duck back as quickly. Surprised, for the child had not been so shy with him in a time, Julian called out, "Good day, Sarah. Have you come to see the kittens?"

She gave no sign she heard, however, and he saw why in the next moment. As Tim led Sampson into the stables, Sarah, her eyes riveted to the stallion, shrank back hard against the stable door.

Her fear struck hard at Julian, and he went to lift her in his arms. "Horses are powerful creatures, Sarah," he said quietly, "and should be respected, but they are good fellows all in all. Come and see. I shan't put you down," he promised, feeling her tense, and she made no objection as he carried her to Sampson's stall.

When the stallion shook his head and whinnied upon seeing them, Julian gave Sarah a knowing glance. "That is Sampson's way of saying, 'where the deuce is my sugar?'" Though the giggle that escaped her was more nervous than amused, Julian grinned as he extracted a lump of sugar from his pocket. "Now, watch how I feed him," he directed quite unnecessarily for Sarah's large, brown eyes were intent upon his every move.

When Sampson had retrieved the lump of sugar his master held out to him, Julian held up his palm to show Sarah he was unscathed. "He is very gentle with me, really. Would you like to try?"

Sarah, despite the evidence of her eyes, began to shake her head, but Julian reached up to stroke Sampson between the ears. "You're a good fellow, Sampson. You will treat the lady gently, will you not?" The stallion whinnied and jerked his head downward. "There, you see?" Julian demanded of Sarah, a twinkle in his eyes.

She could only gaze in almost comical amazement at the miraculous horse that seemed to understand the spoken word, and when Julian held out a lump of sugar to her, she made no protest. Her hand stretched so flat it trembled, she extended the treat to Sampson. No fool, the stallion helped himself with dainty courtesy, and Sarah was so proud she threw her arms around Julian's neck and buried her head in his shoulder.

They repeated the process several times to both Sampson's and Sarah's delight. Then, when Julian's pockets were quite empty, Sampson gave a parting snort before going to bury his head in his oat bag.

"He's not so fearful now is he?" Julian remarked, and Sarah, who by then was sitting upon the gate to the stall, shook her head, a smile lifting the corners of her mouth. "When people are afraid of horses," he went on casually, "it often seems that something has happened to make them afraid." His arm draped around her waist, Julian felt her stir abruptly and knew he'd hit a chord. "I think a horse scared you very much once, Sarah. Can you tell me what happened?" he asked, then tipped her chin up that she must look at him. "Was it Jaspar Willis? Did he frighten you once? If so, you may tell me, for I shall keep you safe from him."

But Sarah pulled her chin from his hold, and when Julian saw her throat working, as if she held back monstrous sobs, he felt the worst sort of brute and immediately lifted the child into his arms. "There, there, Sarah. It's all right, truly. You needn't tell me anything you don't want."

She was clinging to him tightly, her head lying hard against his neck, and when it came, her voice was so soft and muffled, Julian had to listen intently to make out the words. "H-he me-met F-father in the w-woods," she stammered miserably. "I-I d-didn't know."

When she burst into tears, Julian was obliged to allow a sudden spurt of fury to recede before he could speak calmly.

"Of course, you did not, sweetheart." He patted her back gently. "I am certain they did not tell you of their meeting."

"Th-they s-saw me," she went on. "M-mr. W-willis' h-horse r-reared so high and th-then, F-father hit me."

Cursing beneath his breath, Julian held her close. "No one will hit you now, Sarah. It's all right," he soothed, putting aside for the time a grim satisfaction that he had linked Wrexham firmly to Willis. "There, there. I shan't let harm come to you." Though Julian had only the vaguest notion how he might deliver on the promise, he meant to do it, and his conviction conveyed itself to Sarah so that little by little her crying subsided.

"There, that's better." Julian found a handkerchief in his pocket and mopped her eyes. "Do you know," he said as he worked. "I've the most amazing notion you would make a grand rider, Sarah." The remark was intended to distract her from the ugly memories he'd called up and succeeded admirably. Sarah looked up at him as if he had suggested she fly to the moon. Noting that look, Julian nodded crisply. "You are not afraid of horses now, having seen for yourself what a lamb Sampson is, and I do believe that if I could find just the right pony, you would do very well."

When Sarah only continued to gaze at him in wondering silence. Julian cocked his head. "And though we shall, of course, ask her permission to have lessons, we won't tell Miss Isabella precisely what we are about. No, indeed, we'll surprise her with your expertise. I think she will be very pleased."

Julian knew he had succeeded at least in giving Sarah food for thought, when an uncertain smile lit her eyes. "You would like that?" She nodded, albeit slowly, and he smiled.

When he explained that it might take him a little time to find just the right pony, Sarah seemed a little relieved, but before he departed for the abbey and left her to the kittens that had become her playthings, Julian insisted they seal their agreement by shaking hands, a ceremony which made Sarah, to Julian's pleasure, smile outright.

Mrs. Goodbody was somewhat surprised to see her master at the door, for Julian had left word he would be out all the morning with Mr. Cummings, but she duly informed him that

Lady Primley and Miss Isabella were in the formal dining room studying the effect of the emerald wallpaper Lady Primley had ordered.

Julian proceeded toward his study. Over the course of the few weeks that Lady Prim had undertaken to advise him on the refurbishing of the abbey, they had come to an unspoken agreement that suited them both. Julian was not involved in any preliminary discussion as to whether, for example, blue tones of green tones better suited the dining room. Indeed, he was not consulted at all until Lady Prim had made a decision and submitted that final decision to him for what was, in essence, a pro forma ratification.

And, since their brief encounter in his library, Julian had seen Isabella, even less frequently than Lady Prim, and always in company. She had successfully tracked down the disappearance of his three thousand pounds and afterwards had taken on one or two other questions he had put to her, but had managed to communicate with him almost entirely by neatly written notes. Only once had they met face-to-face on the subject of the accounts, and then the estimable Mr. Cummings had sat squarely between them. Julian had, of course, dined several times at Marsh House—the invitation extended by either Lady Prim or the squire—and just the day before had gone to wave farewell when Liza had set off, at last, for London.

Recalling the chaos of the girl's leave-taking, Julian grinned to himself. The dogs in the kennels had bayed, Mr. Buttons had barked wildly, and the squire had roared last-minute cautions all the time it took to load Liza's trunks onto one of the four carriages required to transport the Bashams—for Liza would ride with them—and their entourage to the capital.

Rather to Julian's surprise, Liza, upon seeing her first trunk come out of Marsh House, had burst into tears and run to cling to Isabella. The older girl soothed her with some quiet words and almost had her smiling again when the squire, evidently believing some paternal action was fitting, cuffed the younger girl so bracingly upon the back that the then trickle of tears became once more a flood.

Amused but not entirely untouched, he admitted, Julian stood a little apart, observing the display of Ramsey family feeling until his gaze encountered Isabella's. Whether she was aware of the plea in her eyes, he could not know, but he acted at once and came forward to disengage Liza from her. The moment she realized who it was would hand her into the carriage beneath Ellie Basham's envious gaze, Liza recovered amazingly, even managing to greet Mrs. and Miss Basham with quite a gay smile.

"Well, can't say I regret that's done with!" Liza's father had exclaimed when all that could be seen of his daughter was her little white handkerchief fluttering out the window of her carriage. "Never thought Liza, of all people, would go all maudlin over leaving her Papa, but bedamned if she didn't."

"Now, William," Lady Prim had chided very gently as she dabbed at her eyes with a lace-edged handkerchief. "The dear child has never left home before. It is only natural she should be a trifle uncertain. For myself I'd not have wished her to skip away without a qualm at all."

"Hmmm, well, I suppose not," the squire conceded grudgingly until Lady Prim, believing they were in agreement, smiled mistily up at him. "Oh, well, no, of course not," he added more firmly then. "Wouldn't do at all."

For the second time Julian's eye chanced to catch Isabella's, and this time he knew she was aware what she communicated. Her eyes were alight with laughter and seeing his matching amusement, she had been obliged to turn away to cough, prompting her father to demand if she were not succumbing to influenza.

Lady Prim's voice, pleasant as ever, worked its way into Julian's awareness and awakened him to the realization that he was passing his dining room. Quickening his pace, for there was always the off chance she might think to interest him in whatever it was she considered, he managed to get by safely only to draw up a little farther along before the door to a drawing room that had as yet received only cursory attention from Mrs. Goodbody and her minions.

Maids, he knew, did not wear muslin dresses of lime green, and therefore, he realized, though he had glanced only absently into the rooms, that the young woman teetering high on a ladder wielding a duster over the room's large gilt chandelier could not be a maid, despite the fact that she had covered the front of her dress with a well-used apron and her hair with a coarse scarf.

Why, Julian did not stop to consider, but the sight of Isabella engaged in the menial task infuriated him. He would not have it and strode into the room abruptly, calling out, "Damnation! What do you think you are about!" without warning.

Isabella, even had she expected Julian to be at home, would have been taken by surprise to hear the sudden, harsh query. Whirling about, she forgot she balanced on a narrow rung and stepped off into thin air. Had not Julian acted quickly, she'd have landed in a painful heap upon the floor. As it was, he caught her in his arms.

They were strong and held her securely, but Isabella, understandably, cried out and grabbed onto his wide shoulders. Their eyes met and locked, and the feeling of falling was replaced by the feeling of being held close to a lean, solid body.

It was Julian who reacted first, Isabella would regret to recall later. While she, gazing wide-eyed at him, was just registering the sensation produced by a sinewy arm curving firmly about her soft hips, he withdrew that arm and her feet hit the floor rather hard. In the next instant she was standing quite alone and unaided and feeling somehow at fault, though she could not have said precisely for what.

"You, you startled me, my lord. I . . . did not expect you so soon."

"Else I'd not have found you in here all alone, Miss Ramsey?" Isabella flushed, for in fact it had just occurred to her to regret breaking her own rule, made after her encounter with Julian in the library, to keep to Lady Prim's side when they were at the abbey. "And that absurd costume?" Julian demanded before she could gather her scattered wits. "Have you hired on with Mrs. Goodbody, or have you merely grown accustomed to a maid's part?"

Isabella wished she might sink through the floor. She had quite forgotten her soiled maid's garb. And it was of little help that her interrogator's riding clothes could not be said to be immaculate. Their cut and material was of the finest, of course, and he wore them with such careless assurance, he looked superb anyway. Indeed, the only true flaw to his picture was his hair. It had gotten tousled while he rode. Sourly Isabella noted the result was he could add appealing boyishness to all his other attributes.

Her back stiffened. She would not allow him to cow her no matter how handsome he might be or how he glared at her.

"Lady Prim wished me to judge the effect of her—your—paper only when she had an entire panel in place, and she shooed me out of the dining room; as a result I grew bored waiting, wandered down the hall, and thought to while away the time until Lady Prim should call, when I saw this costume." She waved her hand over her figure and was reminded belatedly of the scarf she wore, when her finger grazed it.

Flustered truly then, for the scarf was quite ugly, she could only think to get it off her head. The knot she'd tied at the back of her neck gave her some trouble, but at last she flung the thing off. Unfortunately with it went her pins, and her soft brown hair came tumbling down.

"Oh!" It was a most frustrated sound that escaped her, and Isabella was careful to avoid Julian's eyes while she set about retrieving her scattered pins. She knew he must think her the veriest idiot, and knew as well she must look the merest schoolgirl with her hair hanging down her back.

Actually she was being unfair to herself. She had thick, waving hair that did not so much hang as flow down her back, and the word "schoolgirl" did not leap to Julian's mind when she, at last, straightened.

His gaze traveled with leisurely appeciation down the length of her tresses to take in, belatedly, the sight of her slender hand stretched out toward him. Recalled to the few pins he had gathered for her, he dropped them into her hand, and glancing up, met her eyes. The look in them dared him to remark further on her appearance.

He was, regrettably, unable to resist. "You look the veriest wanton, Miss Ramsey."

As often happens at such a fraught moment, Isabella was to think later of a dozen clever retorts. At the time, alas, she was far too battered by quite conflicting thoughts to be the least eloquent. Shocked that Julian would refer openly to what it was he tried to make of her, she became confused, for the gleam in his eye was not hot or desirous but rather amused and distinctly friendly. Finally, and most appallingly, she was very aware of a quite sharp flare of pleasure at being likened, by one who should know, to a mature woman not a schoolgirl.

All she could utter, therefore, was a strangled, "Oh." Again. And fly. He stayed her, however, even before she took her first step, saying, "I apologize, Miss Ramsey. I ought not to have teased you so."

Isabella knew she was on very dangerous ground. First she was alone with the marquess. An error, always. And second, her sense of affront was failing her.

"Yes, very well, my lord," she said hurriedly for fear the twinkle that yet lurked in his eye might beguile her into smiling at the absurdity of him calling her a wanton. "But I must go . . ."

"Not just yet," he cut her off, no humor to be heard in his voice suddenly. "I've not had my say on the subject of your dusting. I'll not have you doing menial chores in my home, Miss Ramsey. Thanks to you I've dozens of servants, all paid handsomely and all waiting for you to order them about as you please. See that you do so. Do you understand me?"

She did, and she did not. "Well, I suppose, my lord, but I was only passing the time."

"Isabella . . ."

"Miss Ramsey, Lord Roth, and I do not care to be growled at. Of course, I shan't do anything that displeases you. It is your home after all."

"I am relieved to hear you realize that."

"And," she continued as if she had not heard him, "I shall do as you ask. I was only pointing out that I did not feel, as you may have thought, like a slave with my nose to the grindstone."

"Perhaps I ought to pay you a salary," Julian remarked suddenly in a seemingly serious voice.

Isabella summoned patience. "I said I would do as you wish, my lord. You needn't tease me further."

"I'm not. You are redecorating my home; bringing order to my books; sharing your principal adviser with me; and now cleaning my drawing room. I owe you something in return."

He seemed in deadly earnest. Isabella shook her head firmly, even put up her hands. "No. Oh, no, my lord. You owe me nothing. You are a neighbor, and I am glad to help."

"Don't go and get on your high horse. You deserve some compensation for all you've done—are doing, and cannot deny you need it. Lady Prim was not closemouthed while she sat with me, and she made no secret of the fact that your purse at Marsh House has been strained by ah, several factors."

"Please, my lord!" Isabella cried, too alarmed to think, just then, to be exasperated with Lady Prim. "Our purse can be of no concern to you, and that is the end of it."

"It may be an end for you, Miss Ramsey, but it is not for me." Julian nearly smiled when Isabella's hazel eyes flashed. She was quite lovely roused, but he had reasons other than the picture she made for persisting, and so he added with enough ruthlessness to convince her he meant what he said. "I shall speak to your father, I think it is he who ought to decide."

The threat dismayed her, as he had known it would. Were the matter put to him tactfully, they both knew the squire might not be above accepting a well-flushed neighbor's handout. "You will not, my lord. I will never speak to you again if you do." When her threat did not soften Julian's expression by so much as a fraction, Isabella bit her lip hard. "Very well then! I shall tell you what is none of your affair. When we were betorhted, the Viscount Wrexham generously settled upon me a sum sufficient for most of our needs. We need nothing more. Now, I must bid you good day."

"Miss Ramsey," he waited until she met his eyes. "I meant no offense."

Isabella's heart gave a treacherous little lurch. He looked very penitent. "I did not take any, my lord. It was a generous thought. Only . . . it would not do. I came as a friend, you see."

His smile was slight, but oddly affecting, nonetheless. "A delicate business, friendship. As I am learning."

A moment of silence reigned as they regarded each other steadily. Then, Julian inclined his head and removed himself from her path. "Until later, Miss Ramsey."

A great lump seemed to swell in Isabella's chest, but before Julian could see the tears misting her eyes—and she knew she was a fool for allowing one simple remark to affect her so— she slipped out the door.

Chapter 18

Only a few days later, Isabella received a note from Lord Roth asking if he might call upon her that very afternoon. "I've a question pertaining to the abbey's books that I do not wish to commit to paper. May I ask you to spare me an hour, no more?" It was addressed to "Miss Ramsey" and signed, simply, "Lord Roth."

They would be alone, unless Isabella asked Lady Prim to sit with them, a perfectly proper course of behavior that, however, Isabella did not follow. Lady Prim had accepted an invitation to luncheon with one of her childhood friends, a Mrs. Wright, who lived on the other side of Saxbourne village. The two women did not get together very often but enjoyed themselves when they did.

Isabella had not forgotten, by any means, either the insult the marquess had dealt her or, she admitted, her weakness for him. But he had not in the weeks since he had first kissed her, then proposed she become his mistress, made the least move toward changing her answer. Far from it, he had been utterly circumspect, even aloof, but for the one instance when he had teasingly told her she looked a wanton.

She grimaced at the memory. Likely she had looked the veriest wanton with her hair down, but he certainly had not been driven to the point of abandon by the sight. As she recalled, he had even taken a step back. So he was quite uninterested in her now that he was up and about and could see other women. She need not oblige Lady Prim to postpone her fun. Her father would be about the house, as would all the servants. She could leave the study door open.

The moment Julian entered her office, Isabella knew she had

not judged the situation amiss. There was a light in his eyes, but it was the light of battle and excitement, not the light of lust.

He carried two ledgers but laid only one, the larger, upon her desk. "I thank you for seeing me, Miss Ramsey. I know it must be a bother to you to keep going over my wretched books, but I need confirmation of what I've found from a person I can trust. I wish you to look at this book first," he said. "And by the by, do you object to my closing the door? I should like to keep this conversation between us."

Highly intrigued to see what he had found, Isabella merely nodded. It was not possible to doubt Julian's motives. For one, he was too tense to even sit, but prowled the room while she began to study the ledger he'd given her. She did not need long to see what it was that had so excited him.

"Good Lord!"

Julian swung about abruptly, his eyes alight. "Do you agree, then, that it is the missing ledger?"

"It is certainly a damning one." She looked down at the page before her as if she could not quite believe what she saw. "And so orderly—with every entry labeled. Just look at how much wheat he has planted, far more than the other books show." She turned the page, and her brow lifted. "The rents! The real rents. Good heavens they are exorbitant. Why did the tenants pay them? And where did you find this ledger, my lord?"

"Surprised that Willis did not make off with his own, personal account book?" he asked, addressing the second question and then laughed wryly. "I am sorry to say it was not any cleverness on my part that foiled him but my habit, which you have observed, of strewing things to kingdom come. The first day I was at the abbey, I took all the ledgers from the desk and went out to the cloister garden, for the place was so musty, I needed air. I made myself somewhat at home on those stone benches by the wall, and this one somehow or other fell down to lodge in a hiding place beneath my seat, for that is where Jepson spied it only yesterday evening."

Julian laughed aloud. "Can you imagine how frantic Willis must have been? We'd evidence someone or other was slipping into the abbey at night, but never learned who or why, for Jepson rigged up a few devices he had learned of in Spain, and after one time of having a string of pots come clattering down upon his head, our sly visitor ceased his prowling.

"He must believe I have lost the thing, or he'd not have stayed on. It is most incriminating from the little I can tell. As to the tenants, he has them all in his debt. A little further on, you'll find those entries. I don't doubt he threatened them with debtor's prison unless they paid as much as they could each month and did whatever he bid them without argument."

"I think he is a monster," Isabella declared roundly, and Julian did not dispute with her.

"A greedy one. He'd a dozen schemes to milk the estate aside from pocketing the profits from crops he never recorded planting. You were quite correct about the dikes. He's not made one repair to them."

For an hour or so, they went over the ledger, comparing it with the other, the fictitious, messy one Willis kept for James Montcrief's solicitors in London, a group who would soon be hearing from Julian, he vowed, for he thought they had been criminally lax. "It did not matter to them what went on in Suffolk, because they never thought they would be held to account. They'll find soon enough it was an erroneous assumption."

When they were satisfied they knew all Willis's schemes—the man had even created a flock of fictitious sheep—Julian gathered his ledgers to go, while Isabella remarked to herself how singularly ordinary, if interesting, the interview had been.

He was just beginning his farewells when they heard her father call something to Jack and close the door to his own study. At once Julian's eyes lightened. "Hearing your father's voice reminds me of something, Miss Ramsey. I did wish you to enlighten me on a particular point. You see, I saw your father from a distance in the village yesterday, and though I clearly recall at dinner he once maintained at length that he would never adopt the shorter hairstyle for men, it did seem to me that his hair had been substantially trimmed."

Even as she told herself she was setting her feet upon a path she had found most ill-advised once before, Isabella felt her spirits rise rather precipitately. And she smiled. "In fact, sir, Dobson was prevailed upon to do the honors. But I am surprised to see you look so amazed. I am certain you dined with us another night, when Lady Prim remarked how well she liked the shorter, more kempt style for a gentleman's hair.''

"Ah." Julian's blue-green eyes sparkled. "I do recollect now that you mention it. But tell me, do you think . . . ?''

"Alas!'' Isabella shook her head sorrowfully. "I do believe there is, indeed, interest on both sides, but there remains yet a large, or rather I should say, small, impediment between the interested parties.''

"Never say that Mr. Buttons stands in the way of true affection, Miss Ramsey,'' Julian chided.

"Staunchly, firmly, indefatigably, and what is worse, with sharp, needle-like teeth,'' Isabella replied. The gold flecks in her eyes shining, she related how her father had been attacked in his own study. "He never saw Mr. Buttons reposing most cozily in his favorite chair until too, too late.''

Julian winced. "Ouch! I am surprised I did not hear his roar at the abbey.''

"Likely you mistook it for the baying of one of the hounds,' Isabella said dryly. "Papa's response was quite that loud and every bit as mournful.''

"Lady Prim, I should imagine, was most chagrined?''

"Most,'' Isabella agreed, observing the twinkle in Julian's eye and unable to deny she admired it. "But it was Mr. Buttons who left the field in her arms, looking, I might add, most pleased with himself.''

"Insult to injury for the squire,'' Julian laughed outright. "I do sympathize with his position. To have his lady fair, he is not obliged to slay the dragon as in days of old, but to win the creature's affection—a much more difficult task.''

They both laughed, and then Julian said he'd one more request to make of Isabella. "No, I do not have yet another thing for you to attend to, Miss Ramsey. This concerns Lady Sarah. I wonder if I might make off with her?'' He smiled slightly when Isabella looked her surprise. "I can explain no more, I fear. We, Sarah and I, that is, have an agreement that I shall teach her a—ah—skill, that she will then show off for you as a surprise—which is why I am being so deucedly cryptic about what Sarah and I shall be doing when I make off with her—if you will allow her to go with me that is.''

Isabella could not but laugh. "I am not certain I followed

all that, but I suppose you did not intend me to, and of course you may take Sarah off. She will be delighted.''

Julian came each day for the next week to collect Sarah, who was, indeed, in alt, and generally he did see Isabella, sometimes only to bid good day, but occasionally to ask some question. Once or twice he made some remark on her father, whose clothes were looking remarkably better kept, and she replied in kind. She also had a request or two to make of him, always on the behalf of one or another of his tenants. An elderly fellow, for example, wished to enlarge his vegetable plot to include a portion of Lord Roth's land. He'd a scheme to grow asparagus and sell it in Ipswich where his daughter said the price was astronomical, but he was too in awe of the marquess to apply directly to him.

Imperceptibly as the days passed, Isabella grew easier in Julian's company. It was true, she had a heightened awareness when he was nearby, but the feeling was nothing so extraordinary that she felt fear of it. She did not hold that feeling against the marquess himself, for his behavior continued to be so entirely unexceptional that she found it almost difficult to believe at times that he had once held her in his arms and told her he desired her to be his mistress.

In the middle of the following week, Isabella finally received her first letter from her sister and adjourned at once to her favorite reading spot, a window seat in the drawing room that looked out over the gardens.

"Aunt Carrington is quite the sweetest dear, Bella!" Liza began after the salutation. "Though she is ever so correct and seemed very formidable upon first meeting, I have found she is as soft as butter in July. We have gone shopping at the Pantheon Bazaar . . .''

Liza's handwriting became erratic as she ran on excitedly about the variety of goods displayed in all the shops she had patronized, but Isabella persevered, until she won through to her sister's account of her first assembly at Almack's. "More splendid than any affair I could ever imagine! I danced every dance but the first . . .''

Isabella turned the letter this way and that and finally made out that Liza attributed at least some of the interest she had excited to Julian Montcrief. "When it was discovered that Ellie and I both came from estates close to his, we were besieged with questions about his carriage accident, rumors of which had reached town, and I was not slow to say we had nursed him at Marsh House. How that interested everyone, Bella, though sadly there was not much to say beyond that he mended nicely. Oh, well! Of even greater interest here is Lord Roth's progress at Wynchley and for the most amazing reason. It seems his father, a most imposing, tall gentleman whom I have seen from a distance, has said Lord Roth must work wonders there in only a year. Francis has told Ellie the betting books in all the clubs are filled with wagers as to the outcome, with those believing Lord Roth will fail in his efforts outweighing those who have faith in him. Ellie and I persuaded Francis to enter a wager for us under his name, for we believe in the marquess and hope to win a tidy sum!"

Though she knew it was most improper for Liza to be laying wagers upon anything at all, Isabella could not but laugh aloud, glancing up from her letter as she did so.

"My lord!" she gasped then, quite taken aback to find Julian lounging comfortably in the doorway with his arms crossed over his chest. "I did not see you," she stated the obvious, her wit routed by the thought that his pose suggested he had been observing her for some time, while she, quite unaware, had been reading of him.

Julian chuckled as he pushed himself upright and came to find another wall, the one just by her, to lean his shoulder against. He looked particularly well, somehow, that afternoon, gazing down at her. Perhaps it was the bottle green of his coat, for it seemed to set off his light eyes.

"You were so absorbed by your sister's epistle, I did not dare announce myself as Dobson directed me to do when he waved me off down the hall to find you for myself."

Julian grinned when Isabella began to make excuses for her butler. "Please don't apologize for Dobson, Miss Ramsey. He makes me feel one of the family. 'Ah, my lord,' " Julian said, mimicking the old man to a nicety. " 'Let me see, now. Miss

Bella's here somewheres. Likely her study or the drawing room, mebbe. She did have a letter from Miss Liza.' "

Julian bowed as Isabella laughed. "That was Dobson to the inch, my lord. You could be an actor."

"Hmmm," he murmured, his eyes on Isabella as he marked how her laughter illuminated her face. "One might say I have had quite a bit of experience with acting," he remarked cryptically, then, added, "But not you, Miss Ramsey. You've singularly expressive eyes, and I would wager it was of me you were reading when you looked up."

Isabella flushed, the remark on her eyes unsettling her quite as much as Julian's demonstration of his ability to read her mind. She had already known he could do that. She made a vague, half-reluctant gesture toward Liza's letter. "It would seem you are the subject of some speculation in town."

Julian's laugh was not particularly amused. "As always," he murmured.

Until she had heard Lady Prim's revelations, Isabella had thought Julian half courted the attention of the gossips. She understood now that he had had their attention, whether he had wanted it or not, since before his birth.

Saddened by the thought that the sins of others should have left a defenseless child open to gossip that could only have hurt him, Isabella did not realize for several moments that Julian was studying her closely. Having just had a demonstration of how accessible her thoughts were to him, she ought, perhaps, to have guarded her expression better.

When their eyes met he said coolly, "You know."

Isabella did not pretend ignorance though his expression was rather forbidding. "Yes, most, I imagine. Lady Prim . . ."

" . . . Knew James. I had forgotten. Well, were you as titillated as everyone else to learn I am a bastard, Miss Ramsey?"

Julian's attempt to put her off quite failed. Isabella shook her head slightly. "I was not titillated," she said quietly, "but that may be because I understand you cannot be, my lord. You were born in wedlock, I believe."

"That is cutting the point rather fine, Isabella and you know it."

"Miss Ramsey, my lord," she chastised more to say something light than anything. "And fine or dull, the point is correct. Then, too, Lady Prim was very firm in the belief you are not James Montcrief's son. In her estimation you've too much of the duke's inbred arrogance to be anyone else's son. And I cannot but agree with her, judging as I am by the way in which you are regarding me at this moment."

A gleam lightened Julian's eye momentarily. "And I thought I was being my most amiable self," he rejoined.

Isabella might have let the subject drop then, but the warmth left Julian's eyes as quickly as it had appeared, and she could not. "In truth, my lord," she said earnestly, "it does not matter to me what your parentage is. I can only judge you for yourself."

Her remark, though entirely true, did not have the intended effect. He gave her a cold smile. "How enlightened you are, Miss Ramsey. A pity everyone could not adopt a like sentiment. But this discussion grows tedious. Tell me instead what Liza does other than listen to gossip."

Isabella ignored the directive entirely. "I don't believe you truly care what 'everyone' thinks. It would, I think, be your father's sentiments with which you quarrel, and you must see his position is altogether different from mine."

Julian lifted himself away from the wall abruptly, but before he could put an end to the discussion by simply walking away, Isabella impulsively reached out to touch his hand. It was the lightest touch, but Julian glanced down, arrested. And looked back at her. She wanted to take his hand in both of hers, anything to warm his expression. She did not, of course.

She regarded him steadily. "Thank you for not leaving, for I did wish to say I do not find it impossible to understand how your father might feel, though I cannot condone his actions. Lady Prim has described your brother to me, you see, and I know he was a good enough young man, but . . . slow. For a man as exceedingly proud as everyone describes your father to be, it must have been very difficult to live with the thought that the one boy he knew without doubt to be his, the one who was his heir, was so little in comparison to you."

Too late Isabella realized how completely she had revealed

her own estimation of the Duke of Chandley's second son, and she colored deeply.

Julian's mouth lifted just slightly at one corner, in the merest hint of his lopsided smile. "I think, Miss Ramsey, that you are kinder to both my father and me than either of us deserve."

"That is not true!" Isabella leapt, unthinking again, to his defense. "You . . ."

"Hush." He said it so softly, Isabella might not have known what Julian said, but that he touched his finger lightly to her lips. "This is Thursday, and on Thursday, I ought not to hear flattery from . . . anyone. Please."

Julian took a step back from her, and Isabella, the faintest warmth still lingering where he had touched her lips, blushed at the knowledge he'd had to restrain her.

She was looking anywhere but at Julian, when a sharp, familiar bark alarmed her so, she forgot her tension. "Where is he?" Isabella demanded, certain Mr. Buttons was up to mischief.

Julian chuckled, then said, looking out the window, "There he is with my pupil."

Following the direction of his nod, Isabella found Sarah holding a biscuit high in the air. The reason for her odd behavior became apparent when Mr. Buttons, hidden until then by a low hedge, hurtled himself into the air to win it.

Failing, he was game to try again only to be distracted by, of all people, the squire, who, coming into the garden from the stables and seeing Sarah holding a biscuit at arm's length for no apparent reason, went to investigate.

"Eh, child, what's to do?" he inquired in his most gentle bellow, for the squire was not without sympathy for the shy, little girl.

"Grrrr!" Mr. Buttons let out a low growl, preparatory to leaping the hedge and attacking his nemesis, but Sarah, reacting with laudible quickness, caught him. Understandably Mr. Buttons was not well pleased to be held fast, but Sarah displayed great wisdom and breaking off a piece of the biscuit, popped it in his mouth. Mr. Buttons was instantly appeased.

The squire, no slow top, came forward, a decided gleam in

his eye. "By gad! That's the very thing. Think he'll take a biscuit from me, child?"

Sarah considered the question carefully, then nodded. "I b-believe so, sir. He likes them v-very much."

With an expression to match the gravity of their experiment, for Sarah knew enough of the animosity between the squire and Mr. Buttons to know the squire risked a bloodied finger, she relinquished her biscuit.

Carefully Squire Ramsey extended it, but Mr. Buttons only cocked his head, as if he did not trust a biscuit offered by his foe.

Isabella took sides as the moment drew out, exclaiming in a whisper, "What a little beast!"

"Nay," Julian protested softly, "I should say he is most wise and having read his Homer, is wondering if that is not The Trojan Biscuit your papa extends."

Perhaps Mr. Buttons heard Isabella's outburst of laughter and mistook it for a larger dog coming for his treat, because he suddenly thrust his head forward and claimed the biscuit. While he was occupied with relishing it, the squire cleverly took him from Sarah, who looked on with almost maternal pride as the squire in rapid succession fed Mr. Buttons one biscuit after another.

Finally Sarah's store depleted, the squire leaned down as far as his girth would permit and allowed Mr. Buttons to jump to the ground. This was the true test, and all but the dog waited with bated breath as Squire Ramsey turned toward his house.

He was two steps along when Mr. Buttons fell in beside him prancing lightly.

"I wonder if all the Chinese are so flighty," Isabella murmured as they disappeared from sight.

Julian's laugh was unreserved. "I should say your father would be wise to keep a ready supply of biscuits at hand. But I must take my leave now, for I've a matter to discuss with him before I see Sarah."

Isabella was just turning to bid him farewell when Julian took her hand and lifted it to his lips. His kiss upon her palm was light. "Thank you, Isabella."

That was all he said before he gave her back her hand and took his leave. Isabella understood what it was he meant, however, though she could not find her voice in time to say as much. It did not matter, though. She thought Julian had likely read her understanding.

Chapter 19

"Do come in, Lady Primley." Mrs. Smithby, a faint frown etching her brow, rose from her place among the half-dozen ladies who gathered regularly at the vicarage to sew garments for the needy. "But where is Isabella?"

"Isabella sends her apologies, Mrs. Smithby," Lady Prim's expression signaled sad news, and all the ladies stilled their needles, the better to listen. "Poor little Billy Prewitt has taken a sudden turn for the worse, and as Cora Geddes has a score of other people to see to just now, Isabella has gone to help Mrs. Prewitt with him."

Mrs. Smithby shook her head quite adamantly. "I know that Isabella is the best of girls, but I cannot agree that she should go to that rude hut as she does. Why, I cannot imagine it is even clean!"

Lady Prim allowed herself a small smile, though she, herself, was not entirely comfortable with Isabella's visitations to the poorer homes in the neighborhood. "You needn't worry for Isabella, Mrs. Smithby. Lord Roth allowed the Prewitts to take over the gate house at the abbey some week or more ago."

"Well, that is generous of him!" exclaimed one of the ladies, a trim, bright-eyed woman named Mrs. Thomas. All the ladies voiced agreement, but for Pru Manning, who alone knew of Isabella's particular interest in the Prewitts.

"Was it the marquess's notion, Lady Prim, or Bella's?" she asked shrewdly.

"Isabella did put the matter to him," Lady Prim conceded. "She is especially fond of Billy, you know, and has been most concerned since he contracted the influenza from his brothers."

"I wonder she could ask the marquess such a thing!" declared Mrs. Thomas in some wonder. "I mean I have not met him and cannot know for certain, but I should think he would be quite daunting to speak with."

Lady Prim thought of Julian Montcrief's almost palpable charm and smiled. "I should not say he is daunting, Mrs. Thomas, though I do understand what you mean. He will be the eighth duke of his line, after all."

"And he is so sinfully handsome," added Pru with a rather roguish grin.

The conversation degenerated a moment then, for Mrs. Thomas would know if Lord Roth was truly so handsome, and surprisingly, Letty Smithby found voice first to say, "When I was presented, I thought I might quite swoon away!"

Mrs. Smithby gave her daughter a repressive look, but did confide, though no one had looked to her, "He is quite an attractive man, yes."

It was left to Pru to satisfy Mrs. Thomas's curiosity as to specifics, which she did with enthusiasm, her interest in Francis Basham notwithstanding. "He's quite, quite tall and broad shouldered, and with all that sun-streaked hair and those glorious eyes—they are sea-green, Mrs. Thomas—then he has only to smile to take one's breath away."

"Oh! I should find it impossible to converse with such a man," confessed Mrs. Thomas, whose cheeks had grown slightly flushed during the discussion. "I do think Isabella very brave."

"When Bella has taken a notion into her head, I doubt Prinny, himself, could daunt her," Pru remarked to the general agreement of the ladies busying sewing while they chatted, all of whom had known Isabella all their lives.

Lady Prim did not listen closely as the talk moved on to other matters of interest in the neighborhood. Her needle flashing as she worked, she thought instead of Isabella and how quite undaunted she indeed had been pleading for the Prewitts.

Lady Prim sighed just the least bit. Isabella had fairly flown into the library that day at the abbey, her bonnet dangling from her fingers, her cheeks flushed from haste. "Lady Prim, pray excuse me, will you?" she said at once, politely but with undeniable urgency. "I've a most pressing request to make of Lord Roth."

"Of course, my dear," Lady Prim had replied as she stilled

a desire to send Isabella back to the gilt-framed glass hanging in the hallway that she might, as she ought to have taken the time to do before entering, smooth into place the several wispy tendrils of soft hair that had come loose from their pins when she had removed her bonnet.

Lord Roth, however, when Lady Prim had looked anxiously to see, had not seemed to take Isabella's appearance or rushed manner in bad part. Indeed, as she recalled, he had smiled faintly.

"How may I help you, Miss Ramsey?"

"Oh, not me, Lord Roth," Isabella corrected, and Lady Prim had been a little startled to hear the marquess say almost indistinctly, "No, of course not."

"It is the Prewitts, you see," Isabella had rushed on. "As I feared, Billy has contracted the influenza, and his condition is quite grave. I fear for him, really, and I did think that if, perhaps, his circumstances were improved, he might stand a better chance. I suppose it a farfetched notion . . ."

"Not at all," Lord Roth had broken in to say. "I can imagine it would be healthier for all the Prewitts, were they to reside in a substantial house with real floors and a solid roof. Where is it you wish to move them? Are you eyeing the as yet unused west wing of the abbey?"

Somewhat to Lady Prim's surprise Isabella's lovely smile broke through. "I had considered it, I admit, but decided it would be too musty." Lord Roth had laughed. "Then, in my thoughts, I came to your gate house."

Roth did not seem unduly surprised. "It is not occupied," he allowed.

"There is that advantage," Isabella returned, smiling again. "And I am quite certain Mrs. Prewitt, with the help of a few friends, could have it cleaned up in little time at all."

"I imagine you asked her."

"Well, yes," Isabella had admitted. "I did not wish to assume anything, and she did say as well that she would be quite pleased to act as your gatekeeper. Will it do, Lord Roth?"

"I can see no reason it should not," he said, surprising Lady Prim with his ready acceptance of the notion. "I'll have it taken care of at once."

And he had, pausing only to tell Lady Prim he thought blue

silk on the walls of the saloon would be just the thing. Lady Prim did not believe he had given much thought to her suggestion, but she did not fault the marquess at all. Indeed, she was pleased he trusted her taste so completely. But most of all, she was pleased he had made Isabella happy, for Lady Prim secretly thought the child took too much on herself—or had been given too much. But just then as she departed the room with Lord Roth, Isabella looked the young girl she was. Her worries for little Billy lifted for the time, her fine eyes quite sparkled.

"Lady Primley."

Lady Primley blinked vaguely, then realized Mrs. Thomas was looking inquiringly at her. "Beg pardon, my dear. I fear my mind wandered."

Mrs. Thomas blushed at little. "Well, in truth it was nothing. I only asked if you thought the marquess might ever have an entertainment at the abbey."

"Oh, dear! My mind must be to let today." Lady Prim looked rather undone as she glanced about the circle of curious ladies. "I suppose I have been quite distracted with the abbey and Isabella's worries, too, but to think I nearly forgot to say! Well, to get on with it, the answer to your question is yes, Mrs. Thomas. Only yesterday the marquess revealed he wishes to hold a ball quite soon."

The quite unexpected announcement had a startling effect on the ladies. Some exclaimed, some cried out, the younger ladies squealed, and Mrs. Smithby, evidently undone by such good fortune breathed, "You do not mean it, Lady Primley!"

Lady Primley managed a serene nod, though she'd have rather liked to smile smugly. It was such a pleasure to take Mrs. Smithby aback. "I do, Mrs. Smithby. Of course, only a few of the rooms will have been completely restored, but Roth thought that would not matter."

All the ladies rushed to agree. They did not need much, the general sentiment went, only a ballroom really, just so long as they could be at the abbey, guests of the Marquess of Roth.

It was Mrs. Thomas who voiced the sudden, horrid thought that occurred simultaneously to all the members of the sewing circle. "Does the marquess intend to extend invitations to his neighbors, Lady Primley? Or will he invite only his acquaintances from town?"

"Oh, no," Lady Prim assured her hastily. "I cannot say if Lord Roth intends to invite friends from town, but I can assure you he means the ball to be a welcome to his neighbors." Reassured, the ladies asked a half-dozen more questions, one being the date of the affair. The answer surprised them. "He did say he wished to hold it on the night of the next new moon."

"The next new moon?" demanded Mrs. Smithby. "But there is so little light without a moon, it is more difficult to travel."

Lady Prim agreed. "Yes, but Roth said he'd a notion to celebrate the coming of a new era at the abbey on a night when even the moon was new."

"What a fanciful notion," the vicar's wife exclaimed, clearly uncertain about such a flight.

"Well, he did say," Lady Prim went on, perhaps a trifle defensively, "that he would send torchbearers on horseback ahead of any coach desiring more light."

"Oh, that is romantic!" cried Letty, clapping her hands together, and many of the ladies agreed, though not so effusively.

Not surprisingly the ball, and most particularly the dress for it, was the principle topic of conversation for the remainder of the ladies' sewing circle.

Isabella knew of Roth's plans for a ball, Lady Prim had told her, but nothing was further from her mind that afternoon. Billy Prewitt had seemed to improve after Roth had the family moved to the light, airy gate house. Indeed, when Isabella had stopped by with a basket of food in celebration of the Prewitts' new home, he had come outside to greet her.

Only two days later, however, Billy's condition worsened suddenly during the night. Mr. Prewitt had come to Marsh House the next day seeking Cora, and Isabella had returned with them to the gate house. The child felt on fire with the fever, and his breath rattled in his lungs as if he had to struggle for air.

Cora, after putting her ear to Billy's chest, looked up gravely at the Prewitts, both of whom stood by the boy's bed, and told them what they knew. " 'Tis bad."

Isabella could scarcely believe it. To have the boy who had struggled gallantly all his short life, succumb now, when his family's circumstances had improved so greatly, seemed the most cruel trick of fate.

Cora explained she had seen the phenomenon before. Particularly children, she said, would show brief improvement only to have the influenza flare again with deadly suddenness in their vulnerable lungs.

They all did everything they could, even Mr. Prewitt, whose attitude had undergone a change after the marquess had shown the family favor. Guarded, almost wary in his manner before, he had seldom said a word to Isabella on the few occasions they had met. Now, though certainly not garrulous, he nodded a greeting, a smile in his eyes if not on his lips, and he showed concern for his boy as he had not before.

Isabella believed the man had felt so helpless with Willis's rents draining him and nothing left to finance a move, that he had closed his heart against everyone. Now, given hope, he expanded.

Lord Roth had done that. Indeed he had wrought similar changes over all the estate, in part by lowering his tenants' rents. He did require more in labor than Willis had, but the tenants did not mind as they knew they would have more for their own pockets.

In one day Isabella had seen Mrs. Prewitt burst into tears out of sheer gratitude for the fine, new home she had; had heard two young girls in Saxbourne village say they wished they could get on at the abbey because it would be such a grand house; and had heard from Cora that a new boy born to Wynchley tenants had been named Julian. It was, she had remarked later that day to the man, himself, the supreme honor, and she had added well deserved.

He could not, however, work any miracle for Billy Prewitt. Isabella, equally helpless, had come on occasion to sit with the child to relieve his mother. Such was the case on that particular day, when Cora was occupied with a young wife whose first birth was proving most difficult and Mr. Prewitt was in his fields with his boys as he needed to be.

She feared the child's crisis had come, for his brow was exceedingly hot, and his breathing grew ever more labored. The day dragged on, and as she sponged his forehead or held his hand, Isabella only held to her composure with an effort. The boy's pinched face was badly flushed, and his thin body thrashed as he struggled against the disease overwhelming him.

Twice Billy came awake, asking for water, and each time after he had slaked his thirst he smiled gratefully. That sweetness, when he was faced with death, made her want to cry aloud.

At last there was no escaping the realization that the boy was, indeed, dying and needed his mother. Mrs. Prewitt came, then Mr. Prewitt, returning home earlier than usual. Isabella waited below in the house's small sitting room with the other Prewitt children and a few friends of the family.

They'd not long to wait. Only a little after five, Mr. Prewitt, his eyes red-rimmed, came to say in a few halting words that Billy had died.

With a graciousness Isabella had not expected, he thanked her particularly for her help in easing his child's last hours. Touched, she gave him her condolences and left soon after.

Too drained to think clearly, Isabella drifted out of the gate at the back of the house with no destination in mind. Spring had come to Suffolk. The Soloman's seal, white and bell-like, was in bloom, and small violets peeked up shyly from the woods' floor. Underfoot the ground was soft and slightly spongy, for the drought had broken, but Isabella was aware of none of the beauty.

Her head bent, she saw only Billy Prewitt's small face and tears welling in her eyes, she recalled the two valiant little smiles he'd given her.

That there was someone standing on the path ahead of her, Isabella only realized when her eyes took in a pair of dark objects that her mind at last identified as boots.

Looking up, she found it was Julian before her. She had gone closer to the abbey than she realized and had come upon him as he took a walk before dinner. She could say nothing, but it was no matter. The tears shimmering in her eyes were enough.

Julian's expression tightened infinitesimally as one spilled onto her cheek, and somehow it was the most natural thing in the world for Isabella to walk into his arms.

In her need for comfort she did note how, for the merest fraction of a second, Julian stood very still as she laid her forehead against his chest.

"He was so young, Julian," she said in such a soft voice he

could scarcely hear her. She was not sobbing. The tears simply flowed from her, as she laid her hands flat upon his chest.

"I know," she heard him say, his voice low and quiet and as soothing as the strong arms he wrapped around her.

"And good," she declared, her voice muffled but fiercer too, for some of her numbness had left her. Suddenly she lifted her head. "He was so very brave at the end. You will not countenance it, but he even smiled his thanks when I got him a glass of water!" Before Julian could make a reply, Isabella cried angrily, "I hate death, do you hear? And Willis! He is most to blame."

Isabella hit at Julian's chest with the side of her fists, as if he were Jasper Willis, but he did not seem to mind. Still holding her, his sea-green gaze steady, he asked quietly, "Who else do you blame?"

Her mind having raced on, she could not think what he meant. "Beg pardon?"

"You said Willis was the most to blame which implies someone else is to blame as well."

Isabella's eyes fell away from Julian's, and she seemed to realize her position for the first time. The instant she stiffened, he released her. Perversely the moment he had withdrawn his arms and left her quite as she wished to be, she longed to return to his embrace. She made do with lashing out at a loose rock, though her soft kid slipper was not fashioned for such an activity.

Abruptly as the pain in her toe receded, she said, "I don't know who is to blame. His father, perhaps, for not challenging Willis. Or Dr. Davies for being too old to be of help."

Chiming in, as if he were only adding to her list of those accountable, Julian said, "And Our Maker, of course, for choosing to take the child so soon."

He had struck a chord. Isabella whirled upon him, her hazel eyes sparking with anger. "He might have taken Willis, but He chose a helpless child!"

It was a blasphemous sentiment. Isabella lifted her chin, daring Julian to take issue with her, but he did not. Indeed his tone was decidedly mild as he said, "Willis will be taken in time, I imagine."

Isabella bit her lip and looked out into the woods. "Mr.

Smithby says I rail too much at death. He says I would make myself God.''

She cast Julian a glance then. It was only a brief look, but he saw that though her eyes were flinty, there was, too, a question in them. ''I only know of Mr. Smithby that he married Mrs. Smithby,'' he said.

It was an absurd answer, really, and far below the weightiness of their topic. Isabella stared at Julian a long moment, her response in the balance, until all at once her expression softened.

This time she only nudged the stone by her foot as she muttered, ''Though he may be a fool on the subject of matrimony, the vicar is a good man, really—as you might know, if you attended his church on Sundays, my lord.''

''And endure Mrs. Smithby afterward?'' One side of Julian's mouth curved down wryly. ''Not a chance. And though he may be a good man, he is a fool to say you wish to play God. As I've said before, you've a generous heart and would only see an end of suffering.''

''He looked half his age, Julian.'' Isabella's eyes had clouded again, and biting her lip against another bout of tears, she did not remark how easily Julian's name came to her lips. Only he did. ''Dear heaven!'' she went on. ''When I think how fortunate I am, I, I feel so unworthy.''

Isabella was thinking of the hearty breakfast she'd enjoyed that morning, the warm clothes she had to wear all the winter, the comfortable bed in which she slept. Julian thought of the come-out Liza would enjoy because Isabella had agreed to wed a cold, middle-aged roué of no morals at all.

''Self-pity does not become you, Isabella,'' he said curtly. ''You give more to the people around you than anyone I have ever known, and yet how you would wear sackcloth and ashes. Perhaps your father ought to seek out a nunnery for you.''

''That is not fair!'' Isabella gasped. ''I think all people of sensibility may thank God for their good fortunes, and yet wonder why it is others are not so blessed! I only would make life better for the Prewitts. That is all!''

''Good,'' Julian returned. ''Then you will help me review the reams of applications I have received for the post of doctor in Saxbourne village.''

Isabella stared a full minute, and Julian was hard put not to smile. "You would help us make a living for a doctor?"

Julian nodded, but once again his mood became grave. "People will still die, Isabella, even those who deserve a long life. We can only . . ."

" . . . Do the best we can," she finished for him somewhat sheepishly. "I know. Mr. Smithby has told me often enough."

"Good God! Never say I am becoming a Smithby!"

He was so genuinely taken aback, Isabella smiled. Mr. Smithby was small, thin, wispy, learned, and quite pious. Without thought, Isabella flicked her gaze over Julian's tall, well-made body. "No, my lord," she said slowly, lifting her eyes to his. "I do not think you are in the least danger of resembling our vicar." There was the veriest moment of pregnant silence before Isabella added in a rush, "Except perhaps, that you are both adept at cajoling me out of a fit of the dismals. My thanks, my lord."

It was the truth that after her mother's death, Isabella had had a difficult time and that it had been the vicar who had reached her. Oddly he had said much the same thing about death and God's will as had the notorious Marquess of Roth. Only the vicar had not held her.

She scuffed at another rock. It was time to go. Past time, because she did not want to go at all.

Chapter 20

Isabella stared at the words that seemed to leap out at her from the letter lying on her father's table.

"Rumors have come to me associating your daughter with the Marquess of Roth, and as you well know, I desire my future wife to be entirely above suspicion. I shall come soon to Suffolk to look into the matter for myself. Until then, Squire, I advise you to have greater care for my honor as well as your daughter's.

Isabella squeezed her eyes shut, then reread the words she had not intended to read in the first place. She had only glanced at the letter because it was lying open by the journal she'd come to scan. When Julian's name outlined in Wrexham's hand had leapt out at her, she'd been powerless to keep from reading the whole.

Noise coming from the entryway brought her head up. She was in too great a turmoil to see anyone. Indeed she felt almost ill to learn someone—who could it be?—had gossiped poisonously about her to Wrexham!

It was as well Isabella hurried away, for she'd have encountered her father and Julian had she stayed and might have, in her distress, blurted out her knowledge before she had thought through the proper cause of action to take.

But because she did not stay, she'd no notion her father ushered Julian into his study for the very purpose of reading him the hateful letter.

The squire was quite furious. "It's the outside of enough that the man would question, Bella!" he raged. "I've half a mind to call him out myself but that my girl'd be the one most hurt by the scandal. It'd cling to her even after she married."

Scowling he poured his guest a glass of brandy and then,

settled with his own glass, read the full letter. Julian listened
attentively. It was their second meeting on the subject of
Wrexham. The first had come after Julian had kept watch on
Wrexham's bay the night of the last new moon. The following
day he had gone to describe to the squire what he'd seen.

"A sleek smuggler's ship, sir, was met by half-a-dozen punts
that skimmed across the bay from the marshes like waterbugs
to collect their illegitimate cargo." The squire had gone, for
a florid man, quite pale and Julian had allowed him to drain
a large helping of brandy before he added, quietly, "Squire,
I know that you are involved in this business."

His host's large head had jerked up at that. There had been
a long moment while each took the other's measure and then
the squire had sagged weakly into his chair. "I'd give a great
deal had you not learned it, Roth, though I feared you would.
I'm no liar, though, nor a true smuggler when it comes to it,
though I have reaped the profits of several cargoes."

"Was it Wrexham came to you, sir?"

Had the business not been so serious, Julian might have been
amused by the look of amazed respect the squire had given him.
"How did you guess? Eh, never mind! You're sharp as he is.
Aye, it was Wrexham came to me last summer with the scheme.
My part was to do naught but keep hunters from my marshes—
no difficulty when everyone knows you ought not to hunt
overmuch after two years o' drought. Might hurt the stock for
ages, if you do."

Julian bit back a smile at his evidence of the squire's sense
of responsibility. Ramsey had not meant to amuse, for he was
frowning down moodily at the amber liquid in his glass.

"I needed the blunt. I'll not hide it. I proved the poorest father
my children could have after Betsy died. Without her by me,
I couldn't see things as I ought. I ran through two years of the
estate's profits in a few months. Cards, mostly, but I did come
by a new hunter and two grand bitches. I didn't stop there, I'm
ashamed to say. Went off to Newmarket for a spell with an old
friend, too. I had to borrow to cover my losses, and it was the
greatest good luck Bella finally realized what was afoot. She
stemmed most of the flow, bless her, but she could not bring
back the capital I'd wasted. Two years of drought were no help
there. Suddenly there were no marriage portions for the girls,

and of course no resources for a proper come-out. Nor were there funds for Peter's schooling. Can't say I understand what he wants with a pack o' tomes, bless me if I do, but they're his heart's desire. When Wrexham offered ten thousand pounds in a year. I leapt at it. Never thought what I did 'till you came, boy, and made some mention of a ball you took on the Peninsula. I'd the most awful thought then, though I knew the timing was all off, that it could have been my blunt, the very ha'pennies I scraped together to bring in that first load of the brandy, that paid for your wound.''

Now at this second meeting, with Wrexham's letter before them, the squire again recalled the summer before and how on the same day Wrexham had approached him about the smuggling, he'd expressed his interest in Isabella.

''I was surprised, I don't mind sayin'. Her mother's father was a duke, but Bella's lived a quiet life, and Wrexham has always been high in the instep. I understood better, though, when he reminded me of his first wife, a beauty, but a shrew and unfaithful to boot. Bella'd be loyal. He saw that and that she's got an air about her, when he met her at some do Hortensia Basham gave. Said Bella was a cut above the ordinary run, which proves he's a sharp 'un. I'll say that even if she is my own daughter.

''He couldn't be sure she'd accept him, being old as he is, though, and he'd the notion we should call the profits I took in from our scheme a betrothal settlement. In that way I would account for all blunt I came by suddenly, and Bella would be hard put to refuse him. She'd have denied Liza and Peter too much. You must remember it was not just the boy's schooling was in question, but his inheritance. The man I'd borrowed from was pressing for what I owed. I can't blame him, he's a wife to account to, but I was close to havin' to sell the estate to pay up.

''Egad boy! I'm goin' maudlin on you. Never meant to carry on over past history—and sins. But I thought you should know why Wrexham'd taken this poison's been dripped in his ear hard. He's pride aplenty, lad. He may well be anglin' to call you out. He's the sort who would, and he's a crack shot, you may be sure.''

Julian quite agreed a duel was to be avoided for Isabella's sake, though he believed Wrexham's intended visit to Suffolk had as much to do with brandy as a concern for his honor. Or, Julian smiled grimly to himself, he hoped that was the case.

He'd a desire to take down the viscount for several reasons, not the least of them being he despised the wretch for having harmed the fragile girl who was his only child. It helped, too, that he'd been in battle and seen his friends and men cut down by ammunition that countrymen like the viscount thought nothing of financing. He was pleased the squire had seen the point for himself, if a little late.

There were several parts to his scheme. First and simplest, to deny the man his land route across Wynchley, Julian had had only to move himself and dozens of people loyal to him onto the estate. Next, he had gotten the squire to write his confederate to say, truthfully, he'd lost his stomach for smuggling and would no longer protest his marshes from prying eyes. Deprived of his hiding place, Wrexham was left with little choice anything but to unload his lucrative cargo onto his own land.

To lull any fears Wrexham might have about so bold a move, Julian planned his ball. All the neighborhood on the night of the next new moon would be at Wynchley, leaving fewer ears about to note the sound of laden carts rumbling out of Wrexham Hall's gates.

Finally, because he wanted Wrexham himself on the scene, Julian had, only the day before in a most satisfying scene, fired Willis. Thus he denied the viscount his able lieutenant only a short week before the next shipment was, as Julian strongly believed, to come.

"You are still agreed we shall keep all this from Isabella?" Julian asked suddenly of the squire. "I don't want Wrexham to have the least suspicion of what we intend, and she'd not be able to keep her knowledge from her eyes."

"Aye, lad! There's no use her knowin' yet, and I'd keep her ignorant of this gossip. It would cut up her peace and for no reason."

Julian could not but agree with both points, and so the men went about their business, quite unaware that Isabella's peace was utterly destroyed even though she'd no notion of the smuggling.

She could not forget the way Wrexham had referred to his

honor. Like her father, she believed him the sort of man who would resort to the dueling field in an instant.

Isabella gave no thought at all to her name, to the gossip that would surely slander her if her betrothed challenged Julian Montcrief, her near neighbor and a man of well-known reputation. It was for Julian, she worried.

There could be no question that Chandley would be infuriated should he get word of yet another duel. He had not said directly his son must go a year without causing any scandal, but he had implied it, surely. All Julian had done at Wynchley would be for naught. He would lose his patrimony, though he was entirely innocent.

But there was one not so innocent. Isabella bit her lip. Oh yes, not innocent at all. If Wrexham wished to avenge his honor, it was not Julian he should call out. It was she who betrayed him, though God knew she had not meant to do so. In the silence of her darkened office, Isabella bowed her head so that her forehead touched the pane of the window. The glass felt cool to her skin, and she drew a deep shuddering breath.

The past weeks had been such joy. The least thing could catch her eye and laughter would bubble up inside her. Nothing had tried her patience; no one could put her out of countenance. Not that anyone had tried. The whole world had seemed as giddy and light and playful as she.

She had never felt so before, and at first, she'd not been able to account for it. Or had not wished to. Then her father had told her, one soft, bright spring afternoon, when she had come in from the garden with Sarah, a basket of flowers in her hand, that she looked pretty as the day. "I declare you do, Bella! Never saw your eyes so bright. It must be this grand day that's put that sparkle in them."

He'd not known that Julian Montcrief had lazily supervised her and Sarah as they gathered their flowers. But Isabella had known and had faced the cause of her joy.

She'd not felt remorse, for she could not feel at fault. She had not given her heart away. She had fought her attraction to the Marquess of Roth.

And might have succeeded in her struggle had he been merely a very handsome man. Particularly when she had been so angry and hurt; when she thought him only a deceitful, hurtful rake, she had been safe.

But he had been so very honorable ever since she had read him that furious scold. Even when, grieving for little Billy Prewitt, she had walked into his embrace, he had held her only as long as she wished to be held and then had given her his handkerchief that she might mop up her own eyes.

At Wynchley, too, he had proven himself a far different man from the licentious libertine, she'd called him in her mind. In every respect there he had been an exceedingly generous, hard-working gentleman who could display, and not only with Sarah, that sweetness upon which Lady Prim had remarked.

As for his being a rake, if she could not deny that side of him, Isabella understood it better after Lady Prim's revelations. If his own mother took lovers, and all the women he encountered besides, why should he think there were women who truly held their honor dear? Certainly he would have no interest in marriage where, as he believed, there could be no trust on either side.

And so, understanding and forgiving and finally respecting, she had fallen in love. Sweet, sweet love. The time of reckoning had come, of course, but she could not regret the joy she'd experienced. She would hold the memory of it all her life, though she knew Wrexham must not see it.

How to say to a betrothed, "But, sir, I did not betray you with any act, only girlish dreams. You needn't worry. This other man does not return my affections. He was physically attracted once, perhaps, when there was no other woman about, but that feeling deepened into nothing more than friendship."

No, Wrexham would not be well pleased. And, considering Julian's reputation, it would be asking a great deal of the viscount to believe them both innocent.

But . . . Isabella put her head into her hands. Perhaps it was not fair to marry if her heart was engaged, however futilely, elsewhere. She could find the means to return the settlement, somehow. No! There was Sarah. She loved the little girl too well. And even did she not, what would she say to her? "I am sorry, Sarah, but you must return all alone to your father's house, where I know you were not happy, because I am in love, and if I cannot marry my love. I cannot marry anyone." It was too gothic and self-indulgent to be thought of.

Wrexham did not love her, after all. No, she must lock her love for Julian away in the farthest recesses of her heart. Not my word or deed or gesture would she betray her feelings to Wrexham. She would marry him, and she would make him a good wife. He would have no cause to fault her—or Julian.

Isabella kept her decision to herself. To no one did she reveal what she had read. Least of all did she think to tell Julian of Wrexham's suspicions. Ugly, they sullied the quite innocent— particularly on Julian's part—friendship that had come to mean so much to her.

Too, she feared that if he learned she was distressed by those suspicions, Julian would not allow her to play the meek part she knew instinctively would best appease Wrexham. The marquess did not love her, she knew, but he did see himself as her friend. He'd wish to have the matter aired and would confront Wrexham head on despite the consequences to himself.

And there would be consequences. Isabella knew as surely as she knew anything that an interview between the two men would go badly. Julian would not brook the viscount's arrogance. Nor need he, a marquess with a lineage as ancient as Wrexham's, and Isabella did not need to know her betrothed well to know he would not care for being outranked by a more handsome, younger, wealthier man.

No, a meeting between the two men was to be avoided. And the best way was simply to pull back slowly from Julian Montcrief: to see less and less of him until finally she saw nothing. It would have come to that anyway. When his year at Wynchley ended, Julian would have no cause to linger in Suffolk. The estate was his father's from what she understood. He had a life to live; a wife of his station and suitable wealth to acquire.

The immediate result of Wrexham's letter, then, was that Isabella saw little of Julian that week. She busied herself with other matters by visiting Pru, the tenants, taking Lady Prim to Ardsley, all in the hopes that whoever it was had carried tales would have nothing new to report.

Finally, though, an occasion arose she could not escape. Julian sent her a note to say that Sarah wished to show off her new, hard-won, secretly acquired skill on the next afternoon. Would Miss Ramsey and the squire be available at three o'clock?

Isabella was very glad for her father's presence when Julian strode into the drawing room at the appointed hour. Now she knew her time with him was at an end, Julian seemed very, very dear. He was so alive, so vital and vivid, she might not have been able to cease drinking in the sight of him, had not the squire reminded her why they had gathered.

"Well! Shall we be off to applaud the little one? I've a curiosity to see what it is she's learned. The way the chit talks now I can make out what it is she says. Helped me bring the runt to heel, you know," he added and regaled Julian with the tale he already knew as they proceeded outside.

"This way, Squire, Miss Ramsey," Julian said, leading them through the gardens at the side of the house to a gate that opened onto the nearest field. There he had them wait until he had peeked through to see, Isabella supposed, if the stage were set properly. "Very well, you may come now," he directed.

The squire, naturally, gave way to Isabella, and when she was on Julian's side of the gate, he took her elbow to position her correctly, which happened to be directly beside him. All she could think was that it might be the last time she would stand so easily by him. The last time she would smell the clean, spicy scent of sandalwood, feel how tall he was, how broad his shoulders . . .

"Miss Ramsey, you are not looking, and if you do not see Sarah and smile, she will be quite disappointed."

Starting, Isabella looked up at Julian. "What . . . ?"

"There," he nudged her shoulder so she turned, and an impression of light, dear, sea-green eyes seeming burned onto her field of vision, she glanced around.

"Oh, my!"

Julian chuckled, then stepped away to wave Sarah forward. Sitting very straight and proud, the child made her black pony trot to their audience and then beamed hugely when both the squire and Isabella burst into applause.

"Never thought to see this!" Squire Ramsey declared.

"I am so proud, Sarah!" cried Isabella. "You look quite wonderful."

"She's a very good seat," Julian agreed, then looked significantly at Sarah. At once the child urged the pony to a canter, and off they went across the field.

"Well, boy, you've managed a wonder!" The squire shook his head. "Never thought the child would mount anything with four legs, not after I saw her take to her heels at the bazaar. Thought she'd a fright of horses."

"She did, actually, but it was not an insurmountable fear."

Wrexham was completely forgotten. Isabella's fine eyes were shining more vividly than they ever had. "I think, my lord," she said very softly, "that you've a very large heart."

With a sense of surprise, she realized Julian had been waiting for her reaction. The moment before she spoke, his face had been almost grave and in the next it was lit by a white, flashing smile. "I could wish for no higher praise, Miss Ramsey."

"Eh, now who's this?" At her father's question, Isabella pulled her gaze from Julian's to see the squire was looking along the brick wall that divided the house and gardens from the fields. It was impossible to see the rider from their vantage point, but it was possible to see his dust. "I'll go have a look. Wouldn't do for you, Bella, not to be on hand, when Lady Sarah returns."

Sarah was a very small figure in the distance and would not be back for a few moments, but Isabella could not argue with her father's logic. It was impeccable. Only it meant she would be alone with Julian when she was very susceptible.

"You are pleased, then?"

"Very much so my lord." She wanted to throw her arms wide and run to him. She bit her lip.

"I am glad, Miss Ramsey. I had thought I might have offended you in some way, for you seemed strained by something when I first came this afternoon."

"No!" She had said it too quickly. "No," she repeated more calmly. "I . . . you have not offended me in any way at all, my lord. You . . ." She could not speak, for suddenly her eyes filled with tears.

"Isabella!"

She shook her head as he started to reach out for her. Instantly he lowered his arm, and sniffing, she essayed a tremulous smile through her tears. "It is only Sarah. You have been so wonderful with her, and I, I could not bear for you to think I was offended.''

''Please, don't cry. Here, you need this.''

Again he had reason to hand her his handkerchief that she might wipe away her tears. Only this time she was obliged to bite her lip to hold back the fresh ones that seemed to rise up when she looked back at him.

''We are friends then?'' Julian asked, as if he had reason to doubt it.

Isabella's gaze flew to his. ''I would ever be your friend, my lord! No matter what may come.''

She thought he meant to say something else then, but she was not to learn what it was he might have said, for simultaneously the gate swung open and Sarah pulled up before them.

Isabella gave the child a bright, applauding smile before she turned to see it was Nell at the gate, looking a little flustered. ''Beggin' yer pardon, Miss Bella, yer lordship.'' She bobbed a curtsy toward Julian, then turned back to her mistress. '' 'Tis the squire sent me to tell ye, Miss Bella, he's had a note sayin' Lord Wrexham's to come for tea.''

Even as her hand flew to her throat, Isabella heard Julian say, ''Ah,'' and the single, inadequate syllable was so filled with satisfaction, she looked to him in complete confusion.

But she'd no more than an instant to consider why Julian should be pleased by Wrexham's arrival, for Sarah, upon Nell's announcement, made a sudden, tense movement that caused her pony to shy. Had the child not been distracted, she'd have known what to do, for Julian had had her practice reacting if her pony were startled. Just then, however, all Sarah's lessons were scattered to the wind. Her grip on the reins gone slack, she was thrown to the ground with a thump and promptly burst into tears.

Chapter 21

"It would seem the entire neighborhood has come out to applaud Roth's achievements."

Isabella looked from Wrexham's hand, pale and manicured on her arm, to the long line of carriages extending down the abbey's drive. "The ball has been much anticipated," she said quietly as she turned to face the windows blazing with light.

"And you, my dear? Have you looked forward to it?"

Isabella was proud she did not falter. "Yes, of course. We've few entertainments."

No more was said as they mounted the steps, yet Isabella could feel her agitation mount. It had been much the same all the week Wrexham had been in Suffolk. On the surface he seemed courteous enough in his cool, aloof way. He had dined with them at Marsh House each night and had not once made any overt accusation.

Only, here and there, he had let drop remarks that, while they might have seemed quite ordinary to an uninformed onlooker, seemed to her to be weighted with hidden significance. She'd have preferred the straightforward question. The little darts, coming when least expected, made her feel she played the mouse to the viscount's sleek, watchful cat.

She'd have scolded herself for being fanciful, had it not been so plain that everyone at Marsh House was adversely affected by Wrexham's arrival.

Her nephew had only to walk into the room for Lady Prim to become a fluttery, breathless, ineffectual stranger, who did not, significantly, make the least mention of Lord Roth or the abbey, though she went every day to supervise preparations for the ball that Julian had done her the honor of requesting her to hostess.

It was Wrexham who raised the subject of his aunt's relations with their neighbor, saying suddenly after they had been discussing something else entirely, "Do you know I was surprised, Aunt, to hear you are assisting our neighbor, Lord Roth, to settle into his home. I had no notion you knew the man so well."

A simple observation, really, but something in the way it was said, silkily almost, made Lady Prim flush and dither and get out only haltingly that she had become acquainted with the marquess when he had been nursed at Marsh House after his accident.

"Ah yes," Wrexham said smoothly, his gaze sliding then to Isabella. "How fortuitous for the marquess that he was injured so near to you, my dear. You must have practiced your nursing abilities quite assiduously to have him recover so quickly."

A spurt of anger for the quivering mass to which he had reduced his aunt, stiffened Isabella's spine. "I wish I did have such abilities, my lord," she said levelly. "But Cora Geddes is the one with the healing touch, and it was she who nursed Lord Roth."

For the merest moment, Isabella thought she detected a reappearance of the approving light that had been absent from Wrexham's eyes since he returned to Suffolk, but then her father had spoken up overhastily. "No, no, Bella took on little of the lad's care. It was Millie who sat with him the most, and my-self . . ."

Wrexham's heavy-lidded eyes cooled instantly and the faintly mocking smile that seemed to linger perpetually at the corners of his mouth reappeared. But Isabella excused her father's ineffectual bluster. He was concerned only for her and where she would be left if the viscount broke off their engagement after a duel with Lord Roth.

The worst-affected of them all by the viscount's presence, however, was Sarah, and little wonder. Her father had her brought into his company three times and each time fixed her with such a disdainful look the child had become to Isabella's dismay, quite incoherent. At the last interview, unable to abide even the fifteen minutes he demanded, the viscount abruptly jerked his hand high so that Sarah cowered back, though he only waved it peremptorily and said, "Enough. Make your curtsy, at least you can do that."

Paradoxically Wrexham's attitude toward his daughter, though it repelled Isabella intensely, bound her more firmly than anything to him. She had not seen him with his daughter the summer before, an omission she now saw as significant. Likely he'd guessed she would not wish a man capable of such unfeeling behavior to be the father of her own children. But now, having come to care dearly for Sarah, she could not see how she could break off with Wrexham, even if she could gather together the funds to repay his betrothal settlement. The child, any child, could not endure such a father all alone.

"Miss Ramsey." It was Hudson, a most proper, lofty-nosed butler, imported from Julian's staff in town, who greeted them at the abbey's door. He took their wraps as Isabella's heart began to pound. It would be the first meeting between Julian and Wrexham.

Her father spoke to her then, complimenting her dress, and his patent pleasure with her looks, though it was a small thing, helped. She'd the fleeting, wry thought that whatever lay ahead, she'd the consolation of knowing she looked her best, for Liza had sent her a surprise from town in honor of the ball. "I know very well you've not got a new dess, Bella, and I thought Mrs. Enoch would do nicely by this silk. It is my birthday gift to you," her sister had written.

Isabella had laughed at that, as she was meant to, for her birthday was in the fall, and she had accepted the gift happily. At the time, having not the least inkling Wrexham meant to come for the ball, she had only anticipated what . . . But she must not think of him!

Her thoughts were too easily read, particularly by a man with eyes like the viscount's. Beneath their low lids, they were as watchful as a serpent's.

Isabella bit her lip. She had done it again. She must think of nothing: of the tiny golden beads Lady Prim had lent her for her hair or the delicate gold necklace of her mother's that looked very lovely around her throat.

Or her surroundings. Lady Prim and Mrs. Goodbody between them had worked miracles. Minions in livery were everywhere.

Candlelight reflected off the polished marble floor, and overhead the great wooden beams of the entry hall gleamed with oil. Isabella's eyes went to the head of the stairs.

Lady Prim's blue plumes were visible. They bobbed and dipped and waved as she welcomed Julian's guests. Behind her Isabella could just make out a golden head.

The climb up the steps seemed interminable, yet Isabella found she was not prepared when at the top at last, she turned to see Julian.

He was the Marquess of Roth that night as he received his guests. The ladies' fans fluttered as they batted their eyes up at him, and the men cast their ladies quick, uncertain looks. But in the next instant Julian would turn his charm on them and flushing at such attention, they, too, were won over—at least so long as the marquess's attention did not return to their wives or their daughters.

The understated elegance of his dress suited him. He needed no bright raiment, his looks were dazzling enough. The stark black of his evening dress only set off his golden hair and light eyes, while the white lace at his throat emphasized the entirely masculine beauty of his features. For ornament he wore only an emerald stickpin and a matching emerald ring. Both stones, though large, were simply set in a square of gold.

Isabella glanced at Wrexham from the corner of her eye. He wore a satin coat of crimson, a heavily embroidered, lemon-colored waistcoat that dripped with gold chains and fobs, and an excess of sparkling diamonds upon his fingers. It amazed her that a gentleman of the viscount's sharp eye could not see how much more poweful Julian's more subtle display was.

"My dear, here you are at last! And looking quite as lovely as I knew you would in that pretty green-and-gold Liza sent down. And Nell has outdone herself with your hair! Such a pretty fall of curls."

Isabelle lightly kissed Lady Prim's cheeks. "You are kind to say so, when you, my dear Lady Prim, look positively regal. This presiding over a grand ball suits you. Do you not agree, Papa?"

"Millie!" The squire blinked, coming out of the abstraction in which he had seemed lost since they had departed Marsh

House. "Egad! I scarcely recognized you got up in all that finery. Well, lad, you couldn't have picked a better one to stand by you here at the head of the stairs!"

When he turned to address Julian, Squire Ramsey swept Isabella along with him. She caught the faintest drift of sandalwood, and her heart tripped. It had come, the time for her playacting. She would be the amiable acquaintance, but she could not seem to lift her eyes from Julian's stickpin. It was larger than she had realized at a distance, but in truth, she scarcely saw it. From the corner of her eye she watched as Wrexham turned from greeting his aunt.

She forced her chin up. Julian was looking down at her. "Miss Ramsey. You loo . . . "

"Thank you, my Lord." Isabella sank into a curtsy, unable to hold his eyes a moment longer. A little wildly she castigated him for not playing his role. How could she be remote? If he regarded her so intently she thought he might read her every thought right there before the world and Wrexham.

The viscount was by her, raising her from her curtsy, and Isabella could only be glad she'd had the foresight to rehearse an appropriate line. In a voice made only a little low with the effort to control it, she said, "I think the abbey's spirits must be very pleased this night, Lord Roth."

"A happy thought, Miss Ramsey."

But Julian's expression did not match his words, for he did not smile. Slowly, he transferred his gaze to the viscount. "Wrexham, how fortuitous that you should be in Suffolk at the time of our entertainment." Casually Julian inclined his head to just the correct degree, the very formality of the gesture reminding Isabella that he outranked the viscount.

By her side Wrexham drew himself up, though an imp in Isabella's mind observed that he did so to little avail. The top of his head scarcely reached Julian's chin.

"I'd reports in town of your . . . activities, Lord Roth, and I thought to see for myself how true they were."

It was the catlike Wrexham of the sly, veiled remark. Isabella went as tense as a mouse, but Julian smiled.

"Do you know, Wrexham, I'd not have thought you the sort to listen to reports at all? But as you are, I am glad you've the wisdom to look into the truth of them for yourself. Having been the object of a few reports in my time, I can say that more often than not the spice of them is exaggeration. You must tell me if you do not find the same.''

With a spurt of quite childish glee Isabella could see that Wrexham was not pleased to be outdone at his own game. A single, thin eyebrow arched. ''I shall be certain to do that,'' he returned, his voice cold as ice.

Something dangerous flashed in Julian's eye, but before he could give voice to it, another party came, and Wrexham led Isabella away to the ballroom. She was trembling as they crossed the threshold, for though she had anticipated they would dislike one another, she had not been prepared for such open antipathy.

''A striking man, Lord Roth,'' Wrexham said, and she saw he had been watching her.

There was no point to be gained in denying the obvious. ''Yes. He is handsome,'' she agreed and looking about for some excuse to change the subject, found it presented in the form of Pru Manning.

Pru had never made any secret of her feelings for the viscount and did not do so then. She inclined her head quite offhandedly and said only, ''Evening, Lord Wrexham,'' before she turned a great, bright smile upon Isabella. ''That dress is superb, Bella! I can scarcely believe Liza was clever enough to pick such material. The gold threads make it shimmer and the green quite matches your eyes! She must have had advice from Lady Prim. No! I'll not have you chide me. The child is scarcely able to pick her own colors, much less yours. But I am chattering on only because I am so happy!''

Isabella's smile was, for the first time that evening, unforced. ''Francis Basham has asked for you.''

''Yes!'' Pru's squeal caused heads to turn, but long acquainted with Admiral Manning's daughter, the onlookers shook their heads and turned back to the conversatiaons she had interrupted. ''And we are to announce it tonight at midnight.''

Isabella greeted the news with more enthusiasm than she felt. She had hoped to leave earlier, pleading a headache perhaps. She did not think Wrexham would object strenuously to an abbreviated eveing, as he was regarding the mostly Suffolk born-and-bred guests with only thinly concealed disdain.

As Wrexham led her to a seat, they encountered Mrs. Basham and Ellie, and momentarily, as mother and daughter regaled her with the various triumphs Liza enjoyed in town, Isabella began to think she might get through the evening more easily than she'd feared. Pru returned with Francis that he might receive her congratulations, and she was introduced to a friend of Julian's, Peregrine Alynwick, who was staying at the abbey.

Wrexham condescended politely enough to the Bashams and spoke at least to Mr. Alynwick, whom he knew from town. It was when the dancing began that Isabella reconsidered her optimism.

When the young people moved onto the dance floor, Wrexham escorted her in the opposite direction. "We shall dance in a little, my dear, but I'll not tax your limited enthusiasm for that activity just yet," he said bending close to her ear.

Isabella only just suppressed a shudder. Even his breath seemed cold. She wanted to say she'd been taught to dance since last she'd seen him but, of course, did not. Indeed, with the memory of that dance with Julian and what had followed welling up in her mind, she could not speak at all. She remembered Julian saying he would give her a warm memory to carry to Wrexham's cold bed, and for the first time believed she'd been a fool not to accept him.

Wrexham did not take a seat by her to chat or otherwise amuse her. He remained standing just behind her, their only contact his hand upon her bared shoulder. Like a talon, it seemed, gripping a possession.

"You are not chilled, surely, my dear?" he asked when she shivered, but before she could answer, he said, "Ah."

Something in his tone made her look up. Julian was only a short distance from them, doing a duty dance with Mrs. Basham. His gaze lifted from his partner as Isabella looked to him. Their eyes met for the briefest moment, and then his gaze fixed on Wrexham's hand.

Isabella almost shook off her betrothed's tightened grasp, but already Julian was gone, and Wrexham released her. If she had doubted it, she knew then his hold had had nothing of affection in it. It had been a studied, cold proclamation of ownership and, too, a trap.

Isabella wanted to turn on him and demand that he

acknowledge how he had listened to some unknown party's whisperings, but she did not. It was not the time, though even had it been, she'd have found it difficult to summon the courage to confront her betrothed. She had not admitted it before, but did then. Something about Wrexham frightened her. If she had to live with him, she'd end like Sarah, shrinking from his very regard, much less his cold touch.

Her heart like a stone in her breast, Isabella ticked off the minutes of the night, a smile pasted upon her face when she must smile, for a few of their neighbors did brave Wrexham's faint sneer. Mrs. Smithby could always be counted upon, and, of course, Lady Prim.

The squire came too and even asked for a dance, perhaps sensing in his way that she was utterly wretched sitting on display as the property of Paul Farley. All too soon, though, the brief respite was done, and Isabella again had nothing to do but watch.

And it was impossible not to watch Julian, though it hurt to do so. She'd a half-hysterical thought at one point, as he smiled charmingly down into Mrs. Thomas's quite rapt eyes, that the pain she felt was some sort of divine punishment for having given up her heart to him when she had had no right to be so free. It had only taken the viscount's hand, again, on her shoulder to underscore how little freedom she did have.

But he was not staking her out as a possession now. He was leaning down again. "Shall we dance, my dear?"

As anything would have been preferable to sitting like the marble statue she felt, Isabella inclined her head. On the floor she caught sight of Julian from over Wrexham's shoulder. Now he partnered one of Mrs. Basham's houseguests, a Miss Mortimer. The girl was a trifle short, perhaps, but she'd lush charms nicely displayed in a ravishing silk dress. She and Julian not only made a handsome couple, but danced well together. Watching them, Isabella missed a step. Wrexham was not pleased.

"You have only to concentrate, my dear, Isabella," he chided, an edge to his voice.

When Miss Mortimer made some light remark, and Julian grinned appealingly down at her, Isabella again misstepped. She rushed to mumble an apology, but caught herself in time. He could only turn her into Sarah if she allowed it.

"It would seem I need practice as well, my lord," she said attempting to smile up at her betrothed.

It was a mistake. His eyes were cold as flint, as if he had guessed why she had become so clumsy. Isabella ducked her head to escape that look and did not again allow her gaze to stray to Julian.

At least, she thought, when the dance was done, there was to be some consolation for the excruciating exercise, for enduring Wrexham's touch, for feeling as heavy as a sack of grain. He did not immediately exile them to their isolated seats, but led her instead to the refreshment table.

Belatedly Isabella saw why. Julian was there with Miss Mortimer. He was just placing a lobster patty upon her plate and laughing at some sally she made.

"This is a most sumptuous repast you have laid out for us, Lord Roth," Wrexham said.

Glancing around, Julian flicked his gaze first to Isabella then back to the viscount. "Your aunt, Wrexham, was the one responsible for the food table, and I must agree with you that she's outdone herself. She said lobster patties were your particular favorite, Miss Ramsey. I hope you will enjoy them."

"Thank you, my lord. I am certain I shall."

When Julian turned abuptly away, Isabella thought the meeting over only to find him turning back to her in the next moment, having served one of the lobster patties onto a plate for her. "And a glass of champagne, surely?" he asked, lifting one from a nearby lackey's tray. "I think you'll find they're a natural match."

"Thank you, my lord." She knew the town-bronzed Miss Mortimer must think her a lamebrained fool with no conversation at all, but Isabella could scarcely think with Julian smiling down at her and Wrexham a dark shadow at her side.

He had not forgotten the viscount, however. "Wrexham?" He offered the man a lobster patty and champagne. His guests served, he made certain they were known to each other.

Miss Mortimer dimpled when Wrexham bowed over her hand, but said only in a bored voice, "Yes, I believe we met only the other day," when Julian presented her to Isabella.

Isabella was no more sincere in her courtesy, when a few minutes more of conversation having passed and their refreshments enjoyed, Julian looked to the viscount. "Shall we exchange partners, Wrexham? I should enjoy Miss Ramsey's company, and I know you will delight in Miss Mortimer's."

"It would be my pleasure, of course," Wrexham returned, surprising Isabella with his easy surrender of her until she saw that his eyes followed her as Julian led her onto the floor. He wanted to see them together.

"I wish you would smile, Miss Ramsey. I think you have not really smiled once all night, and I had hoped you would enjoy this ball."

Isabella wanted to cry aloud at the softness of Julian's voice. "Oh, please, my lord," she begged instead of pulling her gaze from his. "It is not . . ."

"It is a night for dancing, and though this is a livelier dance than we are accustomed to, I demand that you will enjoy it."

It was the first time Julian had ever referred to their waltz. She glanced up, uncertain, to catch the lazy, indulgent, teasng light in his eye. "I see you are very much the marquess tonight, my lord," she said, and all but Julian forgotten, she smiled.

"There! Did you know your smile illuminates your face, Miss Ramsey?"

Isabella's cheeks went very warm, but Julian did not allow her to protest the flattery. Holding her hand high, he masterfully swept her into the steps of the dance.

A little later, as they came together again, he said in a low voice meant only for her ears, "I hope you approve the color of your dress."

It was an odd question, and Isabella glanced down as if she might find the reason for it on her skirts. "Why yes, very much," she said still puzzled.

"It is the color of your eyes, you know. Moss green."

Isabella looked up, caught by something in his tone and saw Julian's eyes were dancing. "You did not . . . !"

"I did suggest green, but it was Lady Prim's entirely brilliant thought to conjecture that gold threads in the silk would set off your eyes."

"Oh!"

He grinned, she looked so very at a loss. "They do, you know. You are enchantingly beautiful tonight."

Isabella could not know that the gold flecks in her eyes came alight then. She only knew she wanted to dance forever with Julian while he told her such nonsense in that low voice. Oh, but she could not.

"My lord, you must leave off all this . . . effort to have me enjoy your ball. I do appreciate it, believe me, but Wrexham watches. He'd not understand. He would do you harm, I think."

Julian's jaw clenched. "Leave Wrexham to me, Isabella. He'll not worry you, I swear it."

Isabella was not to have the opportunity to voice her doubts. The music ended before she could speak at all, and the viscount, himself, appeared with Miss Mortimer.

"You look as if you enjoyed yourself, my dear."

Wrexham's heavy-lidded eyes, lifting from her cheeks, seemed to accuse. "Yes, I did. The dance was spritely," Isabella said, steadied by the sight of Miss Mortimer's pinkened complexion. Assuming a mantle of calm, she curtsied to Julian. "Thank you, my lord. I did, as Lord Wrexham says, enjoy myself."

"As did I, Miss Ramsey. And now, if you will excuse us I shall return Miss Mortimer to her party. It is almost time for Francis and Pru to make their announcement."

The festive, joyful air of the two taking their bows could not have made a more striking contrast with Isabella's situation, but she did not allow herself to become despondent. For just a little she lost herself in Pru's pleasure and felt only delight that her friend could plight her troth to a young man she cherished.

The ball became a boisterous affair after that, for the champagne flowed more freely than ever in honor of the happy couple. Only Wrexham held himself aloof from the general high spirits, and immediately after Isabella had congratulated Francis and Pru, he announced his desire to depart.

Quite as eager as he to have done with the night, Isabella sought out her father. He seemed strangely sober to her, considering his taste for champagne, but he professed no desire to join her and Wrexham. "I'll wait to see Millie gets home," he told her. He began to say something else, until he looked behind her. "Ah, Wrexham," he said then, swallowing his words. "See my lass gets home safe, now."

Her father's unusual behavior occupied Isabella very little. The moment she was seated in Wrexham's carriage, a heavy, fraught silence settled between her and her betrothed. She'd have given a deal to read his expression, but he'd not had the carriage's interior lamps lit. At last, the unnatural quiet becoming oppressive, she said the first thing she thought of as lightly as she could. "I am pleased for Pru and Francis. I think they will be very happy together."

"Do you?" Isabella's eyes went wide. His tone was little better than a sneer. "They may be, but only if he keeps her in the country. She is too forward to take in town."

Isabella stared into the dark, unable quite to believe the cool dismissal of a woman he must know was a close friend. "I have always liked Pru's spirit."

She sensed rather than saw Wrexham's shoulder lift, but he said nothing. He had no need. The one gesture said clearly enough what he thought of her opinion.

Isabella sat back on her seat, biting her lip. She simply could not wed herself to this man. But what, then, of Sarah? A throb at her temple indicated how heavily the question weighed upon her. She wanted nothing so much as to be in the quiet of her room, far from Wrexham, to think.

The journey to Marsh House seemed to drag on interminably, and finally, she stirred, glancing impatiently out the window, only to have a pair of stone pillars capped by gryphons meet her disbelieving eyes.

"But we are at Wrexham Hall!" she exclaimed. "Your coachman has forgotten me."

"I assure you, my dear, that my servants would not be so remiss." A mocking laugh punctuated the cool utterance. "You are coming home with me, you see."

Chapter 22

"What?" Isabella gasped. "I, I cannot come to the Hall now."

"Ah, but you can and shall," the viscount replied, his smooth voice filled with venom. "I have need of you."

"What need, my lord?" Isabelle demanded in a voice she made every effort to hold steady. She'd the sense it would be best not to show fear.

She saw the dark outline of Wrexham's head nod. "You are quite exceptional, my dear. Almost . . ." He shrugged, leaving the thought unfinished. "But as a reward for sparing me the fit of histrionics I had feared, I shall satisfy your curiosity. You see, Isabella, you are to be an assurance for me, an assurance that I shall not be denied the profits of the cargo of contraband I intend to smuggle ashore tonight. It is my largest load yet, you know, and along with the brandy my, ah, contacts have included a most lucrative gentleman I presume is a spy."

Isabella pressed her hand to her mouth. Either he was mad or she was. Smuggling? And spies?

"Come, come, you are so quiet, Isabella. Have you naught to say?" Wrexham chided.

That you are the greatest blackheart alive, if this is all true, Isabella thought. Aloud she asked, "How am I an assurance for you?"

Again Wrexham nodded. "So steady you are, my dear. You are an assurance against whatever plot to foil me your lover has concocted."

"My lover?" Her throat gone suddenly dry, the question was a croak.

Suddenly Wrexham's hand snaked out and grasping Isabella by the neck he pulled her hard against him. "I detest false innocence, my dear. I speak of Lord Roth. Your reaction to him tonight was as telling as his reputation had led me to expect. How unforgivably vulgar of you, Isabella, to choose to become one of his many conquests, when you might have been my wife. And do not think to deny what I saw with my own eyes! You have been little better than a corpse in my company, but you came alive in his.''

With a disgusted sound he flung Isabella from him. "This better suits my plans anyway!'' he sneered. "I'd have had to use that pitiful excuse I have for a daughter else, and there can be no question Lord Roth will have a greater care for you, passing fancy though you are.''

Isabella strove to quell a wild feeling of panic that she might think what to do, but the carriage pulled up before the Hall, and Wrexham seized her arm again.

Only two lights were visible. One, stationary, in a high tower overlooking the sea, and the other bobbing slightly at the top of the steps. When Isabella struggled as Wrexham dragged her out of the carriage, he jerked her arm violently.

"Stop that! I've no time for heroics. Rench!''

The shape holding the lantern came scuttling forward.

"Yer nibs?''

"The carts are ready? And the men?'' Receiving an affirmative to each question, Wrexham thrust Isabella into his confederate's hold. "Take her to the tower.'' Though small, Rench was a strong man. With ease he twisted Isabella's arm behind her back and shoved her before him. "You'll watch for the ship's light from there,'' Wrexham commanded. "You know the signal?''

"Aye,'' Rench grunted.

"If I've not come within an hour after the signal, you know what to do with her.''

Isabella had a long, long time as she lay shivering upon the stone floor of the tower trussed like a chicken and with a gag in her mouth to wonder what it was Wrexham's henchman knew to do with her. She did not doubt her jailer would do as he'd been told. She had seen it in his cold, ruthless eyes before he'd doused the light and turned to keep watch from the tower window for the signal.

Another figure kept watch from a window that night. It was

Sarah at Marsh House peering anxiously into the night for some sign of Isabella's safe return from the ball. She had long known she displeased her father, and with a child's logic it followed in her mind that he could not be pleased with anyone who had befriended her. Sarah had watched him hand Isabella into his carriage earlier, and though the squire was there, an unreasoning fear had risen in her to see the man she knew to fear ride off with Isabella.

No effort on Nell's part could soothe her, and she peered out into the darkness for hours, her eyes accustoming themselves to the black night. When she made out the outline of a carriage rattling down the road that ran by Marsh House to the abbey, she leaned hopefully forward, but it did not turn in at the gate.

As time continued to pass and there was still no sign of Isabella, Sarah's agitation grew, until she decided, against reason, the carriage had been her father's, and he had taken Isabella away from Marsh House with him. She clasped her arms about her, shivering, trying to think what she must do, only to hear the sound of horses' hooves pounding down the road from the direction of the abbey. The marquess rode a horse!

With a surge of gladness, Sarah, looking out the window again, saw that the horsemen had turned in at Marsh House. Up the drive they came, six in all.

Whirling around, she ran for her door, threw it open and ran into a dark, hard shape.

Her scream of terror was hushed before it could be uttered. "Nay, hinny. 'Tis only old Cora come to see what ye're about. I heard ye movin'."

Sobbing in fright, Sarah threw her arms around the old woman. Cora patted her, then, hearing the horses, cocked her head. " 'Tis a restless night," she muttered. "There, there, child." She returned her attention to the distraught girl clutching her. "What ails ye?"

It was a few moments before Sarah quieted enough to stammer out that she feared her father would harm Isabella.

"Aye, yer father's a bad mon, but . . ." Cora shrugged. "Ah well, who can say what sooch a one might do? We'll go an' see what's brought riders to our door, eh?"

They were an odd sight to the men tromping through the front door. The child dressed in her nightgown with a blanket wrapped around her for cover, and the old, wizened crone, bent with age, a candle in her hand.

"Whatever are you up and about for, Cora, and with Sarah?"

It was the squire who called out. A match was struck and candles lit. Cora's old eyes identified the marquess and his man. Two men the old woman shrewdly guessed to be in some capacity or other keepers of the law, though they were dressed in servants' garb, hung back by the door, and another man in evening dress stood just behind Lord Roth.

"The child's afeared for Miss Bella. We coome down ta see that all's right."

"But Isabella ought to be here, Cora."

It was Julian's firm voice, and upon hearing it, Sarah launched herself down the stairs, running into his embrace. Julian held her to him, but was only vaguely aware what he did. His eyes were hard on Cora.

"Nay," Cora addressed him, her own voice sharpening. "Miss Bella's nae returned ' ome."

Squire Ramsey's roar might have been heard in London, had anyone been listening closely. "Wrexham left with her half an hour ago! And they were not on the road. We'd have passed 'em!"

Into the general murmur of consternation, Cora said, her voice raised to command attention, "The child did see a carriage pass by the gates 'ere. Fast it's speed was, she said."

Julian looked down at Sarah. "Think hard, Sarah. Was it within the last half hour you saw the carriage?" Her brown eyes almost black with fear, Sarah nodded her head. "Damnation!"

"What is it, Julian? What's afoot?"

The speaker was the gentleman behind Julian. He came forward now into the light. Of about the marquess's age, he was of lesser height and softer build.

"I cannot say for certain, Perry, but I think it possible Wrexham has taken Isabella to the Hall. Come, we must have a council now that our circumstances have changed."

Sarah was crying, and as he led the way into the front room, Julian held her. "You must not worry, cabbage," he whispered to her. "I'll not let any harm come to Isabella. Trust me?"

The child pulled back to look solemnly into his eyes, and after a moment she nodded gravely. As Julian put her in a comfortable chair, the squire raised his voice in question. "What would possess Wrexham to take Bella? I cannot see it, man. They've had an accident. That is all."

"You said yourself we did not pass them. Overturned carriages are difficult to mistake even in the dark. And Sarah saw a carriage pass by here. Damn, but I'm to blame."

"You?" the squire echoed, dumbfounded by the seeming non sequitur.

Julian raked his hand through his hair. "I misjudged him, an unforgiveable mistake. I never thought he'd guess I meant to catch him out."

Julian stood beside the chair in which he had deposited Sarah, and Perry Alynwick was oddly affected when his friend, seeing that the child regarded him with wide eyes, reached down to stroke her cheek. "You'll not be offended if I speak ill of your father, little one? He is not, I fear, a good man." Sarah, mute still, shook her head. "Yes." Julian nodded briefly. "I suppose you have cause to know him. Well then," he turned abruptly to address the five men and Cora, who had seated herself in a chair by the door. "My guess, and it is no more, is that Wrexham intends to use Isabella as a shield."

The squire banged his fist upon a table. "But he would not use my own daughter so!"

"Aye, 'e would. 'Tis a bad 'un, Squire."

Squire Ramsey looked wildly about at Cora. He seemed on the point of protesting either her presence or her certainty, but after looking into her black eyes, he groped for a handkerchief to mop his face.

"I cannot say I know Wrexham well," Julian addressed the squire. "But I would not dispute Cora, and he is desperate for funds. He has continued to lose heavily at the tables all this year."

Perry Alynwick spoke up then. "To my certain knowledge, he lost ten thousand in one night alone."

The squire gaped, unable to comprehend such extravagance, though he, himself, was no stranger to damaging losses at play. "Ten thousand?"

No one answered, for Jepson had spoken at the same time.

"What's ta do, m' lord?" he asked Julian. "Time's passin', an the ship'll be in the bay soon."

"The first order is to get Isabella, then we can attend to Wrexham and his smugglers with a free hand." Julian looked to Cora. "Do you know any of the servants at the Hall?"

"Aye." A smile crept over her lined face. " 'Appen I nursed cook's grandson this winter, milord. Saved 'is life."

Julian smiled back. "Well done, Cora. She'll be the one to tell us where Isabella is. Now, Sarah, you must stay here with the squire and wait for us."

Sarah bit her lip, but it was the squire who roared a protest. "Eh? What's that?" he cried. "You don't think I'd betray you to the scoundrel's taken my Bella, damn his cold hide?"

"No, no, nothing of the sort Squire," Julian assured him. He waved a hand that included the two men dressed as servants and Jepson. "It is only that all these fellows have been trained for fighting, and Perry is allowed by virtue of his ability with a pistol. He's one of the best at Manton's."

Squire Ramsey protested, railed, cajoled, and pleaded his interest in Isabella but to no avail. Julian held firm. "I would fear for your safety, sir, and think of Isabella. She would be distraught, should anything befall you. You must await us here."

Cora did go, however, mounted behind Jepson. Julian included her because she knew the Hall, and when they dismounted at the edge of the woods bordering the estate's lawns, he asked where the kitchens were. "Let's pray the cook's been roused to provide food for these rogues."

Julian gestured in the dark and Jepson grunted. They both saw the man, rifle slung over his shoulder, who prowled the edge of the drive.

"Kitchen's there, milord."

Her crooked finger pointed to the side of the house. "Good, we can use those pines for cover." Julian turned to the men behind him. "Here is what we shall do. Cora and I shall go to the house and find Isabella. You will keep watch here. When the ship comes, allow them to bring the goods ashore and to load the carts, but not to leave. Keep them even if I am delayed. I want to be certain Wrexham and his principal henchmen do not escape. Sprinkle the powder we brought across the drive and hold them with it.''

When everyone understood his role, Julian, Cora following behind him like a black shadow, made his way from the woods to the line of concealing trees.

They encountered two sentries on their way, but saw the men in time to shrink back into the shadows. After a dash across the stable yard, they slipped through the kitchen door and found the room was inhabited by one woman, her back to the door as she bent low over the fire. Cora nodded once, indicating it was the cook she knew, and Julian crossed quickly and silently to her, clapping his hand over her mouth before she could give them away.

"We mean you no harm," he whispered low in her ear. "You recognize Cora Geddes?''

The cook's wildly dilated eyes turned to Cora, and abruptly, she relaxed in Julian's grip. "Miss Isabella's been brought 'ere, by 'is lordship," Cora explained, the hoarseness of her voice revealing she was out of breath after her run with Julian. "Know ye where she be 'eld?''

Bewildered, the cook shook her head. "Nay!''

"Think, woman!" Julian shook her shoulders. "It may mean her life.''

The cook, a small woman with wispy hair unconfined by a cap, shrank from him. "Ah, mercy! I know naught of Miss Isabella, truly, sir. The master took all the men down to the bay, when the signal light came, all but the two in the yard and the one up in the tower.''

"In the tower?" When she nodded, Julian demanded how he might get there unobserved.

"There be none to see, but the back stairs be through that door, there.''

Julian nodded once, then looked at Cora. "Cora, you keep a watch here . . .''

Cora held up a bag. "I'll warn ye, if need be, milord, but meantime I've someat for the men's drink. Fast asleep they'll be, when they drink of it.''

Julian's smile gleamed suddenly in the dim light. "I could have used you on the Peninsula, Cora.''

Despite the cook's assurance that no one was about, Julian ascended the servant's stairs cautiously, and on the fourth floor, the last, flew silently along with his knife before him in what he hoped was the direction of the tower. Turning the corner of the final corridor, he saw narrow, stone stairs winding skyward and smiled to himself.

He had nearly reached them, when a cat darted out of the shadows before him, meowing loudly. Julian ducked back against the stairs just as the door at the top of the stairs was thrown open.

"Eh! 'oo's 'ere?" demanded a harsh cockney voice. In the ensuing silence, Julian heard a pistol being cocked.

There was no hiding place along the smooth corridor, and Julian gathered himself and leapt away from the wall just as the man leaned over the stairs and fired. As the bullet screamed by his ear, Julian threw his knife. The man screamed in pain, stumbled, and fell down the stairs. Julian tied him with a length of rope he had brought, and gathering up the man's pistol, took the stone stairs two at a time.

He gave the tower door a kick, then ducked back against the wall outside. When no shot came, he whirled into the room, pistol ready.

A moan sent him running to the wall by the window. "Isabella! Are your hurt?" Julian demanded, flinging the dirty rag in her mouth aside.

Isabella's first attempt at speech was a hoarse croak and so she shook her head as she cleared her throat. "No. No. I am not hurt, only frightened out of my wits."

Julian, having freed her hands, was untying the rope binding her ankles. "You are safe now, Bella. I won't let anything happen to you."

Shaken as she was, Isabella did not note the pet name he used. "He, he was to kill me, I think, if he did not hear a certain signal from Wrexham."

Julian cursed, fluently and grimly. "I'll see that villain in hell, you may be sure of it!"

Isabella could have taken his handsome face between her hands and kissed him for his fury on her behalf, but Julian was already lifting her to her feet. Deadened from the time she had laid in one position, neither her legs or her feet would work

properly. When she collapsed, Julian caught her about the waist.
"The feeling will come back in a little. Just lean on me."

"But how is it that you are here, Julian?" she asked.

"With a little cunning and a great deal of luck," he said, and
Isabella saw his teeth flash white in the dark.

"You are enjoying this," she accused, suddenly suspicious
that she'd have seen, had there been sufficient light, a reckless
gleam in his eye.

Julian's low laugh turned the suspicion to certainty. "I allow
I find a certain pleasure in meting out comeuppance to a villain.
But we've not the time to debate the matter," he added when
she stiffened, for she was not well pleased to have her ordeal
seen as an adventure. "There's much to do. They may have
heard the wretch's shot on the beach and if so, they'll soon
swarm the house."

Julian hauled Rench up without care for the man's wounded
arm, and shoving him forward, they set out for the entry hall
where they found Jepson.

In a low voice he asked after Isabella's well-being before
turning to his master. "They've the wagons loaded up, but we
've laid the powder like ye said. Jake'll light the fuses at the
first sign o' trouble."

"Well done, Jepson. And Wrexham?"

"Below in the bay with the Frenchies, so Master Perry says.
But ye'll find Willis just out that door on the drive with the
wagons."

In the dark, the line of wagons before the Hall seemed a
ghostly cavalcade until Isabella, looking out a small, round glass
in the door, made out the shapes of several men loading kegs
and tightening straps. Two men stood just at the foot of the steps,
their backs to the door. Even in the dark she recognized Willis's
shape.

After shoving Rench into Jepson's grip, Julian stepped
outside. "Willis!" Wynchley's former land agent whirled into
a crouch, his pistol at the ready. Julian did not flinch. "Shoot
and you'll go up in flames with your wagons. We have laid
powder all around you."

The men by the wagons froze. Isabella heard from several
the cry, "Powder!"

Suddenly a fresh, sharper murmur arose. Peering through her

spy hole, Isabella saw that a man lay slumped upon the ground.

Julians' low laugh raised the hairs on her neck, though she was not his enemy. "Cora Geddes came with me," he called out. "She did not approve her mistress being threatened."

One man gave a wild, high-pitched laugh, while his fellows called out in fear. They were local men, it seemed, for they recognized Cora's name—and her skill with herbs.

Willis attempted to retrieve control of his men, growling loud enough for them to hear as well as Julian. "There's a man above has orders to kill the Ramsey girl if we're attacked. He'll do as he's told."

"I think not, Willis. Jepson, bring out our friend."

His cocked pistol at Rench's temple, Jepson thrust the smaller man out the door before him.

Simultaneously another man fell to his knees, swayed, then toppled headlong into the dirt. Then two others went down by him. The locals still standing had had quite enough. Taking to their heels, they ran for the cover of the woods.

"Don't move, Willis, or you, there, by him," Julian ordered, lifting his pistol. "Throw down your weapons."

With Jepson occupied with Rench, it was two to one, until another man Isabella identified as Julian's friend, Peregrine Alynwick, stepped out from the corner of the house, his pistol trained on the stranger by Willis. The stranger surrendered without a word.

Willis glanced over his shoulder in the direction of the path leading to the cliff. No one was there. Muttering a curse, he threw his pistol to the ground. His speed startling for a man of his size, Jepson leapt out and had Willis's pistol before Isabella could draw breath.

Jepson and Perry had just bound the two prisoners together, when a languid drawl pierced the night.

"Well, well. It would seem you have my spy as well as my men." Though she could not see him, Isabella started nervously. Wrexham had come, and he did not sound defeated. Nor was he. "But as you can see, I've the trump card."

Isabella had not long to wonder what he meant, for Julian exclaimed, "Ramsey! What the devil!"

"Blast it all, man! He had my daughter. I could not sit idly by my fire!"

Oh, Papa, Isabella gripped the edge of her little window tightly, peering in vain into the darkness. He had thought to rescue her and had gotten himself taken hostage instead.

"Lord Roth," Wrexham called out. "You shall allow me to leave with Miss Ramsey and her father, or I shall make short work of the squire here, and I am certain you would not want that."

"I don't give a tinker's damn what becomes of the Squire, Wrexham," Julian returned, his voice hard as granite. "He'd have given Isabella to you for reasons so selfish they are contemptible." Isabella could hear her father protest vociferously, but Julian continued unheeding, "Shoot him for all I care. Or," he paused, and tension seemed to crackle like a live thing in the night. Even the squire fell silent, waiting. "Release Ramsey, and we shall duel for who it is leaves Suffolk alive tonight."

"Ah! I underestimated you, Lord Roth! A nobleman's solution to our dilemma. I accept. A pair of swords hang in the games room. Take the second corridor to the left, the third room."

Jepson passed Isabella, a large, silent shadow in the dark night. It seemed to her he returned all too soon, the swords and a lantern in his arms.

" 'E'll do that fine," he whispered, but Isabella could hardly think for the fear she felt. One of the two men might die, and she prayed to God, it would not be Julian.

She could see nothing now, for the men had all moved from her sight, and unable to bear the suspense, she crept cautiously out the door. Seeing her father's broad back just by the corner of the house, she sped down the steps to shelter behind him.

The duel had already begun. Both men were stripped to their shirts, though the night was cool from the sea breeze. Their swords struck sparks as they thrust and parried, now retreating, now advancing.

Julian was the younger and the stronger, but Isabella could tell Wrexham had the more practice with the outmoded weapon. She let out a soundless scream when he sliced open Julian's sleeve. Julian never faltered, though Isabella could see blood seeping through the tear. Feinting to the left, he drew

Wrexham's attention, then disengaged deftly to draw blood, in his turn, from the viscount's chest.

Wrexham grunted, staggered, then to Isabella's dismay, lunged forward, seeming unshaken. Swordplay followed that was too swift to analyze in the dim light of the lanterns Julian's men had brought. More sparks flew as their swords clashed. Back and forth they went, back and forth, two dark shadows by a cliff's edge. She could hear their groans and grunts, then, suddenly, Wrexham executed a quick step, flicked his wrist, and sent Julian's sword flying to the air. He shouted in triumph, lowering his sword to impale his opponent. Isabella opened her mouth to scream, but Wrexham wavered oddly. His shout became a macabre gurgle, and grabbing the place on his chest where he'd been hit, he fell backward, lost his footing, and before the others could gather their wits to reach him, toppled from the hill to the beach below.

Chapter 23

"Peter! Bella! I shall soon be a countess! Papa has agreed with Aunt Amelia that Chively may pay his addresses."

Smiling delightedly, Isabella began to offer her congratulations, but her brother spoke first. "You truly want this Earl of Chively, Liza?" he inquired specifically of his sister, whom he resembled in likeness, if not in temperament. "I cannot understand your eagerness for the man. I have it on the best authority he cannot abide excessively emotional females."

Liza promptly hit Peter with the fan she carried, for it was a hot day, and fans were so very fashionable. "I am not excessively emotional, you . . . scamp! And anyway, Chively quite dotes on me. He adores me, in fact! That for your plaguesomeness!"

"Peace!" Peter laughed, dodging his sister's wicked licks. "If you'll promise not to coin any more words—plaguesomeness, indeed!—then, I shall vow not to plague you further, particularly as I actually approve your choice."

Subsiding onto the settee beside Isabella, Liza cast Peter a broad smile, but she turned in the next moment a more uncertain look upon her sister. "Bella, you are certain all this talk of marriage does not upset you?"

"Not in the least, my dear!" Isabella replied at once. "I am dazzled by your good fortune, though I am not surprised by it." She squeezed Liza's hand, but seeing that a trace of doubt lingered in her sister's pretty green eyes, she added, "You must know I did not . . . love Wrexham, Liza."

"Ugh!" Peter grimaced. "What a cold fish! I know I ought not to speak ill of the dead, Bella, but I'm deuced glad you're no longer tied to him."

"At least he died a hero," observed Liza. "I do think it was very fine of him to attempt to apprehend a spy!"

Peter nodded but reluctantly. "Yes, though I must say I'd have thought Wrexham the last man on earth to put himself out for the good of his country. And no matter his unexpected heroics, I think Bella can do better."

"Oh, yes!" Liza cried, in complete agreement with her younger brother for once. "After Chively and I are wed, you shall come to stay with us in town, Bella, and we shall find just the right gentleman for you."

Isabella kept her eyes upon the teacup she returned to the table. "I shall let you and Chively settle in, Liza, before I descend upon you." When she glanced up, she changed the subject. "But I would hear more of this gentleman who thinks to marry my own sister. Did you not say you've a friend who is brother to the earl, Peter? Come, tell us whether he beats his siblings."

Liza, quite pleased with the world, could only giggle foolishly, while Peter launched into a sometimes factual, sometimes highly exaggerated, account of what his friend, Arthur Worley, had reported on the habits of his older brother.

Isabella listened rather more closely than her brother's tone warranted, for her question had not been idle. Wrexham had shown her how different a man can be from what he seems. Beneath his cool, contained exterior, the viscount had hidden madness.

Unbidden, that grim, tumultuous night came to her. She could see, again, Wrexham clutching his chest and falling backward. It was her father who had turned first from the group of men staring at the beach below and seeing her, grasped her by the shoulders.

"No, Bella! It is a grim sight."

Staring into the squire's face, she saw confirmation of the viscount's death and cried out, "Oh, Papa!" with such a mixture of feelings, she could not say whether relief or horror were uppermost.

"There, there, my chick." Unaccustomed to her tears, her papa had patted her awkwardly. "He was a spawn of the devil and better gone."

Shivering, Isabella sent up a prayer of thanksgiving for her deliverance and only realized her deliverer approached them when Julian addressed her father. "I hope you will forgive my harsh words to Wrexham about you, sir. I did not wish him to know he did indeed hold a trump."

"No insult taken, lad! I guessed what you were about. The notion for a duel was brilliant, though I'd hazard you did not expect swords."

Remaining in her father's embrace, Isabella twisted to look at Julian. Someone had tied a neck cloth about his arm, but, though his ripped sleeve showed a deal of dried blood, he seemed unaffected by his wound. Indeed, for the merest moment, his smile flashed white in the dark. "You would hazard correctly, on that sir," he replied to her father. "It was not until we began the match, I recalled the viscount had a reputation with the sword. I'm only relieved I had my own pistol with me."

"The premier swordsman of his day!" The squire affirmed. "Killed more than one opponent, as I recall. I feared for you, lad."

"No more than did I, particularly when he did not falter after I landed that hit. I did not know if I could get in another." Julian's gaze fell to Isabella and abruptly the excited tension of battle left him. "But, here! We hold your daughter in this unhappy place with our talk. How are you, Miss Ramsey?"

Isabella marked the formal address far more than Julian's worried tone. She separated a little from her father, but not so far that his arm did not remain about her shoulders. "I am well and grateful to you, my lord."

"It was my foolishness got you into this danger tonight, Miss Ramsey. I'd no notion . . ."

All of Isabella's wits came together then, for Julian sounded genuinely undone. "That is purest nonsense, Lord Roth!" she said sharply into the darkness. "It was the viscount put me in danger, no one else. He was a thorough villain."

When she shivered thinking of what the man had intended for her, Julian shifted as if he meant to reach out for her, but the sound of carriage wheels on the drive just behind them prompted her father to turn, and as he had his arm about Isabella, he turned her, too. "Ah! Jepson!" He declared with satisfaction. "I could do with my bed at last."

Falling into step beside her as her father made for the vehicle,

Julian reminded Isabella of Sarah. "Would you prefer to tell her, Miss Ramsey, or would you rather that I did?"

"She is my responsibility, my lord, though I thank you for offering."

"Very well then, I shall see you tomorrow. There's a great deal to see to here yet."

"But your wound . . ."

" . . . Will be seen to by Cora." Again his smile flashed in the night. This time when he reached for her, Julian was not forestalled. His hand beneath her elbow felt comfortingly strong as he helped her into the carriage.

"Good night, Lord Roth!" the squire slapped Julian hard upon the back. "I'm in debt to you for a great deal, but most of all for keeping my Bella safe. And you've my thanks for sparing me the tongue lashing I deserve. I very nearly queered your scheme, and I know it."

"It was my mistake, Squire," Julian said with a shake of his head. "I ought to have realized how impossible it would be for you to do nothing. Good night, sir, Miss Ramsey."

On the ride home Isabella found she was not surprised when her father confessed he had been allied with Wrexham and Willis in their smuggling scheme. She had guessed there was something unsavory in his connection with Willis. However, she was quite beside herself to learn the betrothal settlement that had prompted her to accept the viscount in the first place had been naught but her father's own ill-gotten gains.

"Nay, Bella!" her father cried when she gave an astonished cry. "You needn't chide me for the lie I sanctioned. Regretted it from the first, but I didn't see how to tell the truth, and I did think 'twas all for the best. We'd such need of the blunt, you see. Ah, but I was a fool! Plain and simple. I truly saw Wrexham as a prize!"

For that Isabella could not fault him. "You couldn't know the truth of him, Papa. None of us did," she said. "And it is all done now. Tell me instead of the ball. How did Ju . . . Lord Roth account for leaving his own fête?"

"He and that Alynwick fellow put it out he'd taken ill, but desired the ball to continue on account of Pru and young Basham. Likely his guests are still dancing at the abbey. Blast!

I've only just thought of Millie. This business will be a blow to her.''

"Yes, it will," Isabella agreed. "And Sarah! How awful for her to have her father branded a traitor. Must the truth be known, Papa? Perhaps Rench and the other men—they were revenuers I think? Yes, they did not really have the look of servants. But why can they not say for Lady Prim's sake and Sarah's that Wrexham died in service to his country?''

The squire brightened. "Well, I cannot see why they should not! I'll have Jepson pass on the thought to his master when he returns to the Hall.''

At Marsh House Sarah was waiting for them along with Nell, whom the squire had roused to stay with the child. Isabella did not think she had ever seen eyes so wide with anxiety and hoped never again to see a face so pale. It took some hours to soothe the little girl and to persuade her her father could not threaten them ever again, then to listen as, on that night of truth, Sarah haltingly confessed how her father had struck her more than once.

Quite drained by the time she climbed into bed beside Sarah, Isabella fell into an exhausted sleep that was, nonetheless, disturbed. Wrexham's face, Willis's, Rench's grasp, and Julian's voice all came to her. She'd the sense of fear and turmoil.

The next morning, she was no more settled. Her future was her own once more, but her thoughts fragmented, she could not seem to think what that would mean except that she was not bound to Wrexham.

One minute she would think it significant that Julian had risked himself to save her, and in the next she would squeeze her fists tightly and upbraid herself for a fool. Her father had explained to her the marquess's deep aversion to smuggling. He had wished to trap Wrexham out of concern for England, and when she had gotten caught in the middle, he had acted to spare her harm. No more.

But she awaited his visit with a tension all her best arguments could not dispel. She was free now. Might that not mean . . . ? That the answer was to be no, Isabella realized when he entered the drawing room where she sat with Lady Prim. He was dressed in traveling clothes complete with a caped coat.

While he turned to give Lady Prim his condolences, Isabella remarked to herself she had been quite as wrong as anyone as to why Julian had stayed in Suffolk. It had not been his father's challenge that kept him, as she had thought, but the excitement of the chase. Now he'd caught his fox, he was off.

But not before he took the time to console Lady Prim in his gentlest manner. "You did not deserve such grim news this morning after all the work you put in to bring off our ball."

Lady Prim dabbed at her eyes with her tiny lace handkerchief, but she managed a weak smile at Julian's use of the plural. "It is so startling. Paul was not a warm man, but he was my nephew, and . . ."

Julian took her hand in his. "And you would not have had him come to such an end, I know."

He nodded as Lady Prim spoke of Wrexham's supposed heroics, and Isabella was glad to see their lie lift the elderly lady's spirits. After a moment Lady Prim recovered sufficiently to take in the traveling clothes Isabella had seen at once. "But you are leaving us, Lord Roth?" she queried.

He kissed her hand then relinquished it. "Indeed, I've left my horses standing, my sudden business in town is so urgent. You will forgive me if I bid you a hasty adieu and then take Miss Ramsey for the merest moment? I've a favor to ask of her you needn't be bothered with."

Lady Prim was no proof at all against Julian. She only nodded rather mistily as he kissed her cheek and then wished him farewell.

Julian rose and then looked to Isabella. "Miss Ramsey?"

Thinking he'd something more to say of the fiction they had created about the viscount, Isabella preceded him from the room. She learned in the hallway before the front door that she was not entirely wrong.

"My business in town has to do with the man we took with Willis. He's a French spy," Julian told her, his voice low but urgent.

Isabella nodded. "Wrexham said he'd a lucrative gentleman to bring ashore."

"Damn! It is one thing to be greedy but another to be a traitor." Julian frowned darkly. "At any rate the man soon saw it was in his best interests to tell what he could. I pried from him the names of his contacts in town, two of whom, I regret to say, are men highly placed in the War Office. I've no choice but to go to London to see to them. There is an opportunity not only to apprehend the traitors but to feed the French false information. Before I left, I wished you to know you needn't worry the magistrate will question you. I left you out of the report I gave him.''

''I am grateful, my lord.''

Julian nodded in understanding. ''That leaves the abbey. I cannot say how long I shall be gone, a month, perhaps more. I spoke to Mr. Cummings this morning, and he has agreed to look after matters there, if you will agree to review the books he keeps. I know it is a great deal to ask, for you are quite occupied here at Marsh House, Miss Ramsey, but I would be most obliged.''

Isabella searched Julian's expression. He was watching her intently, but self-interest alone might have prompted that look. He had not said what he intended after he returned. Then she scolded herself. The man had saved her life. ''Of course, I shall lend my assistance.''

Relief and something else that was gone too quickly to read flashed in Julian's eyes. ''I am grateful.'' A shout from beyond the door informed them the horses were becoming restless. ''You do understand my haste?'' Julian demanded urgently.

''Yes, of course. You must reach London quickly with your spy, if his contacts are not to wonder what has gone amiss and send down to Suffolk to learn of his capture.''

''A great many lives depend upon my speed. You will wait for me?''

Rather unaccountably it vexed Isabella that Julian should demand some certainty of her when he revealed nothing of his ultimate intentions. ''Where would I go?'' she inquired tartly.

To her amazement Julian laughed, though she could not think how she had amused him. '' Nowhere, I hope, my most dear Miss Ramsey. Nowhere.'' And then he caught her chin with his hand and kissed her full upon the lips, though they stood in the hallway and anyone might have come upon them.

It was as fierce a kiss as it was brief. No sooner was Isabella stunned by the feel of Julian tasting deeply of her lips, than she was bereft, because he, after he whispered, "I shall be done by June's end, Bella," was gone out the door.

"Bella, you are lost in your thoughts!"

Blinking, Isabella looked around to find Peter regarding her. "Whatever were you pondering so deeply?"

"That it is mid-July," she replied before she could catch herself. When the oddness of her tone caused her brother and sister to regard her with concern, she struggled to throw off her melancholy. " . . . And time to dress for what promises to be a most festive dinner."

Happily distracted, Liza laughed, while Peter said, "Do you know, I was wondering if there would not be two announcements tonight?"

"Why, what do you mean?" Liza demanded mystified.

"Bella, you have been here with them all this time. Does it not seem to you that Papa and Lady Prim are uncommonly agreeable with each other?"

Even as Liza cried out in some disbelief, Isabella smiled in earnest. "Yes, I should say they are most agreeable."

"But I thought Papa only suffered Lady Prim and Mr. Buttons in his household because you insisted, Bella!" Liza exclaimed.

Isabella chuckled. "In the beginning he did resent having his splendid freedom curtailed, but after a time, Papa found he rather liked having an adoring woman about to blush when he teased her, though her presence meant he could not smoke his cigars in the drawing room or wear his muddy boots into dinner."

"Will you mind Lady Prim taking your place here?"

Isabella looked at Peter in surprise. She had not considered fully what a marriage between her father and Lady Prim would mean to her. Of course, Lady Prim would want the running of the house. "No, no," she said to her brother. "Lady Prim and I get on very well."

Which was the truth Isabella told herself stoutly when she went to her room. Weary of the heavy spirits that had plagued her since June had gone by without any word or sign of Julian, she put all her attention to dressing. It was as well she did, for

Sarah came running in well before the hour the family was to gather. The young girl had gained much confidence in the past few weeks, and her timidity, as well as her stutter, had all but disappeared. After exclaiming with gratifying wonder, ''You look so pretty, Bella!'' the little girl tugged on her arm. ''Come, I've something to show you.''

''But I've not got my shawl,'' Isabella protested.

''It is warm, Bella! You won't need it.''

''Well, at least allow me to arrange my neckline.'' There was need to do that, Isabella thought, for the dress was one Liza had brought down to her from town and was cut rather low for Isabella's tastes. A very becoming shade, the color of daffodils in the spring, the thin muslin dress revealed the swell of her breasts and though she was not voluptuous, it seemed to her more was on display than ought to be.

She tugged twice to little avail, and Sarah, who was also dressed in a new gown of sprigged muslin, could wait no longer. ''You must come, Bella!'' she pleaded, fairly skipping in impatience.

Isabella admitted defeat in the matter of her high-waisted gown. It fit so snugly just below her breasts, it would not be lifted.

''What is it you are in such a great hurry to show me?'' she asked Sarah, as the child hurried her down the stairs at an alarming pace. ''Has Mr. Buttons got your kitten?''

Sarah had brought one of Julian's kittens home from the abbey, and as might have been expected, Mr. Buttons had taken instant umbrage. There were frequent skirmishes, all inconclusive, for the kitten was adept at escape. Only occasionally would he climb higher than he realized, obliging Sarah to fetch him down or to find someone taller to assist him.

Sarah shook her head. Isabella saw her smile, but she hurried on, before more questions could be put to her. On the first floor, they did not enter the drawing room but hurried on toward the back of the house. They passed Dobson. He was, to Isabella's surprise, beaming fondly at her, but she was not allowed to stop and ask what had made him smile so. Sarah actually jerked her hand, and they fled by Cora whose black eyes seemed to gleam with a certain smug light. Mystified, Isabella stepped through her own study door as Sarah motioned her inside.

"What is it, Sarah?" she asked as she heard the door close behind her.

"A surprise. A pleasant one, I hope," Sarah replied, as she slipped out of the room before Isabella could protest.

Isabella swung about, gasping. "Oh!"

"I said I would return by June's end and almost got it right."

Julian levered himself away from the wall where he had propped himself until she was in the room. When Isabella stood staring as if transfixed, he smiled slowly. "I hope you don't mind my sending Sarah after you. I wanted our first meeting to be very private, and when I explained my dilemma to Dobson, he was so good as to devise a solution."

Giddy, her knees feeling as if they were fashioned of jelly, Isabella could scarcely credit it was Julian standing there looking even handsomer than she remembered. His dark gold hair was a little touseled from his ride, and his sea-green eyes were alight.

"I think Dobson treats you most familiarly, my lord."

"I hope he'll not be the only one to do so," Julian replied softly, coming to stand just before Isabella so that she could see it was not merely humor that lit his eye but a gleam of such intensity, she caught her breath.

Her heart leapt as he traced the line of the blush on her cheek with his finger. "I have missed you, Bella, mia."

As I have missed you, Isabella thought but did not say, for already Julian was drawing her into his arms, holding her tight against his lean, hard body, and she was lifting her soft lips to meet his.

It was a long, heady, passionate kiss that left her breathless when Julian broke it off to kiss her cheeks and her nose and her brow. "I love you, Bella. I love you so," he whispered, his eyes, their aquamarine color heated by passion, dazzling her. "Those words are new to my tongue, but I would practice them often. Will you marry me, my lovely Isabella?"

He was so amazingly handsome gazing down at her, all golden looking with the sun's last light playing over him, that of a sudden, Isabella lost all her courage. "Oh, Julian, are you certain? I . . ."

"You are lovely and loving and wise and warm and everything I want in a wife but had never thought to find." He kissed her lips slowly, caressingly. "And I want you, Bella," he added in a far huskier voice. "That has not changed, and God help me, it has been the purest hell being so honorable."

She laughed at the sheer wonder of his admission. "I thought you had not the slightest interest in me after that one kiss, my rakish lord. You were so very correct."

"I was determined to win your good opinion." Julian's hold on her tightened of a sudden as he looked down intently into her hazel eyes, eyes that hid so little of her feelings. "Bella, can you forgive me that unforgivable proposal? I wounded you deeply then, and I've no excuse. It was often my experience women would betray almost anything for little more than a rogue's smile, but to think such a thing of you, Bella. It shames me that I did."

Isabella was as earnest as he and took his face between her hands. "I forgave you long ago, Julian. You did win me honorably, you see. You were everything I wanted in a husband, and when I thought I could not have you . . ."

"That is another thing you've to forgive me! I did not tell you what I knew of Wrexham and let you go that entire, wretched week . . . and the ball, thinking you would wed him. I wanted you entirely free of all obligations and ties to him before I spoke to you of anything between us. He had stood between us once, Bella, and I could not have that again. Do you understand?"

"Yes, Julian. And had you told me, I could not have played the dutiful betrothed, as I suspect you'd have wished. You did think to take him by surprise upon the beach at Wrexham Hall did you not?"

Julian's expression hardened. "I did, but Willis warned him I might know something of their smuggling scheme. I'd have been better advised to haul that scoundrel before the magistrate for his misdeeds at Wynchley. I contented myself with threatening him within an inch of his life, should he ever return to Suffolk, because I feared he might retaliate against us all by falsely naming your father as his accomplice. I was a fool to think my threat enough. The villain had too much to gain by being here and went directly to Wrexham. And as a result of my misjudgment, you nearly were . . ."

Isabella put her hand over his mouth. "You did what you thought best, Julian, and you came for me in time. I was quite unharmed, and, though it is a dreadful thing to say, it has turned out better this way for Sarah. She is so very happy now she's no need to fear her father again.''

"I am glad for that. And now that we understand one another very well, Bella, mia, will you marry me?'' More urgently, he added, "You do love me? You have not said it.''

She almost laughed aloud at the thought Julian could doubt she was madly in love with him, but beneath the smile in his eyes there was the smallest question and so she did not laugh. "Yes, my lord. I do love you very, very much.''

Her eyes shining, she lifted her lips to his for a very long kiss. Then it was Isabella who drew back to ask a little breathlessly, "But what of your father? I am not . . .''

Julian cut her off with a full laugh. "I have spoken with him, and am pleased to say that, for the first time in my life, I rendered him quite speechless. He could scarcely credit I meant to marry at all, but then, when he learned whom I'd chosen, he was truly astonished. It seems he knew your mother rather well when they were young and admired her. All he could say for a time was, 'Well!' At last, when he did find speech he managed very nicely, for he said I had all his respect, which is saying quite a deal for Chandley.''

When Isabella could only say, "Well!'' herself, they both laughed and as lovers' will laughed again for the sheer pleasure of laughing together.

"Hark,'' Julian whispered, his forehead resting on Isabella's, and his lips hovering tantalizingly over hers. "I hear the sounds of a Ramsey gathering. The squire is bellowing . . .''

" . . . and Lady Prim is chiming in gently.'' Isabella laughed low as they listened to voices in the hallway. "That is Peter, home from school for the vacation.''

"And Liza is home as well,'' Julian added, for they could hear her chiding Peter.

Julian looked a question at Isabella when a deep matronly voice sounded. "Lady Amelia accompanied Liza. The Earl of Chively has lost his heart to my sister, and our aunt came to put his case before Papa.''

"An interesting approach. Have the girl's aunt do the asking.''

"No more outside the bounds than yours," Isabella retorted, though her sparkling eyes belied her tone. "You have spoken to me before you spoke to Papa."

"Ah, but I know his reply."

Isabella grinned. "Conceited man!"

"Actually, I made certain he would favor my suit," Julian whispered as if he were confiding a great secret. "I kept back two kegs of the brandy for him."

"The smuggled brandy?"

Julian's eyes danced. "Well, I could not see that it would further our effort against the French to pour the brandy in the Thames. Your father's throat seemed quite as fitting a receptacle."

"Such a lack of respect!" she protested only to ruin the effect by laughing.

He kissed her, because she looked very lovely when she laughed, then said very softly, "The truth is, I have done the whole thing quite properly. I asked your father long ago, when I enlisted him in my scheme to ensnare Wrexham."

"And he said nothing all this time?"

"On the contrary, he embraced me at once." Julian grinned when Isabella cuffed him rather caressingly for teasing her, and trapping her hand, he kissed it. His eyes took on a hotter gleam then. "I like to do my own wooing, Bella. You do not mind overmuch, I hope?"

"No, oh, no, my lord. I, oh, I do not mind at all," Isabella replied, the timbre of her voice becoming huskier as Julian nibbled her upon her ear and then bestowed a trail of soft, lingering kisses down her neck.

"And you will marry me?"

The question was the merest warm breath in her ear. Isabella shuddered with pleasure and turned large hazel eyes that seemed more gold than green up to him. "Your wooing is so very effective, my lord, I would wed you as soon as ever we may."

It was some time before Julian and Isabella adjourned to the drawing room to receive the by turns delighted, tearful, and enthusiastic congratulations of her family. The squire, happily, had had the time to drink down several exceedingly satisfying toasts to the general good fortune that had, through no fault of his own, befallen both his girls, and his countenance was almost as flushed as his eldest daughter's when he lifted his glass to her a final time. ''Here's to you, Bella. And to the lad who's wise enough to see what a splended wife you'll make. May your life together be as satisfying as the sparkle in your eyes promises it will be.''

ROMANTIC ENCOUNTERS